In All Things

Marta Curti

Aleteo Press

Aleteo Press
www.aleteopress.com

Publisher's Note: This is a work of fiction. Names, characters, places,
and incidents are a product of the author's imagination. Locales and
public names are sometimes used for atmospheric purposes. Any re-
semblance to actual people, living or dead, or to businesses, companies,
events, institutions, or locales is completely coincidental.

Interior design by Marta Curti
Interior sketches © Trish Nixon, used with permission
Cover design and photographs by Marta Curti

In All Things / Marta Curti -- 1st ed.
ISBN 978-0-9970406-0-9

For Maria,

the strongest woman I know

PROLOGUE

On the day I was born, an albatross spread her wild, wide wings to the north-blowing wind. With a single flap she was lifted smoothly and silently, as if she were one lone feather and not hundreds drawing her together in a mingling of contour and down. As the years passed and I took my fledgling steps and as I learned to navigate my youth, she continued to soar through her great vast life, rising up and up in homage to her almost weightless bones.

But nine years later, as this hook-billed pilot finally settled her body onto a large pale egg which had sat, heavy in her abdomen, for many long weeks, I had no choice but to watch my own mother slip from me. And due, perhaps, to her impending death, or her long-held belief that there should be no secrets between mother and child, it was also the year I learned one of my fathers (for I have had three) was a rapist. I am not speaking of my biological father, nor am I speaking of the only man I ever called father. I am speaking instead of the man who fathered the idea of me; the man who planted the seed of realization inside my mother's heart that sprouted and grew and blossomed into me

She used to say, "In all things, there is beauty...even in that *moment because it brought me to you." The moment she spoke of was the moment of her rape, though she would never use that word. It was a name I would assign to it, years later, when I truly understood. Now, some may think it strange that a mother would speak to her son about such things. But in the end it is as much a part of my story as it is hers.*

Part 1

hollow bones

I am 47 years old. Up until today I had never seen snow. I had always believed, however, that it, like death, is cold. But as I lie here now, fully immersed in both, I feel nothing but a gently nagging warmth radiating from my bones. Because now, I finally understand everything that has brought me to this one place, to this one time, to this small window of space between angels' wings and the silky darkness of ravens. And as I look up at the two faces gazing down upon my own—that of my son, who has taught me more than I ever knew I needed to learn and that of the man who I have loved since long before—I realize this: I know, finally, what I will say. I know what I will say when I walk through heaven's doors and glimpse the shining face of God.

CHAPTER 1

AUGUST WAS NOT YET BORN, less than five months in the forming, when I learned the secrets contained inside his heart. There was the physical secret—that it beat too fast against the narrow bones of his rib cage, that it would always work twice as hard as it should to sustain the coursing of blood through his veins. But his heart held another kind of secret too. The kind bound so tightly to our own, we dare not imagine the possibility of it. His heart's secret was in the knowing and the freeing of other people's secrets—secrets of loves gained and (almost always) lost. The erratic, syncopated beats of my son's heart had the power to draw stories from the ordinary-hearted with the ease of a magician pulling a rainbow-colored scarf from the innocent hollows of a young girl's mouth.

And for some, the sharing of their stories (the remembering, the re-living) was enough. Whether the experience filled them with joy or comfort or only a sadness so great they had to pull away from my son for fear their sorrow would consume them, the fact that their tale had been told was, for them, a burden lifted, a weight shed, a freedom gained.

But there were others. Others who somehow had a need for something…else. And my son's heart easily obliged. These people would get to see, at last, the full truth of their own stories: how each heart connects to the next, how it looks from the other side (to feel what others felt, to know what others knew) to finally understand.

This was the secret that would draw people to my son or push them away—a burden and a relief wrapped into a tiny fisted muscle keeping him alive, though by all rights he should not be.

The day I learned these secrets was an otherwise ordinary day. I had left work at the flower shop early, had eaten lunch in the park, and had maneuvered my way, as usual, through L.A. traffic. The ordinariness of the day fell away only when I lay in the examining room—my belly exposed and my heart mesmerized by the pointillism portrait of my son (my son!) on the small monitor. To temper the anxiety I felt during this, our first ultrasound, I let everything fall out of focus—the kind doctor with her long, dark hair and full lips painted frosting pink, the almost life-size poster on the walls mapping the female reproductive system in color-coded objectivity, the counter with glass jars holding cotton swabs and tongue depressors, even the stale air and sterile smell possible only within the cold, pale walls of a doctor's office. Everything fell away, except for the image of my child on the ultrasound monitor. I focused only on his metamorphosis. I tried to make out the shape of an ear, the slope of his forehead, the minute arcs of his feet. All of which told me: YES! He is here; he is alive. There is still a chance. And then I heard it…the tinny beat of his heart.

But, I had only just begun to hear its soothing rhythm beating softly—tiny wings tapping against the walls of my eardrums—when the doctor pulled the probe from my belly as though it were hot and we were both in danger of getting burned.

"What's wrong?" I asked.

"I'm not sure," the doctor said, her hand moving to her chest as if suddenly reminded of her own heart. Color spread up her cheeks, and a silence flooded the room and I felt I might drown in it. I stared up at this young doctor, awkward in this news she now carried, awkward in everything she did not want to say.

The only sound was my own heart, beating furiously now, as if trying to claw its way out of my rib cage.

"Your son's heart is still growing, changing, but, still it's…not right. Something is…different."

She shook her head as if trying to purge the thoughts that swam there. After a few moments, she regained herself, the crimson color draining from her cheeks.

"I'm afraid your son has an accelerated heart rate, Ms. Rose. His heart beats at a pace much faster than normal."

"How much faster?"

"About three times too fast. It sounds, well, I don't know. I've never heard anything like this before."

"What does that mean?" I asked, panic rising in the back of my throat, leaving its bitter, metallic traces on my tongue.

"We'll need to keep close tabs on this, monitor you both very closely. I would like to call in a specialist. But, the important thing right now is for you to remain calm. Look, I just need one minute. I'll be right back," she said and quickly left the room.

And with nothing else I could do, I waited for her to return, waited for her to say everything I feared she could not. Would she tell me my son would not live to see anything? Would she smile sadly and say *with this heart he has been given, he should have been dead long ago*?

As had happened many times before, I felt myself suddenly losing contact with the objects around me. I no longer felt the rough surface of the sheet beneath me but hovered just slightly above it. I desperately gripped the edges of the examining table trying to keep myself from floating away.

§

I was five years old the first time I lost control of my own gravity. I had been living with my new foster family for only a few months. The woman, Charlotte, was so large entire rooms shrank in her presence. *Her smile*, her husband Mark used to say, *could tame a pack of wild wolves*. What I remember most about her though is that

I never saw her cry. I never saw her on the verge of her own life. I, on the other hand, cried for any reason, or for no reason at all. She jokingly chided me for this.

"You're a sweet kid," she told me, "but way too sensitive. Will you try not to cry so much?"

"I'll try."

"Promise?"

"Promise," I said over and over. But each time I felt wronged or out of place, or simply unloved, the tears came, and I unwittingly broke my promise to Charlotte.

The day I finally kept my promise was also the day I first drifted out of myself like a seed caught among the ripples and tides of the sea. I had been playing among the brown and golden leaves that had collected beneath the trees in our backyard. I crinkled them in my fingers. I tossed them in bunches and watched as they drifted, twirling to the ground. One leaf in particular caught my eye. When it settled to the floor I realized it was not a leaf at all, but instead a single bird feather—long and slender. I grabbed the end of it between my fingers and held it before me—amazed at all the colors, the blues and greys, purples and greens. The entire feather was perfect, and its fragile iridescence drew me instantly into the imagined life and death of its owner. Now, I had never seen death up close. I had never felt its pointy finger worrying the bones of my spine, but, in my limited experience, I believed death must be a lonely enough endeavor. I thought it only fair and right that this bird be laid to rest with all its feathers intact. I became obsessed with finding whatever else remained of it.

I searched the garden looking for telltale signs of the departed: more feathers, its slim and hollow bones, perhaps even the small, curved frame of its skull. I scrambled beneath the recently watered rosebushes—nothing. I pushed aside the soggy leaves and dirt covering the roots of the lemon trees, but there was not a sign. I parted the overgrown grass like curtains and came up empty handed. The less I found, the more determined I became. Finally, after hours of looking, I failed to find any other evidence that this bird had once lived and died somewhere in the vicinity of my life.

Frantic, I stumbled up the back steps and pushed myself through the kitchen door, feather held firmly between my fingers.

"Charlotte! Charlotte!" I called. "I found a dead bird. I found a dead bird!"

Charlotte came bounding into the kitchen. She took one look at me, at the dried leaves in my hair, the feather clutched to my chest, and the mud covering my hands, my knees, my shoes and now the kitchen floor.

"Well, that's a shame, dear. It was probably eaten by one of those damn neighborhood cats! They're always creeping into our garden," she said, pulling the mop from the closet, setting the bucket, tilted to fit, into the kitchen sink. She opened the tap and let the water run. It made a harsh, violent sound as it hit the bottom of the empty bucket, and I began to cry.

I cried, not only for the death of this bird, but also for its absence from my world. I have since learned too well that *that*, after all, is the problem with death. It has not so much to do with the dying, but with the ones still left behind.

Charlotte approached me and knelt down to look me in the eyes, her hands cupping my shoulders.

"Come on. Don't cry. Remember what we talked about? You promised. Look, we'll get you cleaned up and give your feather a proper burial."

I wiped the wet from my eyes, my cheeks, my neck and breathed deeply.

"Okay," I smiled.

"God has a plan for all of his creatures. It was this bird's time is all."

"Did God kill this bird?" I asked.

Behind my words, came the *rush, rush, rush* of water as it filled the bucket and began to overflow, splashing onto the linoleum floor.

"Shit!" yelled Charlotte as she scrambled to the sink. Her socked feet hit the puddle of water sending her skidding inches across the floor. She fumbled for control and came to a halt against the sink. She pressed her hand to her chest to soothe her pounding heart.

"Whoa, that was close," she said and smiled as she turned off the tap.

The incessant rushing of the water now the slow *drip...drip... drip* of a leaky sink.

She turned back toward me, and one leg, caught off guard by its own ineptness, slipped out from underneath her. She tried to grip the sink for balance, but her hand caught the edge of the bucket instead, sending it down, tumbling over her, spilling its liquid guts until it seemed as if a giant river had erupted, bubbling up from whatever depths lay beneath the kitchen floor. As she fell, her head made contact with the edge of the stove. There was a crack like an eggshell against a glass bowl, and then her body hit the floor. I watched the blood—murky and dark—ooze onto the tiles, mixing with the water, diluting it to a soft, swirling pink. Charlotte just laid there, her eyes wide open. Unblinking. Unseeing.

Charlotte! I tried to say her name but found I could not will my voice. I could not force my tongue. For five years I had evaded it, and now death had come twice to my door. I looked up at the wooden cross hanging above the kitchen window; the person suspended there stared back. I refused to cry. I would not disappoint Charlotte again. This time, I would keep my promise.

I shut my eyes and swallowed hard against the building in my throat. I bit down on my lip and forced myself to breathe.

Don't cry, don't cry, I repeated over and over in my head. And I didn't.

Looking back now, I suppose the fear, the loss, the guilt—everything I felt right then—had to go somewhere. If I would not release it, it would find its own means of escape.

It began with a lifting of pressure from the soles of my feet and the sensation of sharp pin pricks at the tips of my fingers. Slowly, I became aware of each pore of my body, tiny holes that let the pain in. And I felt myself rising—not the same as flying—not a willful act with a purpose or a destination. I was just floating. I tried to grab onto the door jamb, to push myself against the wall to make it stop. I dropped the feather and watched as it floated, arcing and drifting, past my torso, my mud encrusted knees, past my shoes; it continued to fall, past where I stopped and before the floor began. I floated like a balloon on a string, inches above the ground, my feet a-dangle in shoes that slipped, just vaguely, at the heels.

I don't know how long I was there, suspended between myself and nothingness, when I heard the door creak open. Mark, Charlotte's husband, entered the room—a cry warbling in his throat.

That was enough to send me crashing back to solid ground. I hit the floor hard and ran.

Days later, I was sent away. Mark was there to see me off with a hug. As I was leaving he pulled a feather, long and fine from the left-hand pocket of his jacket. Without words he held it out to me. I cupped my hands, and he placed it in my palms. It was weightless and blameless. I held it there as I walked down the steps and entered the car. I held it there for the entire car ride and all the way out of his life.

§

Years later, I went to the library to try and identify the former owner of this feather (for I had kept it hidden in a cardboard box). That was when I learned birds molt their feathers every year, and chances were good that this bird, this maker of my feather, had not died that day. Perhaps it was still flitting through the trees, showering children's gardens everywhere with its jeweled feathers—its emeralds, its amethysts. I wondered if Charlotte had known this simple fact. From then on I began to collect found feathers, though

I rarely could identify the bird from which they came. To me, they were no longer a symbol of death but one of beauty, of mystery, and of renewal.

§

There was a knock, and the doctor timidly entered the exam room, closing the door behind her. She once again turned on the ultrasound machine and set the probe against my abdomen. I braced myself for the sound of my son's heart, for the cadence that could signify yet another child who would not make it beyond the confines of my body. Another child lost to me before he was ever mine.

"Okay, this is it," she said. And I heard the *thump-shuffle-whisper-thump* of my son's irregular heart.

The doctor involuntarily inhaled sharply.

"There is something you're not telling me. Please, I need to know."

"It's just..."

"Tell me."

"It's crazy..."

"If it's about my son, I have to know."

She looked down at me and sighed. "No, it's..." she laughed. "It really is crazy. The sound, the beat of his heart, I swear it reminds me of a sound I haven't heard in a very long time. But that's not right either. It *is* the same sound. I'm sure of it."

"Tell me."

"If anyone knew I was even thinking this, much less considering saying it out loud, I think I would lose my license."

"Whatever you say stays between us. I promise. I have to know."

"Okay." Then she inhaled purposefully, deeply, closed her eyes, and let out a long sigh.

"I've heard the exact same tone and rhythm, the exact same everything before." She lightly, almost unconsciously, touched the lines of her neck. Red crept above her collar coloring her cheeks to match her poorly chosen lipstick.

She placed her hand gently on my belly. I waited, watching for the words that were there, teetering on the edge of her tongue. When she parted her lips, I waited for those words to spill like drops of water tumbling from the sky, slowly growing heavier and heavier with their own weight before falling, breaking into a million more of themselves each time they hit the ground.

But she did not say a word—or if she did, I heard nothing. I was only keenly aware of the flat of her palm resting, forgotten, on my abdomen, and I felt, suddenly, a prickling sensation creeping up the base of my skull. I tried to still my heart. But the more I tried the faster and more arrhythmic its beating became. The doctor placed her other hand over her own chest and I could hear both our hearts now, distinct in the secrets they kept, but now beating, *thump-shuffle-whisper-thump*, in perfect unison with each other and in perfect unison with my son's.

But while our three hearts moved faster, everything else seemed to wind down, to slow; the second hand of the clock on the wall taking much longer to tick down each second, until everything stopped.

Except for the sound of our beating hearts.

CHAPTER 2

FOR A MOMENT, EVERYTHING WENT BLACK. A breeze began to stir, and the unmistakable smell of horses wafted into the room. From the darkness, I saw a flash (in the particular way sunlight has of reflecting off a metal surface) which gradually dissipated into a soft, hazy glow. Then clearly, I could see the spinning wheels of a wheelchair with strands of hay caught in its spokes. With each turn, the hay caught, making a *thump-shuffle* against the spoke, then a *whisper* as the wheel made another revolution, again, again and again—a continuous *thump-shuffle-whisper-thump*. A young girl named Emelia (who would one day become a doctor, a wife) sat in the chair, her hands working the rims as she raced along the pavement. I watched this twelve-year-old girl laughing easily as the wind ruffled her hair. Just ahead of her, I saw a boy, his back against the rough mottled bark of a tree, cheering her on. Suddenly I felt everything she felt. I knew everything she knew, as if all these memories were also my own.

I knew that every weekend she went to the racetrack with her father. I knew she always wore a bright yellow sundress (fingering its hem whenever she felt nervous) for the occasion. I knew this choice of wardrobe came at her mother's insistence. *Yellow stands out*, her mother told her. In a yellow dress, her mother believed, she would not be easily lost among the crowds of strangers, laughing, pushing, cheering; couples walking arm in arm; men smoking fat cigars.

I knew her father was young, perhaps too young for the responsibilities that lay before him. But despite this, or because of it, grey hairs had etched themselves in his beard and coffee-colored hair. I knew one of his hands rested on his daughter's shoulder while the other rested inside his coat pocket against the silver flask whose contents made it possible for him to get through each day without hurting himself or someone he loved. I could see him there—feel the excitement he felt as he watched the horses racing, their lean muscular bodies sweating against the strain, the pounding of their hooves spraying up mud behind them.

Equal to her father's excitement was Emelia's boredom. Her restlessness was so strong that after a few minutes she would slip from her father's distracted grasp and go wandering through the crowds. While she was mildly entertained watching the women with their too big hats and matching pastel dresses, their filtered cigarettes stained with various shades of lipstick, they were not what Emelia longed for. What she loved most (what she most wanted to see up close, to smell, even perhaps, to touch) were the horses. She knew she was not allowed in the back, where they were kept. But with each visit to the track, she cautiously tested the ability of the signs warning "employees only" and "no entry" to actually keep her away. They were only words painted on metal, after all. She dared them to do their worst. And one day, when she finally garnered the courage to defy them, she was surprised at how easy it was. As she walked towards the stalls, none of the adults seemed to take much notice of her, despite her wardrobe. *So much for my mother's theory*, she thought.

When the scent of hay and fresh manure filled her nostrils, she was not repulsed, but drawn forward, as was I. I watched as she made her way down to where they kept the horses, rows and rows of them, some black and white, some chestnut, some dappled and grey, all looming above her in their stalls.

I watched her as she snuck from stall to stall, not getting too close, but lingering just out of reach of each horse's nose. I knew she was still too afraid to actually touch one. She would save that for another day. After much time had passed, she reluctantly turned back, fearing her father would notice she had gone. That was when she first spotted the boy.

His back was to her, and a line of sweat soaked his shirt between his thin shoulder blades. He was in an empty stall, shoveling out old hay, rotten and reeking, clumped together with horse piss and shit. As he worked, he balanced himself on two wooden crutches resting just in the crook of his armpits. With each area he cleared, he re-adjusted his weight and then continued on in one seamless motion.

When he finally turned and walked toward her, she saw that his legs were crooked and slight, like those of a long-legged bird. He shuffled past her, his eyes straight ahead. Sunlight streaming in above the rafters lit his red hair. Right then, she knew she loved him.

§

I felt her anxiousness as she began to look forward to each weekend, sneaking off from her father's side as soon as she could, her body a nervous jumble until she could see the boy again. She watched him, secretly, as he calmed the horses by rubbing them high up on the throat, as he fed them carrots and sliced apples when he thought no one was watching, as he fearlessly entered the stalls and brushed down each horse's coat until it shone.

When she finally did approach him, his back was to her and he was cleaning one of the stalls, legs resting, but arms and back moving beneath the weight of his work. She tapped his shoulder and felt the dampness of his shirt where the sweat had soaked through. She wanted to rest her head there, against his sweat, his scent. He turned to her and smiled. They were friends from that moment on. He taught her the names of all the horses, how to gently coax up their legs to check their hooves, how to feed them treats on a flat open palm so as not to get bitten. She taught him the Portuguese words for all of these things: horse (*cavalo*), hoof (*casco*), apple (*maçã*). She helped him with his chores so he would be done faster and they could claim their time together freely. After they placed fresh hay in the stalls they would sometimes lie down in it, his hand on the small of her back and her legs tangled over his so that someone looking in on them from above could not tell where she ended and he began. In those moments she felt alive and beautiful and capable of miracles. She felt safe inside this cocoon that was him, trusting fully that he loved her back.

In the summer, she urged her father to go to the races almost every day. She knew her mother would protest, her parents would fight, and her mother would cry, but in the end her father would win out. He always did. And even at twelve years old she knew, somewhere deep down, she was sacrificing her mother's happiness for her own. But it was only for a little while, she told herself. Once at the track, she snuck off to meet the boy, Paul, as soon as her father began paying more attention to the horses than he did to her. She and Paul spent hours together working, talking, laughing. Every once in a while his lips brushed against hers, or he wrapped his arms around her and she couldn't imagine ever feeling afraid again, couldn't even remember what fear felt like.

One day, toward the end of summer, Paul showed her his wheelchair. It was what he used to get around in almost everywhere but the stables: at school, at home, helping his mother with the grocery shopping.

It makes people more at ease, his mom told him, *to see a young boy in a wheelchair. Nobody wants to see you hobble about. It makes people uncomfortable.*

Only his dad encouraged him to use his legs. At night, when everyone else had gone home, Paul's father let him slide onto the smooth, strong back of an old mare. Paul, his legs twisted awkwardly on either side of the horse, would clutch her mane and whisper in her ear. *Run,* he would say. And she would, slowly at first, but faster at each turn. He felt he could ride forever on those nights. He felt strong and alive and whole. This was a secret he shared with his dad. They never told his mom. Instead, they brought the wheelchair to the stables every day to placate her. They left it sitting in one of the old barns so if his mother asked, he wouldn't have to lie completely. He could tell her, *yes*, he did use the wheelchair at the stables, though he would not tell her (not yet) that he used it as motivation to heal himself, to push himself to build his muscles so he would one day walk without "hobbling about." He dreamed about the day his mother would wrap her arms around him and tell him how proud she was of him. She would kick one wheel of the old rickety chair (the chair was always rickety in his dreams) and say, *we don't need this thing anymore.*

Emelia, almost two decades away from the woman she would become, took in the wheelchair. Its gleaming, silver-spoked wheels reminded her of the symmetrical lines of a nautilus shell she had found at the beach once. She walked over to the chair. She ran her hands along the cold metal. She settled into the seat. She adjusted her legs into the footrests.

"I bet you could beat this stupid wheelchair any day," she laughed.

Paul smiled down at her with a look of uncertainty. But then he yelled, "You're on!"

They lined up on the cement path leading away from the stables to an exercise yard: he—strong and beautiful on his crutches, she—with body folded into the chair.

"One, two, three..." they recited together and then it began— he spun his legs and crutches as fast as they would carry him, she propelled herself forward awkwardly as her arms pushed those metal wheels forward, her breath expelling with more force at each revolution. As she turned the wheels, a *thump-shuffle-whisper-thump* echoed in her ears.

At the finish line, he was triumphant. Sweat glistened off his forehead. His smile was so big Emelia felt she could peer right down into his mouth and see right through to his insides. She felt her heart flutter in her chest. She had never been this happy.

As they were resting in the shade, in silence, she reached down absentmindedly to pluck out the hay tangled in the wheels.

He gently placed his hand on hers. "Leave it," he said. "I keep it there on purpose."

They reminded him of the stables when he was at school or at home, he explained. They gave him something the other kids didn't have. Those other normal, sure-legged kids didn't have straw in their wheels, didn't have horses that ate from their hands, didn't know the trembling of an anxious mare and how it felt when her skin twitched against the back of your thighs. So the hay remained, and each time they raced (for it became something they did often from that day forward) it rubbed against the metal, making a swishing, thumping sound with each turn of the wheel.

And it was this sound (the sound of my son's beating heart— the sound hay makes when caught in the spokes of a young boy's wheelchair) that revealed her secret: the secret of a young girl's love for a boy with bird-like legs—damaged and weak before he could even walk. And it reminded her of his promise that as long as they were together, no harm could ever come to her.

§

By the end of the summer, Emelia's parents were on the cusp of divorce, and months later Emelia and her mother would pack up their things and head half way across the country. But that, in and of itself, would not have been obstacle enough to keep Paul and Emelia apart. She would have refused to go or would have run away or would have called him every day and talked for hours, until her mother could no longer afford both the phone bill and to keep a roof over their heads so long as they were living anywhere Paul was not. As it was, Emelia went eagerly, anxiously, stopping short only of begging her mother to take her as far away as possible.

No one knew what had happened exactly. No one had been there to see it. They said things like *the horse must have spooked*, or *it crushed his head with one kick. He probably died instantly,* they said.

When Emelia walked into the stables and heard the news (hours too late, the ambulance had already come and gone), she fell to the ground as if her bones no longer had the strength to hold her. Then somehow her dad was there, pulling at her to stand up, his hands forcing her away from all that was left of the boy she loved. And though she wanted to scream, nothing escaped her gaping mouth but a rush of air and every belief she ever held in her heart.

§

The doctor pulled her hand from my stomach. Instantly, my heart began to slow to its normal rhythm. I opened my eyes and was surprised to find myself still on the same examining table.

Emelia and I stared at each other trying to find the words to express what we had just witnessed.

"Are you okay, Ms. Rose?"

"I'm fine. Are you okay?"

Emelia stood up, quickly wiping her eyes then her hands along the length of her white coat.

"Would you like to take a walk?" she asked.

§

We were barely aware of moving at all, but our feet propelled us forward out of sheer habit. The direction didn't matter. We were just two women carried along by the power and meaning of memory.

"I haven't thought of Paul, I mean, really let myself think of him in such a long time."

I glanced down at her hands. Her silver wedding band shone up at me. She looked at me and smiled, holding up her left hand. "I love my husband," she said, "I do. And I know he loves me. But unconditionally? Without question?" She shook her head sadly. "You know, on the day Paul died I knew I would never again be truly safe. I knew the bad things would always, somehow, find their way in."

I looked at her then, at her tear-filled eyes and somehow saw my own. So I told her about my other son.

CHAPTER 3

I NEVER WANTED A CHILD. Not at first. As a child myself, I never played with baby dolls. I never wrapped my stuffed animals in blankets and fed them imaginary milk from plastic bottles. When I saw other girls play like this I turned my head in sad disgust. As I got older, this sentiment only grew stronger, hard like a stone inside my heart. But it was not for all the reasons most childless-by-choice people proclaim: they do not want to bring a being into this doomed world or there are too many people on the planet already, though valid arguments all. My reason was this: I believed I was wholly incapable of love.

In all my life I had never known anyone long enough to completely love them, and as far as I could tell no one had ever loved me, even just a little. I believed that before I was born, as my body formed and grew, violent mutations attacked my cells, or cancers quietly ate away at my heart, leaving it feeble and dry like the skeleton of a long dead bird. Though I appeared physically whole, I believed I was lacking the one thing which makes us human. I had been born without the love gene; for I was convinced there must be one. Though my deformity was on the inside it was perfectly visible to me every time I looked in the mirror. Perhaps my real mother, upon looking into my eyes for the first time, saw this lack and recognized it immediately.

In one of her greatest acts of cruelty, Annelle, the woman I lived with between the ages of 10 and 17, told me my mother had killed herself. "Shot herself straight through the head right there in her own hospital bed the day you were born."

But at ten years old, I refused to believe something like this could happen. I knew if it were true, it would mean I had driven my own mother to death, and that my crippled, infant heart had been the cause.

So I fought and I argued. "Why didn't the nurses stop her?" I asked.

And, "She was right there in the hospital. The doctors would have saved her!"

And finally, "Well... well, how did she sneak the gun into the hospital, then?"

This question came from desperation and from no real experience of my own, but from watching too many late night television programs with Annelle's boyfriends.

But Annelle only sighed, "In those days, fear was simpler," as if this were any explanation at all. Then she turned her back to me, her face briefly catching the shadows being thrown by the kitchen curtains mocking me now with their colorful patterns of ducks and flowers and false cheer.

Suddenly and acutely, I became aware of my hair follicles coming loose, my skin dissolving, the marrow of my bones falling away like leaves from an old and brittle tree. I felt myself rising, floating through the room, dissipating bit by bit, fated to be absorbed by the peeling wall paper and ceramic figurines. Surely, I would have disappeared for good had Annelle not chosen that very moment to notice the disastrous state of her kitchen sink.

"How many times do I have to tell you?" she bellowed, without even turning her head to look at me. "You never, never leave dirty dishes when I have guests coming over! Are you deliberately trying to embarrass me?"

The force of her voice sent my particles racing back together and my body, now intact, back to solid ground.

"I've got a date coming over in half an hour. You get yourself to your room, *Two-by-Four*."

Two-by-four. Two-by-four. Those pre-cut slabs of pine or cedar you can pick up at any hardware store—straight, flat boards that no longer resemble the jagged, lively trees from which they were cut. Long before my eleventh birthday, the kids in school called me by that name. And for most of my life, I believed I was flavorless and hard in body and in spirit, and this nickname was my proof of this; proof of more than just how cruel (yet unimaginative) adolescent American boys can be. In the days when I believed Annelle and I could be friends, I had confessed this shameful nickname to her. She had used it ever since.

Without a hint of protest, I turned from Annelle and headed to my room. I didn't bother to mention that her latest boyfriend had called twenty minutes before to say he wouldn't be stopping by after all.

§

That night, I dreamt of my mother for the first time. It was a dream that would return to me often. It played in black and white. In it, I saw my mother still and silent, frozen as if in a photograph. She was caught in mid-run on a wet and glimmering street. Snow-flakes hung in mid-air all around. Her hair was wild and flowing, and the hospital gown she wore was open at her sides like wings. She was naked underneath and her bare back and the curve where her buttocks met her thighs was visible. As she ran, I could see the bareness of her feet, with their deep arches and the dark creases lining the pads of her feet. They were exactly like my own.

This was the only picture, dreamt or real, that I had of her, and no matter how closely I looked, I could never see her face. She kept it always turned away, as if even in death, she could not bear to look at me. As if she believed to look upon the face of her only child, born with an empty heart, was still too much for any decent person, living or dead, to demand of her.

It took me twenty years to learn I was not hollow after all; no cancers had eaten away at me, no mutations had affected the inner workings of my heart. I came to recognize my own ability to love in a moment of so much fear and hideous malice (a torn dress, a crooked tree, a small and fleeing sparrow) there had to be beauty hidden somewhere deep among its cracks, something to cling to, to keep me from drowning. And a few weeks later, like a leaf gently pushing the soft folds of its own flesh, this beauty revealed itself to me, and I was saved. Not just from that moment, but saved, I felt, from my own life.

§

That moment...well, I can't call it a rape. Not a rape, really. After all, I had allowed it to happen. I knew what he had planned. How could I not? I had heard the rumors floating across campus. He searched out those women—young and old, rich and poor, beautiful and plain—who needed what he could offer. Some may have been surprised at the beautiful ones, surprised that they too fell for his trickery, but not me. He made them all believe, for a short moment, that he loved them: young freshmen from wealthy families, lonely professors' wives, even, if one was to believe the rumors, a visiting poet from Argentina. But as the story so often goes, once he had his so-called "way" with them he never spoke to them again.

I watched him for weeks, waiting, imagining the first words I would say to him. He had an easy way about him. He was handsome but not beautiful; fierce but not book smart; smooth with an almost imperceptible jaggedness that lay just beneath his skin. He also had the uncanny ability to say and do the one thing each woman most needed in the exact moment she most needed it. It was as if he had a secret window through which he watched the panorama of their souls—secret wishes, private dreams, lurking fears or hovering insecurities. If one woman felt uncomfortable with her body, with the thickness of her thighs, say, indicated by the slightest of gestures, hands draped casually over her lap when she sat, he took

note and let his hands, his fingers, his lips linger there to show her
that her thighs were a place worth lingering in. If another sat every
day in class (a light sweat on her upper lip, her eyes never meeting the professor's) paralyzed with fear because she might be called
upon to answer a question or explain her point of view and because
if she opened her mouth everyone would realize that she had nothing at all to say, he made off-hand comments like, "I don't think half
the class knew what was going on today. That professor couldn't
teach his way out of anything." And they would laugh together at
the professors who expected too much and the students who only
pretended to understand. And she would feel comforted.

Perhaps it was the way he had of saying these things, or the
women's desperate need to believe him, but they trusted him and
let him in. And despite hearing the others talk—that he had done
the same to them, only to break their hearts in the end, each new
woman believed that *this* love (that *she*, that *this* time, that *he with
her)* was different. And though I knew he was faking sincerity and
concern, I truly believed he could see into these women. I hoped he
would see into me and would know exactly what to say and exactly
what to do to make me feel like a person somebody could love.

Alone in my room, I carefully wrote my name and phone number on a clean sheet of paper. My name—the curve of the *y*, the fine
loop of the *p*, stared back up at me. If words could smile, this one
did. I carefully folded the paper and left it on the windshield of his
car. I imagined the words, *Penny, I love you*, and my heart danced
inside my chest. Of course, I knew his reputation. I knew he would
not love me. But I felt that my heart, after twenty solitary years, was
in danger of atrophy, and if nothing were done to help it along it
would stop one day soon of its own accord. I believed my physical
life, my very survival, depended entirely on three simple words: *I
love you*, spoken to me if only just once, by anybody.

Two days later, I entered his apartment. He came in behind me,
closing and locking the door. He took two steps toward me. Later I

would think of his movements like a cat's—not one on the hunt, but one that has already made its kill.

He grabbed my head and began kissing me, his tongue hard and rough in my mouth. I instinctively took one step backward.

"I…" I muttered, not yet understanding why he seemed so angry. Why didn't he give me what I most needed, as he had all the others? Why didn't he smile or flatter?

"This is what you came for, isn't it?" His words and his body both pinning themselves against me, my back cold against the wall.

"Won't you tell me you love me?" I asked coyly and immediately regretted it.

For of course, it wouldn't be that easy. Of course things could not work that way. He let out a sharp, hiccup of a laugh, and in what seemed like one blurred motion lifted my skirt and brought my panties to my ankles. The pink ones I bought especially for that night.

I had hoped he might notice their sheer material and fine lace, the feel of them against my skin. When getting dressed earlier in the day, I had stopped to gaze at myself in the mirror—clad in pink panties and a bra to match. I gazed at my straw-like legs and the red, raised birthmark high up on my thigh, which resembled quite closely in size and shape, the print of a grown man's hand. I looked at my small breasts and thin arms, and I tried to imagine what he might say to me when he saw me. Would he tell me how beautiful I looked or how happy I made him feel? Weren't those the things men said to women they loved, even if they were only pretending? Wouldn't he be able to see into me and know exactly what I needed to hear?

Over the underwear, I had slipped on my favorite dress. It was long and blue with white terns spiraling across the front of it as though poised to fly off in a flutter of wings and breath. When I had first seen the dress at the store I wondered if the blue was sea or sky. Was I gazing upwards at birds in flight against a deep blue heaven or looking down at a flock of terns soaring over blue ocean waves, perhaps how God might see them? That question prompted me to buy the dress in the first place.

But there was no comment on the panties or the dress. He had merely grunted as he opened his apartment door to me, followed by silence as I brushed my way inside.

And then, suddenly, like a poorly edited movie (scenes spliced, dialogue cut) he was on top of me, my dress and its white birds bunched up at my waist (was God looking down on them now?). Like a booming inside my head, I heard each groove of his zipper unlocking as if in slow motion. I pushed my arms against his chest, trying to force him away, to lift his suffocating weight from my body.

"I don't want this! I don't want this!" I begged. But he would not relent. With one hand, he easily pinned both of my wrists (so slight, so feeble) over my head. He ripped at my dress to get at my breasts. With his one free, roving hand, he raked at my nipples. I felt a sharp pain, and then he was inside me.

"This is your fault," he repeated over and over in my ear. "This...is...*exactly*...what...you wanted," he whispered, slowly, deliberately, emphasizing the word *exactly* so that it landed sharp, cutting into my soul.

But this...this was not what I had come for. So I lay motionless through it all, like driftwood on the sand—wooden against the pungent odor of him, his dripping sweat and reptilian tongue.

With head barely turned, eyes half open, I noticed through the window a small courtyard dotted with a single bent tree. And just there, separated from me by a pane of glass that appeared so thin I thought my hand could glide right through to the other side, was a sparrow. It was hopping back and forth chasing up insects or crumbs from the grass. As I watched, I could make out the details of each feather, the different shades of brown against brown, tan and grey. The dark almond color of its small, round eye. The thickness of its bill coming in and out of view as it bent into the grass, up and down, up and down—its legs as thin and weak as straws. When it opened its wings as if to fly my lips parted against my will. I held my breath and…

There was a sudden lifting.

And he was off me. He hadn't even cum. He pulled out of me angry and limp.

"Fucking you is like fucking a god-damned piece of wood!" he shouted. *Two-by-four…two-by-four.* He yanked on his blue jeans and stumbled into the bathroom, slamming the door behind him.

I rose, shakily, and sat on the edge of the bed, hugging my knees to my chest. Afraid to move any more than this, I scanned the room—still unsure of what I had done wrong. And then I saw them, strewn like an afterthought, on the floor in the corner of the room. Card after card, note after note, a few hastily opened boxes partially covered with wrapping paper adorned with hearts or roses or the word LOVE like a slap in the face. I didn't need to get any closer to know these were all gifts from the other women, the ones I had overheard crying, begging, wishing for him to love them still. It was then I believed I finally understood his rage. Unlike the others, he hadn't used his skills to tempt me. He hadn't had to hook me like a fish with well-placed words and smiles (the bait covering the glinting, wounding barb). Had he felt cheated and bored with me? Did mere physical domination pale against the thrill of the real, lasting control he exerted over the others? Did he believe physical rape was for monsters or amateurs? In his mind, was he neither? Had his skills been sorely wasted with me?

One minute passed.

Three.

Seven.

"Are you still fucking here?" he shouted from behind the door.

I stood. I picked up the panties (twisted and crumpled) from the floor. I balled them into my fist. With the other hand, I gently smoothed out the wrinkles of my dress, pulling the torn pieces to-gether—an ineffectual shield across my breast.

Barely aware of the trembling in my legs, I opened the door and stepped out into the dim light of the hallway. I glanced one more time through the living room, out beyond the window. My eyes searched the individual blades of grass. I stared into the branches and leaves of the crooked tree just beyond the window. But I was too late. The sparrow had already flown.

§

Weeks passed. One day stacked meaninglessly upon the next as time moved at its unfaltering pace. I continued to go to class and to work, though each day I felt myself growing transparent and hollow. Was I eating my own flesh with grief? Was I stripping my lungs, my heart, my intestines from my body as I slept? I awoke each morning half expecting to find them piled neatly beside my bed. Who could I tell what had happened to me? My dorm-mates, nothing more than practical strangers? A professor who most likely didn't even know my name? How could I reveal what I had done?

When my heart stopped beating for seconds at a time, or when my bones ached and my breasts felt wrong in the bras I tried to con-tain them in, I believed it was my body rebelling against me and all I had put it through. It took me a while to realize just the opposite was true. I was not shrinking but growing, and someone else's cells were dividing and multiplying inside of me. Soon, I could imagine the feel of this small stranger's soft skin, as thin and transparent as dragonfly wings.

In class, I found myself stroking my belly, humming melodies beneath my breath. Did he even have ears yet? No matter. On the weekends I sat beneath the oak trees on campus, imagining his soft face, the gentle curve of his spine, his small fingers and toes. And when I caught glimpses of my face in the mirror, I was often sur-prised to find myself smiling. At night, sometimes, I woke up laughing from a dream I never could remember.

Though not a miracle, or even a biological wonder, the fact that I became pregnant from this uncompleted act was a sign. God had been watching, and at last he understood.

§

The miscarriage occurred in the first trimester.

"Well, this really is the best time for something like this to happen," were the consoling words of the campus nurse. "You're only a sophomore, you have plenty of time for children," she said as she placed her damp palm upon my arm.

A few spots of blood.

An open hand against my skin.

My uterus, empty and fragile as glass.

§

For the second time that day, Emelia and I stood in silence for a long while—unsure of what more could be said. She finally cleared her throat, "I need to get back to the hospital." Then she squeezed my hand gently, "I'm going to set up an appointment for you with our best pre-natal specialist. I promise you she will do everything in her power to make sure your baby is alright."

"Thank you."

She hugged me. "I'll stop in once in a while and check on you," she said, though I knew she would not. I understood, as did she, that these small embers of memory were still too strong and, if we weren't careful, could burn our hearts to the ground.

§

After Emelia left, I sat down on a park bench to rest for a moment. I placed my hands on my belly and lay my head against the backrest. I looked up into the trees and caught a slight movement in the branches. It was a hummingbird hovering wildly above me.

Its red throat shimmered like rubies in the sunlight as it jerked its body quickly from side to side, before flying away into the L.A.-blue sky.

I read once that a hummingbird, with its fragile almost weightless body, has a heart capable of pumping 1,000 times a minute, while the average human heart (with its capacity for intense compassion and equal cruelty) may beat a mere 60 times per minute at rest, like a clock set perfectly to count down its own hours one second at a time. And yet my son's tiny heart was raging inside me at a pace somewhere in between.

Suddenly, I wanted to stop Emelia. I wanted to tell her, *please, do come by and see us.* I wanted her to promise she would. I stood as quickly as I could and looked in the direction she had gone, but I could no longer distinguish her from the rest of the crowd.

CHAPTER 4

ACH DAY, AS AUGUST GREW INSIDE ME, I felt his heart's capacity for "knowing" becoming stronger. When strangers accidentally bumped into me on the street or customers at the flower shop I co-owned with a woman named Brinda brushed their hands against mine as I passed them bouquets meant for lovers or friends or as appeasements to grief, I would pick up on a word (*tomorrow, forever, please, yes)* or a scent (ripe apricots, burning leaves, chlorine on cocoa-buttered skin) or a feeling (of acquiescence, of surrender, of longing, of calm). And these fragments of secrets which belonged only to these strangers, however briefly, became mine.

Though people, at the first hint of remembering, pulled away from me instantly, every once in a while someone would linger a bit longer in the moment, bringing breath and life back into those memories that would, perhaps, cause the heart to burst if it tried to contain them for too long. In my son's heartbeat, a middle-aged nurse heard the sound of the old fan in her baby's room. She felt its cool air on her face, just as she had when she rocked her infant daughter back and forth during long nights when she couldn't sleep for not wanting to miss a second of her daughter's life, which, in the end, would be prove to be too short. The man who bagged my groceries one afternoon—a balding, rail of a man—heard the precise sound of popcorn popping. He tasted its buttery flavor on his tongue, just as he had years ago when he made this treat for his daughter every night after her mother died, only to lose her, too, to a husband he didn't like and a job 2,000 miles away. Still others

heard the beat of rain on a tent; the fluttering sound of quail startled
from the undergrowth; the sound of handfuls of buttons slipping
between fingers into small glass jars.

I could never tell who would let me remain with their secrets
and who would shut me out. It was always a surprise. Brinda, a
short, round, grey-haired woman of Indian descent who I considered a friend as well as a business partner, pulled away from me
instantly, running from her memories like a lizard scurrying into
dark crevices. But Mariam, a woman I had barely known, readily
let me in.

Mariam walked into the flower shop one day looking for a job.
The moment I saw her, I sensed an air of unshakable sadness about
her, so I hired her immediately. She had been working part-time at
the flower shop for over two months, and though she always made
time to ask about my day or to talk in a light way about her own,
I knew very little about her. I knew she was beautiful and married
to a doctor. One afternoon when her husband came by to pick her
up, she gathered her things and casually remarked, "I wanted to be
a doctor once," as she headed out the door. She worked hard (un-
loading boxes, putting together arrangements in such a way they
always held a small surprise: Japanese anemones peeking out from
the center of smooth-petaled tulips; the strong, sweet aroma of a
stargazer lily mixing with the earthy scent of spider chrysanthe-
mums; white carnations mingling casually among the freesias and
hyacinths). She was never late and never missed a day of work. On
Wednesdays, when she knew we would be in the store together,
she brought along small gifts: squares of thin, individually wrapped
chocolates for me; a water color set and a bright purple teddy bear
for my unborn child.

Once I caught her staring at my belly, and she commented in an
off-hand way on how much she wanted another baby, how she and
her husband, Amal, had been trying.

"It took me a long time," I told her. "I know how hard the waiting is."

"My husband doesn't talk about it, but I think it breaks his heart too. Do you mind?" she asked, reaching out to touch my stomach.

I took her hand and placed it on my abdomen. Though I knew what would happen, it still came as a sudden jolt to my heart each time a new secret was revealed. As our hearts began to race in unison, the beat pulsing in our ears, Mariam cocked her head to one side like an owl listening for voles beneath the snow.

"Oh my God," she said, "I would recognize that sound anywhere."

Forgetting I was in the room with her, forgetting even where she was in space and time, she let everything go and simply listened to the *thump-shuffle-whisper-thump* of my son's restless heart.

I heard it, too, and felt the beat of my own heart racing to match his. Our three hearts raced together while everything else slowed into darkness. Then through the darkness came a pinhole of light, dim and yellow, which slowly grew bigger. I watched myself step through it. Immediately, I felt an oppressive heat. In the moonlight, I could make out a rust-covered car idling noisily in a parking lot otherwise devoid of people. I stepped closer. Inside the car, I saw Mariam's fingers, young and smooth, gently nudging the car's air conditioner knob to full blast. This extra burden on a machine years past its peak caused the car to rattle even more, and the AC *thump-shuffle-whisper-thumped* as it worked to pump cool air into the car and refresh the young couple inside, lost in a fit of giggles at their luck to be in love in a car whose AC sounded like a poorly rehearsed percussionist on opening night. The shaking was so intense, it caused the whole car to clatter and jangle so much that they only half joked that the car might soon fall apart around them. First the wheels, then the side-view mirror, then the whole corroded door, exposing their intertwined bodies for everyone to see. *Wouldn't our parents be pleased?* Amal laughed, as he hugged Mariam tighter to him.

And once again, I knew. I knew they had met as undergraduates at UCLA while attending a college football game. As they got to talking, they discovered that both sets of their parents were from Lebanon, that neither of them really liked nor understood football, and that they both had dreamed of becoming doctors for as long as they could remember. They made love for the first time after the game and, to the delight of both sets of parents (who were concerned about the type of people their children might meet in America), were married three months after graduation. I knew how they struggled to put themselves through medical school and how their old, south-facing apartment got so hot in the summer that one night, as a joke at first, they calculated it would be cheaper and cooler to run the car's AC when they made love than try to cool themselves off with the old fans in their apartment. So, when their desire to touch each other could no longer be outweighed by the suffocating heat, they would run, hand in hand, and crawl into the back seat of their car, starting the engine and immediately cranking up the air. It was on such a night they conceived their one and only child. They lay for a long time after, bodies damp with sweat. When they grew tired, they were soothed to sleep by the lullaby of the car's old air conditioning unit.

This was the last year they were truly happy. Soon, the stress of raising a child and being in school became too much. During the day, they talked about the possibility of one of them going to school part-time or dropping out completely. But at night, once the baby was asleep and they had a few moments to relax, their passion for each other (and for medicine) was renewed. Though their lovemaking was no longer fast and ardent, it had taken on a slow, comfortable rhythm which allowed each to forget their exhaustion for a while, and it satisfied them both.

One night, after their minds and bodies were settling in for sleep, Amal took his wife's hand and said, "I've been thinking about this a lot. I promise, as soon as I get the first year of my internship under my belt, I'll make sure you go back to school to finish your degree. I won't let you not finish."

Then he kissed her lightly on the lips, rolled over, and fell asleep.

She wanted to shake him from his dreams and shout, *Why me? Why am I the one to drop out? Why can't it be you?*

But as the night wore on, she convinced herself it was the right thing to do. She was the woman: a wife, a mother. This was what wives and mothers did for their families. Wasn't it?

Since she could not bring herself to utter the words "I'm quitting" out loud, she simply stopped showing up for class. She screened incoming calls from concerned friends and fellow students, letting the machine pick up, and never bothered to call a single one back. After a while, the calls stopped.

In the second year of her husband's internship, things were even more hectic than before and money was tighter. They never found the right time for her to go back to school. But every day without fail he took her face in his hands and promised once he became a full-fledged doctor he would pay for her to continue school. He would not let her give up on her dream.

Several years later Amal made good on his promise. He bought her a new car, a new home, and hired the perfect nanny after months of searching so she would feel comfortable leaving their son at home while she studied. But when he asked for her opinion about one of his patients or tried to get her to talk about her professors or what she was learning, she kept her mouth pinched and tight. She had wanted to be a heart surgeon, but by the time she made it back to school, she was too old and too tired. She sat in the back of the room, acutely aware of the fine wrinkles spreading out from the corners of her eyes when she smiled (which was rare these days), and the first strands of grey hair she had noticed just the week before. She became preoccupied with all the kids in her class (faces smooth, hair grey-free). They all appeared to possess more energy than she could ever remember having. So she quit. She quit and pretended she was happy as a doctor's wife and the mother of a doctor's son.

Eventually, the envy that had been cooking in her heart for all those years came out as resentment: hot, crisp, and burnt around the edges. And though it scorched her mouth to do so, she swallowed a bit more every day until the jealousy and bitterness filled her completely, leaving no room for anything else. Though they remained married and though she knew Amal still loved her, she made no secret of how much she hated him. They finally lived in an expensive home where the temperature was perfect every day of the year, yet they no longer felt the need to touch each other at all.

But as all things must, Mariam's heart continued to evolve. She was absentmindedly loading the washing machine one day, when she caught the scent of her husband's cologne. She held his shirt to her face and inhaled deeply. It was then she realized her bitterness had taken on a new form; like a caterpillar emerging from a cocoon, her bitterness had morphed into the fragilely winged twins of loneliness and longing. The very next morning she applied for the job at my flower shop, to get out of the house a few days a week while her son was at school. On the days she wasn't working, she caught herself dreaming of having another child. And on those nights when she felt particularly alone (despite her husband awake and reading in the bed beside her, despite knowing her son was asleep in the next room), her mind would conjure up unbidden memories of the last night she and her husband were happy, the night they spent making love in their car; the night they conceived their child. She thought of the sound of an old air conditioner pumping cool air onto their bodies (*thump, shuffle, whisper*), and it reminded her of a husband and a wife she knew long ago, who were happy once, who were in love once, who were hopeful. Once.

So, one night, despite everything she believed she felt for her husband, she reached for him in the darkness and silently begged him to give her another child, to give her someone else to love. And as her hand touched his, for just a second I somehow felt the presence, the secret of another heart. For a moment, I saw what Amal saw, I felt what he felt. And in his heart beat three words—regret, longing, shame. Then everything went black.

§

Mariam had pulled her hand away. "I've got to get going," she said, nervously gathering up her belongings.

"Mariam, wait."

She waited.

"I know what it is to long for something to fill the empty spaces," I told her. "I had a miscarriage in college. I thought I would never recover. "

"I love my son," she said. "I do. I can't imagine life without him and I know having a child was our decision, but…I've never admitted this to anyone…I think of what life would have been like had he been born just a few years later. I'm a good mother. I know I am. But for a long time I resented Sammy for being born. But now I'm ready to have another baby. Am I terrible?"

"You're not terrible," I said. "Just human."

§

That evening on my drive home I thought about the emptiness Mariam felt. The emptiness we all must feel from time to time, and the sometimes desperate, tragic ways we go about trying to fill it. For me, after the loss of my first child (after the loss of so many things), I took to wandering the neighborhoods around the university, sometimes walking for hours; whether walking away from one thing or toward something else, I never could decide. After about my fiftieth turn past the *Oops, A Daisy! Flower Shop* with a "help wanted" sign hanging in the window, I decided to go in. I immediately felt at peace surrounded by the sweet scented lilies, the gaping yellow of the sunflowers, the twisted petals of roses waiting for just the right moment to reveal themselves.

Brinda hired me on the spot, and not long after I was left to manage the shop on my own. It felt nice to be alone—I guess I had become accustomed to it in many ways. It was soothing somehow not sharing the space with anyone, not having to make idle conversation with someone just to ward off the silence, as if it were lurking at every turn as sudden and irreversible as death. Even on the days when Brinda did come in, she remained in the storeroom for most of the time wandering among all the flowers, as if searching for something she had lost there years ago.

But no matter how much time I spent among the flowers, the moment I stepped outside the shop doors, I began to feel nervous. My hands would shake, my heart would quicken. At home, I couldn't eat but felt as if I were always about to burst open, as if I were filling up on emptiness. My heart felt flimsy—an old balloon inflated with stale and apathetic breath. I tried to think of ways to feel safe again, to feel whole again, to know what it was I wanted. The answer came on a Thursday, when a young boy entered the store and picked out a birthday card for his mother. He fished 79 cents from his pocket (carefully counting out loud) and placed the coins on the counter.

As I watched him leave the shop, proudly showing the card to his dad who had been waiting outside, I knew I wanted another child. With this knowledge, I felt an immediate and sweeping sense of relief. It was as if I had been holding my breath for all those years and was finally able to exhale. The only question then was how I would ever find someone to be the father.

CHAPTER 5

I BEGAN WHERE I BELIEVED a lot of other women begin: at a bar. I had never been to one but had seen my dorm-mates in college dressing for such occasions. One evening, I mimicked them as best as my wardrobe would allow. I approached the building with its large wooden door and neon lights. Even from outside, the thump of the music vibrated through my arms. As soon as I entered, I was sure I would disappear amidst the smoke and pumping music, the women in their high and low cut dresses, lipstick smudged at the corner of their mouths as if in anticipation of being kissed. I gripped the back of a bar stool in an attempt to keep myself from going adrift. I could already feel myself lifting off the floor, my legs slowly forgetting the feel of their own weight. A man dressed in a blue suit, with drink and cigarette in hand, glanced up at me and said, "Fuck, lady, are you tall!"

With those words, I fell backward and knocked into two women. Their glasses crashed, spraying sharp-scented liquid onto the wooden floor. I mumbled an apology and ran to the door. Outside I tried to catch my breath and was startled to find the man in the suit standing beside me.

"Hey, are you okay?"

I looked up at him. He had a dark moustache and long hair. His right hand appeared surprisingly smooth and well-manicured as it reached out toward me, stopping just short of touching me. I swallowed hard and turned away, catching sight of myself reflected in the bar window— my skinny frame, my thin wispy wrists, my hands long and slight as ferns. I wished at the moment to weigh 200 pounds. I wanted my flesh and my muscles, even my bones to expand, to give me some true weight. I have always believed there is safety in so much flesh. And there is beauty too. And power. Power to keep yourself planted on the earth—your own body anchoring you to life.

Turning away from my reflection, I was surprised to find the stranger still beside me.

I turned to him and said, "Do you want to come home with me?"

He smiled and gripped my hand.

"You seem a lot shorter," was all he said during the short walk home.

§

The night was nondescript. It was not love. This was my own brand of thievery. He asked the inevitable question about birth control, and I gave him the standard answer: *you don't need to worry.* Then I let him into me, and he came and went in just under half an hour. I couldn't wait for him to leave. When he did, I hugged my belly and wished for sleep to come. But it didn't. I got up and ambled to the bathroom. In the dim glow of the streetlights entering through the window, I could just make out the shape of my body reflected in the bathroom mirror. I flipped on the light and stared at my face, my hair, the ridges and shadows formed by my sharp and angular collarbones. I pressed my fingers to my nose, my cheeks, trying to imagine what my child might look like. Which characteristics would he inherit from me and which from this man I barely knew? Would he inherit my eyes and perhaps the man's hair or his nose (which, when I thought about it honestly, was a bit small, too feminine for a man)? Would he have my ears or his father's?

His father.

It was then I realized all I did not know about this man; all that could be passed on to my child—things I could not see. Had some disease coupled with his genes generations ago? Was some cancer, some mental illness already fated to be passed on to my child? Was this man prone to anger or to deep sadness? Did he beat his wife? Did he have a wife? Was he fearful? Dishonest? Most importantly, was he kind?

Had I, with my carelessness, already doomed my child to a life more difficult than it ought to be? When perhaps it was too late, I wondered—*how do I choose the father of my child when love is not involved*? If kindness could be passed on in genes, this is the trait I most wanted for my son. For I believe it is very easy to be a boy in this world but hard as hell to become a good man.

When my period finally came I wept with relief. I had been given the chance to do things right or as right as I could. I decided then and there—no more lies. I did not want my child conceived out of an untruth (like a crop planted under a bad moon or a mutated fish birthed into a polluted sea), for I feared this lie would cling to the furrows of his soul, un-shake-off-able, hovering always on the fringe of his life like a wasp, buzzing and always threatening to sting.

From then on I took my time with the others, got to know them—these potential fathers—and actually dated a few. But I never allowed myself to open my heart to any of them, even though most had been kind and beautiful in their own ways. I did not want to love them. I didn't know how. In my most hopeful moments, I convinced myself I had never really loved anybody only because I had never known anyone long enough to love them. I had been in and out of foster homes the first ten years of my life, spending a few weeks or a few months with a family before being sent back to the orphanage. The other kids, too, were rotated in and out just as quickly. I overheard someone describe us once as randomly shuffled records spinning in a dusty old jukebox, in a place where no one came for the music.

True, there had been Annelle, my foster person for seven years, but…no.

And then there had been the time, I was around twelve years old, when I vaguely remembered feeling a hint of what love must be, of feeling completely safe with another person. But then from one moment to the next, this person literally vanished (like subtle ash into murky waters) and I was never sure if he had been real, if he had ever really existed at all, or if I had simply imagined him into being.

But then…but then…at twenty years old I did feel love—a strong, overwhelming love for a person (a half person really, a tiny undeveloped thing with few distinguishable features but a functioning heart connected directly to mine). That baby, in its short life, taught me that I was gleefully and unequivocally able to love. And when I allowed myself to really think about it, what I was forced to finally admit was this: though deep down I knew I was capable of love, I still did not believe anyone could ever be capable of loving me in return. Except for a child.

A child does not set conditions on love. A child does not love only those mothers who are physically beautiful. A child does not love only those mothers capable of witty repartee and interesting party conversation or mothers whose legs are always shaved, whose hair is combed and styled, whose cuticles don't peel and bleed.

So I did not let myself love those men, and I would not let them try to love me because I was afraid. For it is one thing to believe you are unlovable, and another thing entirely to have it proven, beyond any doubt, to be true.

So I withheld my love, but gave them truth instead. I told them all exactly what I wanted (to have a baby) and exactly what I didn't (everything else). As you might have guessed, many walked away. But some did stay. And as they entered me, one by one, after HIV tests came back negative and condoms remained untouched on night stands, I waited for the moment when the possibility of love would no longer be something to fear.

CHAPTER 6

IN THE NEAR decade-and-a-half since graduating, I had not once gotten pregnant. But despite all those years of trying; despite all the visits to my doctor, who assured me my body was in working order; despite the false hope of a late period; despite the crushing disappointment when, a few days later, I felt the wetness of blood seeping into my underwear, I refused to give up.

The day I met my son's father was like any other. The sun lifted itself up on its golden haunches and settled itself gracefully into the sky. Clouds formed and parted as they moved across the same blue backdrop. Bodies stirred and began to rise in preparation for their day. Children went to school, and the employed went to work. Wars raged on; people fell in love. Traffic crept along; smog swallowed the city. Stores opened, people shopped, the homeless silently begged for change on street corners—their tattered cardboard signs sadly saying nothing you haven't read before.

§

It was a Friday evening. After leaving the store, I had planned on driving home as usual. But the Los Angeles blue sky had turned ashen grey, and heavy clouds had been unburdening themselves with a slight but steady rain for most of the afternoon. Despite having lived through enough rain showers and the occasional hail storm to know better, most Los Angeles drivers seem to expect interminable sunshine, as if they live in the Hollywood-movie version of their own town. They become slightly scandalized by any unscripted changes in the weather. Precipitation in any form triggers the onset of a mild case of panic among them, like cattle brought to a standstill by the menacing presence of a child's red rubber boot left behind accidentally after an innocent afternoon making mud pies. Thus, the normally horrendous traffic was much worse, so I decided to walk around the neighborhood and do some window-shopping while waiting for the highways to clear.

As I walked, night set in and lines of blinking brake lights illuminated shimmering wet cars all along Ventura Boulevard.

I walked three blocks.

The rain was light, and I was fine with my coat and hat. If it had stayed that way, I might have walked a bit more then turned back. As it was, the rain, almost a mist, became a drenching downpour without warning. I quickly ducked under the awning of the nearest building as two couples—just teenagers—exited. They were dressed in dark clothes, colorful tattoos, and earrings which hung from untraditional places. They walked arm in arm, laughing. As they disappeared into the oncoming darkness and their laughter faded into the sounds of L.A., I turned to look at the building from which they had come. The door was swinging slowly shut. I just had time enough to make out long lanes waxed to a brilliant shine, rows of white bowling pins, a gaggle of giggling teenagers, a few overweight men, and a group of women in bright yellow jerseys and faded high-waisted jeans.

I walked inside. The fluorescent lights, the constant rumble of balls tumbling down wooden alleys, pins having the balance knocked out of them, the familiar jukebox music, beer served in plastic cups, and everyone dressed in the same shoes (this last detail, somehow, brought me the most comfort) made me feel instantly as if I were right where I belonged.

I ordered a beer and watched.

§

I returned to the same bowling alley several nights a week, never playing, just observing. One group of three men was there every time. They were jolly with great bellowing laughter. They were silly like boys. I liked them immediately. After several weeks, they must have noticed me watching them.

"Come on and play with us if you want," one said. I picked up my beer and walked over.

"Thanks. I'm Penny."

A tall, solidly built black man gripped my hand and shook it firmly.

"I'm George," he said with a sideways grin, "retired army captain with a bum leg and twelve grandchildren who only seem to remember I'm alive on their birthdays and all major U.S. holidays."

"This is Al," he pointed to a balding reed-thin, red-haired man seated with legs up, plastic beer cup in hand.

"Al's an accountant who lives for bowling and Neil Young, but only during his Crazy Horse years. He is a perpetual bachelor—but would give it all up the minute any one or all three of The Pointer Sisters call and declare their undying love for him."

Al responded with a gentle nod, a smile, and a subtle wave of the wrist. "Pleasure, Penny." Then he added, "Don't worry, I am aware it's 1995. I'm only stuck in time musically and romantically."

Then, gently gripping the third man on the shoulders and turning him around to face me, George said, "This is Ernest. Ernest is still madly in love with his dead wife."

§

I began to bowl with them regularly. It was a full three weeks before I took Ernest home with me. He pressed his lips to mine, and I tasted traces of beer on his breath. Almost shyly, he licked the corner of my mouth and I smiled. We kept the lights off and as many of our clothes on as possible, as if in agreement that being totally naked was more intimacy than either of us could bear.

He placed his arms on my shoulders and ran them down the

small of my back. I felt relief and kinship in those arms. We moved to my bed. I sat down and pulled him on top of me. As he slipped off his underwear, I felt him only semi-erect against my thigh.

"Wait." I said. I hadn't yet told him why he was here, and for a moment, I wasn't entirely sure myself. Yes, I wanted a child, but there was more. His was such a deep sadness that, baby or no baby, I felt an almost overwhelming desire to relieve his hurt in the only way I knew how. I could have said nothing. I wanted to say nothing.

"I'm trying to get pregnant. I don't want any involvement from the father. Well just this part, of course, the part I can't do on my own." I laughed nervously.

He sat up then but did not leave. Instead, he stayed at my side, his hands resting in his lap. I told him about the miscarriage. I told him about the way I had imagined my child, how his toes would have been (long and sturdy) and how his skin would have smelled (clean like almonds). I told him I knew what I would have bought him for his first birthday—a map and a compass—though he would be too young to use them for many years. With these gifts, I explained, I would raise my son to be bold and free and unafraid. In other words, nothing like me.

In the stillness that followed, Ernest said, "I feel like I'm cheating on Anne. She is...*was* my wife."

"How did she die?"

"She...." he choked, and I thought he might cry.

"Sorry," I replied. No more questions. I did not want or need to know.

But Ernest must have misunderstood my "Sorry" as a "Sorry?" Or maybe he just felt he needed to explain. Perhaps he just wanted to talk about the woman he loved.

"My wife loved Christmas decorations. Her mother was a Jehovah's Witness which meant Anne was never allowed to celebrate any holiday: not the 4th of July, not Christmas, not even her birthday. But her dad...well, he was of no real religion really, but he loved his daughter. Every Christmas Eve he would pick her up, and they would drive for hours on end, in and out of neighborhoods, looking at all the decorations. After her father died, she kept up the tradition. One night a year beneath those lights, she told me she could believe her father was still alive. On our third date we wandered around the streets of Brentwood looking at Christmas decorations. You might not believe it, but it was one of the best dates I'd ever had in my life. We got married two months later, and every Christmas Eve after we prowled the streets looking at decorations. It got to be our thing."

We both laughed, lightly.

"Anne believed how a person chooses to decorate, or not, on any given holiday says a lot about who they are. She once told me," and here he chuckled, "a person's entire psychological profile could be summed up based on the exact number and type of decorations they put up each year. I guess you could say she was a bit obsessed with it all. It was one of the reasons I fell in love with her.

"Three years ago, we were on our way to one of our favorite neighborhoods. She had had a rough couple of years. We were trying to get pregnant, and we just kept losing the babies. We lost three in all before she woke up one morning and just gave up. I don't mean gave up on the idea of having children, but it seemed to me like she just gave up on life. When Christmas Eve rolled around, it was all I could manage to get her dressed and out of the house. I thought it might cheer her up."

He looked at me, and I nodded for him to go on.

"Anyway, we got to Beverly Hills and one of the first houses we saw, I swear, lit up half the street. Anne got so excited. It was the first time I had seen her that way in a long time. The house *was* amazing. Its entire frame was lined with white lights. The front yard was covered in fake snow, and it was so windy the snow was flying all over the place. It felt like we were in a giant snow globe or something. All around the yard were pine trees covered in red ribbons. Each tree was topped with a gold star; you know the kind that flicker, like a real star twinkles when you stare at it long enough? *It's breathtaking*, she said. I remember I joked with her. I said, *it looks like a landing strip for a UFO*. She smacked me lightly on the arm. That was the first time I had seen her smile in months."

He hesitated for a moment then. I squeezed his hand gently and waited for him to continue.

"Personally, I thought it was way too overdone. I mean, how did the neighbors sleep? It was like daylight 24 hours a day. Not to mention the electricity bills must have cost this guy more than I make in a year. But, as I said, Anne loved it. And I loved watching her. The most unusual thing—and this did catch my eye—was a life-sized Jesus strapped to the branches of one of the trees. He was made out of mirrored glass and his face was frosted on. I thought it was tacky. Anne was mesmerized and wanted to get closer. Despite her mother's best efforts, or maybe because of them, Anne was not a religious person. But she stood there just in awe of that Jesus. She walked onto the lawn and stood beneath it.

"I told her to come back to the sidewalk. People in L.A. aren't exactly friendly when they find strangers standing on their front lawns, even if it is Christmas Eve. But she wouldn't budge.

"I remember the wind blowing her hair so I couldn't see her face. The trees swayed, and Jesus rocked. And Anne just stood there. She never moved. Not even when Jesus, with those open arms, broke loose and fell straight toward her. I started to run to her, but I wasn't fast enough. I saw her raise her hands, trying to shield herself, but at the last minute, I swear she opened her arms, almost…almost as if she had wanted—no—as if she had willed it to fall. And then, as Jesus toppled from the sky, she took one step forward."

Ernest's voice cracked, tears and mucus ran in rivulets down his face. I handed him a box of tissues from the night stand. He wiped his eyes and his nose between deep and sobbing breaths.

"She didn't die right away. She couldn't talk, and she wouldn't look at me. She just stared at her reflection in the damn thing. She watched herself die. I tried to cover her eyes, to make her look away, but she wanted to see. To this day, I wonder—did she see her life flash before her eyes as they say, and if so, was it reflected in the glass, backwards and hard to read? Or was everything perfectly clear to her? This probably sounds crazy, but do you think it's possible pieces of her life went missing; were they contained somehow in that mirror? Were important memories trapped in the tiny slivers of glass all around her?

Ernest stopped and inhaled deeply. I thought he was finished, had said everything he wanted to say. But then he continued.

"You know, I still wait for her to come home every day. I know she is dead, but if she walked through my front door tomorrow I can't say I would be surprised. I expect it. I anticipate it. At night sometimes, well, our old house creaks. When I hear the creaking floorboards, sometimes I call out because I'm convinced it's Anne, bringing up the bowl of ice cream we used to share every night. I want to shout down to her to bring the chocolate syrup because tonight I'm in the mood for chocolate syrup, but then I remember. She is only a ghost haunting my heart.

"I know. I know. These are foolish sentiments from a middle-aged fool who believed the words *for better or worse 'til death do us part* guaranteed me my wife for more than eight years."

We sat for a while in silence. My hand groped for his in the dark.

Then he said, "I know what it is to lose someone you love. I can't bring my Anne back, but I want to help you...only I don't want to know either way. I don't want to ever know there is someone out there I could love that much again. I think it would kill me. Can you understand?"

"I do."

He climbed on top of me, and I felt his erection, hard and full—of sexual desire perhaps—but also of a desire for forgetting and maybe even for forgiveness.

He stayed with me for the rest of the night and left early the next morning, saying nothing, but kissing me sweetly on the forehead before leaving. I knew I would never see him again (though I would go looking for him years later). And my only hope for him was that one day he would empty his heart of ghosts and make way once again for the living.

§

Over the next few months, I thought about our night together often. And as the power of my son's heart grew stronger, I wondered what had been passed between Ernest and me. I wondered what is really passed between any two people in the instant when two bodies collide—whether out of love or desire, beauty or rage, violence or apathy. What do we keep? What do we give away? What is passed from body to body, from cell to cell, from one essence to another? And if a child is created, what then? What elements, what pieces had come together to form my child's heart? Besides the obvious (seeds and eggs, our own private chromosomes and double-helixed DNA), was it possible for our injured hearts to manifest themselves in our son too? Did he inherit from us a heart literally broken and yet still capable of the extraordinary?

CHAPTER 7

I WAS SIX MONTHS INTO MY PREGNANCY when people I had barely known, who in my mind were unknowable, began giving their stories away to me. People I had lived next door to for years, who had only said *hello* or *how are you* as we crossed paths, people whose names I knew and not much else, suddenly somehow were pulled to me. It was as if the beating of my son's heart drew them in, just as migrating birds are drawn by instinct or by desire to the one place they need to be, the one place their bodies are driving them to go. But these people were pulled, not by the desire to mate or find food, but by something as key to their survival: they were pulled by the need to finally tell their secrets, to free them, to let them grow wings and fly.

And something changed inside me, too. Before, most of the stories, for me, had been fleeting—mere glimpses of one moment in a lifetime of moments. But now, I began to feel linked instantaneously to these people, and they to me. We felt so strongly connected, it was as if their lives became mine and my life became theirs. And over the years we would defend each other's happiness as fiercely as we defended our own.

I really met Peter for the first time on a Friday, as I was coming home from work. He and his cat, Puppet, had lived in the apartment directly above mine for the past three years. Occasionally Peter and I greeted each other coming or going. And in the evenings after work when things were silent outside, I would rest my eyes and listen to the low rumble of his footsteps as he paced back and forth above me for hours. I believed he had walked far enough to span entire continents without ever having left the four small rooms of his apartment.

I knew he was 24 and worked a couple of nights a week cleaning office buildings. I knew Peter took Puppet outside every afternoon for a dose of fresh air, which consisted of Peter leashing the cat up and placing him squarely in the center of the oak tree growing from a patch of grass just outside my window. There, Peter allowed the cat to climb, but not too high, for fear he might fall and break a leg, or worse.

"You know, Peter," I told him that day, "cats are known for their ability to climb and fall. I think he'll be fine if you let him move a little. You have him on a leash. He can't go anywhere. It'll be okay."

Peter, slightly pot-bellied, crinkled his nose and his freckles bunched together, "Cats always land on their feet."

"That's true," I agreed.

After a few minutes Peter scooped Puppet gently into his arms.

"That's enough for today," he whispered into the cat's ear as they made their way up the stairs. When he reached his door, he turned to me and asked (as if we were old friends), "Would you like to see my pictures?"

Growing up, Peter had lived for adventure. He was raised on surfing, rock climbing, dirt bike racing. His parents were wealthy and encouraged his interests. They bought him skateboards and skis and skydiving lessons for his 15th birthday. Though they were not close in a traditional sense, they bonded over travel and adventure. He and his parents took a trip every year to some place exotic. By the time Peter had hit his teens, he had been to every continent of the world. When I set foot into his apartment I was drawn to the pictures on his wall—images of him posing atop the Great Wall of China, climbing Mayan ruins in Guatemala, snow-shoeing in the Alps, and sailing in the Caribbean. But the ones I found most captivating were the pictures of Antarctica and its stark whiteness so bright it burned my eyes just to imagine being there. I wondered out loud, "What was it like? What were they all like?"

Peter looked at me with such sadness then and said, "I can't really say."

He explained to me that he remembered the moments themselves: the long boat rides, the hikes, the views, the sequence of events, the people he encountered. Yet, he could not recall the pounding in his chest when he took his first step into nothingness; when his left foot, followed immediately by his right, lifted off the edge of the plane and stepped into air; the wind suddenly rushing up to meet him, pressing his face into a permanent grin. He could not remember the feel of his feet locked into skis as he let gravity carry him through blinding snow. It was as if he had watched all of those moments on TV or read about them in a book but never really experienced them for himself.

In his "old life," as he called it, he had wanted to be an architect. He had once admired words like *angle iron* and *apse, joist* and *scuttle*. Now, towering Ionic columns and buildings jutting out at odd angles against the sky frightened him and made him long for the neat, square walls of his small apartment. As a teenager, he used to take apart car engines and radios and then put them back together again just for fun. But now, even the wires connecting the speakers to his stereo caused him to have nightmares of twisting eels that devoured his brain.

He knew all the information had once been there, tucked neatly into the folds of his mind, but now it was gone—lost—and he preferred not to think of it at all. His only reminders were the pictures which his parents insisted he keep on the wall, as if they were trying to say *this is our son, here in these photos, the one with the charming eyes, quick wit and strong body*. And when they visited him in the apartment they paid for (they had wanted him to live somewhere fancier, more expensive, but Peter insisted on living here. He was tired of fancy, tired of expensive, tired of pretending those things still mattered), they spent more time visiting with the photos—recalling each moment, each adventure—than they did getting to know the new person before them, the person who, in some other life, had been their son.

§

I stared for a long time at those photos—at Peter as a much younger man (made older by loss and not so much by years)—a different person than the one who stood beside me. He leaned in closer to point out the raw and sullen beauty of the Atacama Desert, and his arm softly grazed my own. Neither of us moved.

Again: the darkness, the pinhole of light, and three quickening hearts. I saw a bone-shaped dog tag banging against a red leather collar, *thump*, and falling again, *whisper*, and banging again, *thump*, and a dog's heavy panting, *shuffle, shuffle*, in between. I saw Peter taking his dog Quinn, a large mixed breed, for a jog in Griffith Park. Peter held the leash lightly in his hand, their six feet tramping the dirt as they strode in and out of shadows cast by verdant trees. I stood there, too, my feet in the reddish dirt, the sound of dry leaves twisting among themselves in the wind.

And again, I knew. I knew the physical thrill Peter felt as his blood pumped and his sweat dripped. I saw the tiny indentations in the dirt as droplets of his perspiration hit the ground. I knew in a few hours, he was supposed to go on his first date with a girl he had been dreaming about for months, and yet he wasn't feeling the least bit nervous. I also knew Quinn. I knew him to be a dog of high intelligence and amazing obedience skills, both of which were quickly forgotten at the first sight of any small furry mammal. On this day, I watched as two particularly annoying squirrels ran across the road in front of man and dog, with their tauntingly twitching tails and incessant chattering. It was as if they knew Quinn was on a leash and couldn't get to them. But Peter had not been paying attention. He had been thinking about the girl—Sophie was her name. So when Quinn suddenly pulled too hard, the leash slipped with one jerk out of Peter's hand. Quinn took off in a long and powerful lope. Ignoring Peter's calls, he went barking and bounding after the rodents, the leash trailing behind him, flipping and darting like a hooked fish. Peter, aware of the acute deafness Quinn seemed to acquire in the presence of small, annoying animals, took up chase.

"Quinn!" he shouted as he ran after dog and squirrels. "Quinn, get back here!"

"You should keep your dog on a leash" someone yelled as he ran past, "there are leash laws, you know."

Ignoring this, Peter rushed on. Rattlesnakes were prevalent in this area, and as a puppy, Quinn had been bitten but had miraculously survived. Peter wasn't sure they would get so lucky if it happened again. Adding to Peter's worry, Quinn was now running down the trail, and if he kept going it would lead him right onto Los Feliz Boulevard where traffic could be hectic. He had seen enough smashed squirrels in the area to know they didn't have enough sense to stay out of the road, and Quinn wouldn't be any better.

He would chase a squirrel through a burning building if given half the chance, Peter thought. *I should have held onto his leash tighter! Shit!*

Peter picked up his pace when he could no longer hear Quinn barking. He thought he heard a horn blaring and the sound of squealing tires. He imagined Quinn hurt and bleeding beneath the wheel of some asshole's black Corvette and ran faster.

I watched his muscled legs spinning across the dirt, his breath coming in heavy gasps. I saw it before Peter did—a large root twisting up out of the dirt (not an inconsequential thing really, a root; a thing meant for the uptake of water and the anchoring of stems). Peter's right foot hit the root, and the toe of his shoe caught but only for a second, only for a split second (less time than it takes to even say *split second*). But it was long enough to throw him off balance. He fell and somersaulted through the shrubs lining the trail, gravity forcing him down and off the edge of a small ledge. His body hit the ground with such force the air was knocked out of him. He lay there, unable to move. Twenty-three minutes later Quinn returned, unscathed. He sat at Peter's side, his lips curved into a smile only dogs can muster—drool pooling at the edge of his gum lines. Peter remained in the ravine for a long time. His left leg was broken in several places. He had fractured two ribs and cracked his wrist. All which would have been nothing but a good story to share with his friends over a six-pack, if it hadn't been for the perfectly placed stone at the bottom of the ravine. Peter hit his head at just the right angle and with just the right force to cause just enough brain damage to render him incapable of many of the things he did in his past life. He would say later he had lived 20 years without an accident, as if it were all being saved up for that one day.

Hikers found him just before nightfall, thanks to Quinn's incessant barking. Peter's outward injuries healed (though he still walks with a slight limp), but his mind, the person he used to be, never fully recovered.

My brain limps too, he used to say, *and they don't make crutches for that.*

He remained in the hospital for four weeks—metal rods and screws holding his bones together. His parents stayed with him the whole time. They spoke to him of ordinary things, refusing to acknowledge anything at all had changed. They spoke of their next family vacation (perhaps water skiing in Tahoe); they wondered aloud when he was going to ask Sophie for another date (*she would be the luckiest girl in the world*), but when they tried to speak to him about Quinn, he only grew angry.

"I don't want to see Quinn!" he shouted at them.

"Baby, Quinn's not here. But he misses you. He's waiting for you at home."

"I don't want to see him. I don't want to see Quinn," he said over and over, his body convulsing with each sob.

And here, unexpectedly, like a knock at the door or a hiccup, or the incandescent body of a butterfly settling onto your shoulder, I saw the other hearts, the ones needed to complete the tale, the ones necessary to bind the ties. I expected Peter to pull away, like Mariam did at the sudden and unexpected appearance of Amal's heart in her story. But Peter did not shy away. He let his parents' hearts remain. He (we) listened to what they had to say.

It was the sight of their grown son crying (they couldn't remember the last time they had seen him cry, but he had surely been just a child then, only four, maybe five) that brought them into this tale. His mother (a heart full of weeds) felt as if she were suddenly being held underwater by a great force; to his father (and his feckless heart) it felt more as if someone had thrust a knife into his chest and pulled out his beating heart. But the realization was identical: their son had changed, both in body and in mind, and he would never be the same again. For the first time, they both understood this simple fact, though neither was ready to accept it as truth.

And now, they would have to find someone to take care of Quinn until Peter was ready to see him again. It broke their hearts even further to get rid of the dog—their son's best friend since he had been 17. They had given Quinn, just a puppy then, to Peter as an early high school graduation gift—back when they had such big dreams for their only child; when they were sure he would find fame, fortune, happiness, and adventure; when he was still the son they had wanted to have. Giving the dog away meant, somehow, giving up on the idea that Peter would ever be Peter again. Though it took some convincing (it wasn't easy to find someone willing to care for a dog as large and energetic as Quinn), Peter's father managed to get his business partner, Jim, to take care of Quinn "just until Peter is ready to take him back."

The day before Peter was to come home from the hospital, his parents piled Quinn, his water bowl, and his favorite toy into the car and drove him to Jim's place. They both knew what this meant, though neither would admit it—not even to themselves. Instead, they assured each other they had done the right thing. They were sure that Quinn and Peter would be reunited again, within a week or two. Three at most, they decided.

"Peter won't be able to stand it without Quinn; he'll want to get out and start running with him again as soon as he can," his father said.

"Oh, yes. Yes. I'm sure of it," his mother replied, absentmindedly fingering the gold pendant she wore around her neck as she stared, unseeing, out the car window. "I'm sure of it."

§

When Peter arrived at his parents' house he hobbled straight to his old room. His parents had kept it exactly as it had been on the day he left for college. While he was in the hospital, they brought everything from his old apartment just off the UCLA campus in Westwood—his car, his bike, his clothes, his cell phone, his stereo— to their house in Crescent Heights.

"It's all here for you, Son," they told him, "whenever you want to go through it."

But Peter didn't respond. He spent the better part of the time in his room. He barely ate. He did not speak. He sat by himself, asking the same questions over and over *"Why didn't Quinn listen? Why didn't I hold the leash tighter? Why didn't I wait for him to come back to me instead of chasing after him like an idiot? Why... why...?"*

But one day, months after his cast had come off, his parents awoke to find him rummaging through his things in the garage with all his old buddies.

"I called the guys over," he said when his parents found them there.

"That's great. That's great," they said in unison and disappeared back into the house.

Peter gathered all his outdoor gear (boards of all kinds: snowboards, skateboards, surfboards, plus skis and poles and helmets and knee pads) and gave it away to "the guys," people he once knew as friends, but who he unequivocally understood would stop calling him as soon as an acceptable amount of time and enough *sorry mans* and *don't worry, nothing's gonna change, we're still best buds* had been said.

When the remnants of his old life (of his old self) had been given away—handed over to young men still sound of body and mind, Peter marched (as best he could with his damn limp that months of physical therapy could not get rid of) into the kitchen and said, "Ok. I'm ready to see Quinn now."

"We'll go get him now. Right now." His dad quickly threw a coat over his pajamas and grabbed the keys to the car.

During the entire drive back from retrieving Quinn, his father could not stop smiling. As he watched his son, his beautiful boy, laughing in the back seat with his arms around his dog, he couldn't help but wonder, *could it be? Could it really be? Was there hope Peter would once again be normal* (and here he shuddered inwardly, his smile twitching slightly at this word: *normal*)?

§

In the days that followed, Peter was anxious to go running again with Quinn.

"Just take it slow, Son," his dad cautioned. "There's no rush."

But Peter wouldn't listen. He didn't want to take things *slow*; everything around him seemed to happen too slowly, as if his brain were mired in quicksand struggling to get out.

The first day Peter went hiking with Quinn, he picked an easy trail which sloped gently into the hills. But Quinn wasn't used to taking it easy and pulled and strained at his leash. Peter, frustrated and still in a bit of pain, turned around after only ten minutes.

"That's okay, Son," his dad said when Peter returned to the car where his father was patiently waiting. "We'll do better tomorrow."

But, despite their efforts, they were never able to do any better. Tomorrow and the next day and the day after that were proportionately more frustrating: Quinn was simply accumulating days of pent-up energy, while Peter gained sore muscles and a heavy dose of resentment. But Peter would not give up just yet. On their final walk together they had just passed a short trail heading first around the manicured lawns of a picnic area (where families dined on chicken and warm potato salad, where couples kissed on wrinkled, grass-stained blankets, and children—celebrating someone's birthday—took turns beating a pony piñata with the hopes of exposing its candied guts). They headed to a slow rise up into the hills. Quinn did fine, at first. But on the way back, with a small down slope before him and his senses on full alert, Quinn insisted on running. He pulled as hard as he ran, literally dragging Peter behind him, causing Peter to fall.

Embarrassed and angry at his own weakness, Peter stood up as soon as he gained his footing again.

"Stop Quinn! Just fucking stop!" He yanked the leash back hard.

Quinn startled for second, but, as dogs are wont to do, he didn't dwell too long in what had already passed. A moment later, he wagged his tail, barked joyfully and began to pull with equal force.

Peter yanked again, this time jerking Quinn up off his front paws. He held the leash up close to the collar, Quinn's weight barely resting on his back legs.

"I fucking told you to stop!" Peter screamed as he shook Quinn. "Why don't you ever listen you stupid fucking dog!"

And to his surprise (and perhaps equally to Quinn's) Peter lifted his foot and kicked Quinn. "Why the fuck didn't you stop?" he shouted over and over, releasing his grip on the leash, his fists now pounding into the soft flesh of his best friend. Quinn whimpered and cowered, his tail tucked between his legs. A small stream of urine stained the soil.

Suddenly, Peter stopped. He dropped to the ground shaking.

"Just go! Get the fuck out of here!" he screamed. But Quinn did not run away. Instead he crawled expectantly into Peter's arms, licking his face and whimpering slightly. Peter wrapped his arms around his dog and wept. "I'm so sorry, I'm so sorry. It's not your fault, Quinn. It's not your fault."

They sat there together on the trail for hours, until Peter's father became worried and hiked out to find them.

On the way home Peter said, "We need to send Quinn back. I don't belong to him anymore."

§

When Peter and his father dropped Quinn back off at Jim's house, Peter held Quinn's face in his hands and promised, "I *will* come back for you. One day, I'll be ready. Knowing you're here waiting is going to help me get better. I just know it."

Then he reached down and began to unfasten the dog's collar, trying to remove the small, bone-shaped tag with the name QUINN engraved in tall letters and Peter's name and cell phone number etched below.

Jim turned to Peter and said, "You leave that on Quinn, now. He's your dog. We're just holding on to him for a little while. "

Peter smiled up at Jim, hugged Quinn one more time, and hobbled back to his father's car, whispering softly to himself, "You can do this, you can do this," over and over.

CHAPTER 8

SHORTLY AFTER BEFRIENDING Peter, I met Joe. I was walking from my car to my apartment with armloads of groceries. Joe, with his dark hair, almond eyes, smooth skin, and high cheek bones typical of many of Native American descent, was sitting inside a classic convertible Buick. His head was leaning back, left arm hanging out the window, eyes closed while the vibrant melancholy of Pink Floyd piped from the radio. It swirled across the parking lot, and I felt it might carry me away, like a pile of leaves in a windstorm.

As I passed his car he opened his eyes and smiled. Then, seeing me struggle with the weight of the shopping bags, he quickly lunged up and over the door and landed squarely on the asphalt.

"Let me help you with those," he smiled and gently lifted the bags from my arms.

"And who do we have here?" he asked glancing down at my swollen midsection.

I patted my stomach gently. "This is August."

It was the first time I had said my son's name out loud to anyone but myself.

He bent down, placing his eyes at belly level and said, "It's nice to meet you, August. I'm Joe."

At my door, he set the bags down.

"This is where I leave you…um…" he said expectantly.

"Penny," I replied.

"This is where I leave you, Penny. I'm Joe. You can find me in apartment number eight or the third parking space from the left. If you ever need anything."

I met Alice, his girlfriend of 14 years, several weeks later when we ran into each other again in the parking lot. I was going to work, and they were just coming back from somewhere, walking hand in hand.

"We've been together since we were nine years old," Joe declared proudly. And, though I felt jealous—possessive of something which was not mine to begin with—the feeling was merely fleeting.

I continued to run into Joe almost always when he was in his parked car, music swimming out from the speakers. But for all the times he sat in his car, I never actually saw him drive anywhere.

At first I suspected he didn't know how to drive yet and was sitting in the car imagining the day when he could feel the wind blowing through his hair, the sun at his back, the open roads of America intersecting with his life at last. However, my theory was blown when I saw him several weeks later pulling deftly (but illegally, I would later discover) out of the parking space and easing his car into L.A. traffic, clearly comfortable behind the wheel. I wondered if perhaps he and Alice couldn't afford a stereo, and the car was the only place where he could listen to music. But I ruled this out the first time I was invited to their apartment for lunch and saw the compact stereo in the living room.

One weekend afternoon, while having iced tea with Alice, I blurted out the question. Perhaps my curiosity got the best of me, or maybe my pregnancy made me restless and bold.

"Alice, why does Joe sit in his car all the time, without going anywhere?"

"He hasn't told you?"

"No. And I've been too shy to ask."

Without hesitation Alice replied, "I have sex for money, Penny."

I was momentarily startled into silence.

"So Joe...?" I started to say.

"Joe loves me," she said. "I don't mean it like it sounds, like I treat him like shit and he loves me anyway. It's not like that. This is just a job. He can't be here when it happens, obviously, but he refuses to leave the apartment complex. In case something...in case I need him."

She took a long sip of her tea.

"Follow me," she said grabbing our glasses.

I followed.

She stopped at a small room in the back of the apartment. She opened the door. On the back wall hung a portrait of Alice. In it, she was naked, lying on the floor, her back to us, her head defiantly turned upward.

"Joe painted it, didn't he?" I asked and imagined him with his dark hair falling in front of his eyes, paint smudges forming along his cheeks as he wiped the sweat from his face with the back of his hand. I could picture Alice, too, her young body and confident smile, the trust they must feel for each other emanating from their skin.

"It's beautiful isn't it? But it isn't what I wanted to show you. Look out the window."

She gestured toward it with her hand, the ice clinking against the glasses. She passed my glass to me, and our fingers touched momentarily. I had a brief flash (sacrifice) before she moved away. I pulled back the curtain and looked straight into the empty parking lot, the third space from the left, where Joe always parked his car. It was filled with bright orange cones to prevent others from taking his spot.

"He arranged it with the manager to always park in the same place. When I work, he sits out there. He keeps his music loud enough, but not too loud. From there, he could hear me scream if a client got rough. That's why Joe sits in his car all the time."

I felt ashamed for wondering if Alice washed the sheets each time, and if she and Joe made love together in the same bed she used for work.

As if she could read my mind, she told me, "I know it's a hard thing to understand. Believe me. But it's a job, that's all. I have sex for money. Joe, when he can find the work, installs wall-to-wall. He lays carpet. I lay strange men. It's our joke. We joke about it." She smiled and let out a slight laugh.

"Look, I don't do anything without a condom, and I get myself tested every three months like clockwork. It started with one guy. Now I have about a dozen steady clients. I hung the painting there because it reminds me of Joe. I keep the door to this room shut whenever he is home. We sleep in there," she said and pointed to another room just off the first.

"Joe and I met when we were nine. He told you, right?"

I nodded.

"But he didn't tell you how we met? It was a few days after my ninth birthday. I was in the hospital for my own shit. Joe was there because his dad beat him so badly he nearly died. We spent as much time as we could together while we were both in the hospital. It was like nothing else mattered. We just felt protected when we were with each other. After I got back home, we sent letters to each other every week. I've saved every one of them. They fill two dresser drawers.

"I had no idea..."

"How could you know? Don't worry," she assured me, before continuing on with her story.

"Joe was just a little kid when his older sister died. Drowned. That was when his dad started hitting him. About a year after his sister's death, Joe overheard his mom one evening on the phone. He didn't know who she was talking to, but she said, *I swear it's like he wants to kill Joseph now, before God does, as if to get through all the pain of losing both children at once.*"

"My God. Poor Joe."

"We both knew he had to get out of there, or he wouldn't survive. When we turned thirteen we decided to run away together.

Since Joe had been in and out of hospitals for most of his childhood, he never learned to read. He still can't. We were just two kids on our own. We were scared, tired, and hungry, and no one would hire us to do anything. We needed the money. The opportunity presented itself, and I took it. It seems like such a long time ago. The truth is I know Joe wants me to quit. Hell, I want to quit. But I'm terrified I'm not qualified to do anything else. Anyway, it was something I did to keep us together. It's not pretty, but this is us. And through it all, we have each other. "

"Alice, I don't know what to say."

"Don't worry. You don't have to say anything, "she smiled. "You know, when I told my mom I was running away with Joe she didn't try to stop me. I guess she knew she couldn't. But she warned me it would be hard. *How will you live? Where will you live? How will you eat?* she asked.

"I was so proud of my answer. I told her, *It doesn't matter. We love each other!* And my mother got this look on her face I had never seen before. Not even after my dad died. She looked, literally, as if all the life had just been taken out of her. I will never forget it. She hugged me and said, *You know, love isn't always enough.*

"The truth is she's right, Penny. Love isn't always enough. But sometimes, just sometimes, it is."

I stared at Alice, unsure of what to say, unsure of what I should feel.

"Do you want to see some of the letters?" She quickly got up and disappeared down the hall. A few minutes later, she came back with a stack of envelopes cradled in her arms. She opened one, unfolded the paper inside and handed it to me.

My eyes scanned the page, and my breath caught. "This is exquisite," I said. The "letter" wasn't comprised of words at all. Instead, the page was covered in a collage of drawings, pictures cut from magazines, a dried leaf, a yellow feather.

"Like I said, Joe can't read so well. So these are our letters. We talked on the phone whenever we could, but from the time we were nine years old, this was how we communicated with each other."

I stared at the pages for a long time, absorbing what they meant: the love, the trust between two kids that had endured for all these years. I knew right away I wanted to do something to help my friends. Only two things occurred to me.

"Alice, if you ever want a job at the flower shop, it's yours."

Alice grabbed my hand. "Thank you, Penny. Thanks."

And then I blurted out, "I'd also like to teach Joe to read." I immediately felt embarrassed at my boldness.

"Joe likes you a lot, Penny. He's ashamed he can't read. I've tried to teach him, but he resists it when it comes from me. He trusts you. I think he would be really pleased to learn from you."

A few days later Joe and I began his lessons. While Alice worked, he and I sat together in his car, pouring over the children's books I had gathered from the library. At the end of one of our lessons, Joe said, "So Alice told you everything."

"Yeah."

"Everyone thinks I'm stupid for loving her."

"I don't think loving someone is ever stupid," I replied.

"Did she tell you? She saved my life."

He placed his hand lightly on mine.

Immediately, I felt the tingling at the base of my skull and the now familiar sensation of everything around me, of time itself, slowing down. Only the sound of three quickening hearts remained.

CHAPTER 9

FROM THE DARKNESS, A SMALL PINHOLE OF LIGHT. Through the light, I saw a pair of knitting needles moving furiously in polished hands. Metal clashed against metal (*thump*), and then I clearly heard the shifting of the yarn as it was looped over a long silver needle (*shuffle*). Then, the needle gently pulling the yarn through (*whisper*). Metal against metal, looped yarn, needle pushed out and lifted; metal against metal, looped yarn, needle pushed out and lifted—over and over in a continuous motion. The *thump-shuffle-whisper-thump* of my son's heart echoed in the sound of the purl stitch executed by the capable hands of Joe's mother.

The pinhole grew, until I was once again surrounded by light. When I looked around the room, I saw them all. I saw them all and I knew them all. I somehow knew all the hearts in this story, all the hearts connected to this event, all the hearts changed by what was to come. I saw Joe's mother knitting on the couch, while Joe and his sister were splayed out on the floor, reading. A fire burned in the fireplace. It had been a cold winter, and I felt the chill raising the hairs on my arms. That morning, Joe's father had gotten up early to catch the morning light against the snow. He made a decent living selling his stark black and white photographs of people, animals, and leafless trees with branches outstretched like the hands of fallen angels reaching for one last grasp at heaven.

As with all the others, I knew. I knew Joe and his sister were anxiously waiting for their father to return. I knew that to Joe, his dad's job was a mystery. Joe didn't understand how his father could go out into the world, the same exact world Joe lived in, and come back with pictures so beautiful they didn't seem to belong to this ordinary place in which the rest of us existed. Joe had seen some of the people and objects (a rusted car with a bird nest inside, a collapsing barn in a field of flowers) his father had photographed over the years, but they always looked plain and regular when they weren't frozen inside a frame on a sheet of glossy paper. Joe wanted to learn the secret of taking ordinary things and making them seem otherworldly. Though he wouldn't admit it to his sister, Joe secretly hoped it was magic.

Kelly, on the other hand, was merely bored stuck inside the house with her baby brother. They exchanged a look, a mere glimpse, and each knew what the other was thinking. They were going to make a break for it. They knew their mom, who lost all track of time when she was knitting—distracted by what she perceived as her own personal art—would not notice their absence for at least a good ten minutes. So they nonchalantly crept from the living room into their bedrooms to get ready before sneaking out the back door.

To prepare for the day's adventure, Joe put on his down coat, gloves, and a cap and scarf his mom had knitted for him last Christmas. Kelly, apart from her warm clothes, packed a backpack full of snacks, a sketch pad, some colored pencils, her favorite book on art given to her by their father for her birthday one year, and a tiny makeup case containing a small mirror, some blush, and lipstick.

"That looks heavy," Joe said eyeing his sister's backpack. "Why do you have to carry all this stuff anyway?"

"If I'm going to be an artist one day," she said, picking up the bag and threading her arms through each strap, "I definitely need to carry my art supplies with me at all times. What if we run into a herd of deer just begging to be sketched? What kind of artist will I be if I let a chance like that slip by?"

"And the book?"

"I might need to look for tips on how to perfect my shading. If the deer are moving, I won't have much time to capture them and I want to get it just right."

"And the makeup?"

"There are other cabins across the lake. You never know what cute boys might show up to watch me sketch my very first master-piece."

"Oh brother…"

Once outside, they followed their father's footsteps through the snow. They walked for about 20 minutes before they found him. He was standing in the middle of a frozen lake, sure-footed atop the slippery surface. He had such a bold, confident way about him it seemed no earthly forces applied to him. Joe's grandparents even used to brag, *our son must have a pact with God Himself. He has never been sick a day in his life.*

And it was true. He grew up on the Chumash reservation in southern California and had a childhood typical of anyone who grows up with nature as a playmate. He climbed trees; tracked roadrunners along dusty paths; played war games with his friends among the boulders; and trapped lizards, toads, and even once a rattlesnake to keep as pets (all of which his mother made him set free the instant she discovered their presence in her home). The days of his youth passed without even the minor but common problems his classmates seemed to face: a few missed days of school due to a bad cold; an arm fractured from falling out of a weak-limbed tree; the normal scrapes and bruises of childhood games. When he gradu-ated from high school, he left the reservation and decided to test his luck in the larger world. He met a beautiful woman, got mar-ried, moved up north, and had two wonderful children. It seemed that every single day of his life had been perfect. Now, when he thought about his parents' words he conceded that maybe they had a point; for as an adult, he believed he could walk across this ice with a hundred men at his side and he alone would not stumble, he alone would not fall. He stood without fear or doubt. And whether he really did have a pact with God or not (and who can say for sure), one thing is certain. God chose that day to reveal just how much one person can lose in a single day. Whether God reneged on a deal or no pact had existed in the first place, it didn't really matter. The result was the same.

§

As Joe watched his dad, he took in the colors and the morning light illuminating the ice and snow. He tried to memorize exactly how it looked, so he could compare it later with his father's photographs.

Their father, meanwhile, didn't notice them at all. His back was to them. He was leaning into his camera mounted onto a tripod, focusing on the dark shapes moving across the snow.

Kelly inhaled and exhaled rapidly, letting out a low *ooooh* sound.

"See," she whispered, "what did I tell you?"

Joe turned and saw three bucks walking on the other side of the lake, occasionally stopping to look around and sniff the air. Though it was the middle of winter, these three deer had not yet shed their antlers, and they looked magical, with their dark fur, warm and rich, contrasting with the white snow.

"I'm going to sketch those deer. You wait here."

"Dad's going to kill us if he finds us!"

"Then be quiet. He won't even notice us if you keep your mouth shut."

Kelly walked gingerly onto the ice, holding her arms out at her sides for balance, catching herself as her feet threatened to slip out from under her.

Joe—never one to pass up an adventure—trailed behind her. He loved the feel of his feet slipping and sliding on the ice as he tried to keep up.

When they were quite a ways out, but still a good distance behind their father, Joe heard a strange sound—a loud drawn out

snap, like a cowboy cracking his whip but in slow motion and re-
versed. He continued to move forward. He didn't notice that Kelly
was standing perfectly still, as frozen as the ice around her. She held
her arms out like a tightrope walker trying to keep her balance. Her
eyes swelled with tears. Joe noticed none of this until he bumped
right into her.

"Don't...move..." she whispered softly. Joe could barely hear
her.

Right then, their dad turned and saw his children on the lake.
He yelled, "Don't move! The ice is cracking."

He took two hesitant steps (a father's heart, a protector's heart
but a coddled heart all the same. A heart unsure of its place in tragedy). His arms stretched out to them, when first Kelly then Joe disappeared into the deep icy lake.

Beneath the water, Joe felt as if a force was holding him under
and poking tiny needles into his body, his chest, his eyes. Water
seeped into his clothes, and he felt heavy, unable to move. But before he could understand what had happened, he felt a firm tug on
the back of his jacket and then felt himself rising from the water. Air
entered his lungs, and he gasped—painfully at first and then with
relief. He felt the warmth of his mother's arms as she hugged him,
briefly, tightly, before she began peeling off his clothes just as deftly
as he had seen her, dozens of times, peel the skin from raw, dead
chickens. When he was naked, she wrapped him in her down coat
and set him on the ice. Then she plunged her hands into the water
again, screaming out her daughter's name.

She had noticed he and Kelly were not in the house only minutes after they had left. She knew just where they were headed, and
she also knew their father would not be pleased. She quickly bundled up and headed out into the deep snow, thinking about how
she would punish them, well, in her way anyway. A half hour of ab-
solute silence (no talking, no playing, definitely no music) was their
usual punishment, which was as strict as she could be with these

two children who brought her more happiness than she believed was possible. She knew what would happen though. During the 30 minute silence, Joseph and Kelly would make strange faces at each other trying to get the other one to laugh. And she, their mother, would have to try to hide her own smile behind her knitting or the latest fashion magazine.

As she walked, she decided she would make some hot chocolate with marshmallows for them, well, after the 30 minutes had passed of course; maybe then they could bake some cookies and have them ready for their father when he got back from work. As she approached the lake, she was running the list of ingredients in her head, mentally checking to see if she had everything they would need for a big batch of oatmeal raisin cookies. She was just contemplating whether to add cinnamon or pecans when she heard her husband's shouts. She looked up to see a big dark hole in the ice where her children had been just a moment before.

And so she ran, sliding, falling, rising again, until she reached that dark place which held all her secret fears. Fears so strong that some nights she dared not sleep. She remained awake, listening, paralyzed with the belief her children would stop breathing in the night, though they had long outgrown the age when this was a real risk. She worried someone would abduct them from the front yard; she feared God would take them early, for she did not have the faith her husband had. She knew all things, good and bad, were possible.

But once there, staring into the icy darkness and faced with the real possibility of losing the two people who meant more to her than her own flesh, than her own blood, she confronted those fears and plunged her arms deep into the abyss. She felt the cold embrace her arms. Her hand fumbled in the water, reaching for something to connect her to her children. When her hand glanced against something, she did not know what, she clutched her delicate knitter's fingers into a fist and pulled with all her strength. She fell back, and Joseph, her beautiful Joseph—blue and cold, fell beside her. Once he was safe, she returned to the gaping hole (a horrible grinning mouth, gnashing teeth) where her daughter still remained. She plunged her hands in again, and this time the water did not feel as cold. By this time, Joe's dad had arrived, his breathing harsh and shallow. He was side by side with his wife, their voices rising together in a wail, screaming out their daughter's name, "Kelly! Kelly!" while they knelt on the ice, hands frantically searching the water.

With no sign of their daughter, Joe's father quickly removed his boots and coat and jumped in. He dove under and came up for air, over and over, each time empty-handed, until his wife convinced him he would die if he didn't get out of the water. The human body can only stand so much.

But Kelly (a young heart, a girlish heart, a heart that wanted to kiss a boy, a heart that wanted to paint the world) was not one to give in as easily as her parents. Though the extra weight she had been carrying in the backpack had caused her to sink faster and deeper into the darkness and though she was terrified, she wisely managed to struggle out of the heavy pack and her coat and swim upwards toward the light, towards her brother, her father, towards warmth.

But when she arrived at what she thought was the surface, her hands touched solid ice. This was not what she had expected. Now panic began its steady creeping into the chambers of her heart. She began to swim, one hand on the ice, looking for the hole they had made when they fell in. She didn't know which way to go, and the silent, murky waters offered no clues.

All the while Joe remained curled up in his mother's coat against the hard ice. He could not move but just lay, staring at the thick clear sheet of frozen water beneath him. And then he thought he saw movement, there, just below him. To this day, he knows it was her. He could see her; he felt he could almost touch her, as if the only thing between them was a thin pane of glass, easily broken. If he listened hard enough, he believed he could hear her heart pounding inside her chest.

Joe tried to scream, *Dad, Dad, she's here,* but nothing came out but a soft groan, a hoarse whisper. All he could do was watch her beneath the ice, her eyes wild with fear and her two hands pressed up against the solid surface. She was kicking trying to propel her body through the ice with sheer force of will. When she opened her mouth in a silent scream he saw the bubbles trailing from her mouth, and he had a sudden urge to pop them all. He closed his eyes against the tears. When he opened them again he saw her falling, falling into the deep and frozen darkness, her long hair trailing up behind her like the branches of the leafless trees in his father's photographs.

§

Though to Joe it seemed like he had been on the ice for days, from the time he and Kelly had fallen in to the time his parents had truly given up, less than seventy minutes had passed. As they walked, the three of them bundled together as one, Joe raised his head from where it rested on his mother's shoulder. The three bucks, with their defiant antlers, were still there, having moved off only a short distance from where they had been when he and Kelly had first seen them. They had not been scared off. Being creatures of the wild they were used to death and all its mayhem. As long as it didn't directly affect them, they were free to look on with a timid nonchalance; for, often, some other creature's death brought them a few more days of living. But they would never venture too close. For it is never wise to tempt death by reminding it you are still among the living.

Joe drew his eyes from the deer to the black camera mounted on a black tripod like a memorial to the dead from the living and wondered if there was enough magic in there to bring his sister home.

§

Joe spent the next few days in the hospital. He had almost died. If his mother had not come out looking for them, his father would never have made it to him in time. Even after he was sent home (with a clean bill of health from the doctors), it would be years before he ever truly felt warm again. He spent many winters, springs, and even summers dressed in the sweaters and caps his mom knitted. She did little else but knit after Kelly died, and Joe ended up with so many scarves and hats he could wear a different one each day of the month and still not wear them all. But this suited Joe just fine. He usually wore several caps and scarves at the same time, because he never felt warm enough. He lived his life with a chill in his bones that would not abate for many long years.

§

They did not hold a funeral for Kelly; there was no body, nothing to bury but their love for her, which they were not ready to let go of just yet. Instead, they packed up and moved back to southern California, where the temperature never dropped to freezing and where bodies of water flowed year-round, gloriously free of ice. Despite the much warmer temperatures, his mother continued to knit and knit. But after a while, she gave up on trying to actually make anything concrete like a sweater or mittens. Instead, she knitted one continuous piece about ten inches wide. When she ran out of yarn in one color, she would just switch to another. When she ran out of yarn completely, she sent Joe's father for more. Very soon she had what appeared to be a scarf designed for the unimaginable girth of God's neck.

And because her heart (a mother's heart, a fearful heart, a heart in pain from loving too much—a human heart after all) could not keep itself alive, could not muster the courage or the energy to beat without her daughter, she had no choice but to shut it down completely. To turn it off like a light, to plunge herself into darkness. To take the "mother," even the "human," out of the equation. And with this precarious plan in place, when Kelly's name would come up in conversation, when Kelly herself or the ghost of her at least would spark embers in her mother's ashen heart, she would draw a certain comfort from the knowledge that, although her daughter was dead, although they had been too late, at least she would never again have to worry. Never again would she feel cold dread rising into her chest, never again would she have to fear someone could one day hurt her daughter. For all the anguish and loss, she drew comfort from this fact; from now on, Kelly would always be safe, and no harm could ever come to her again.

§

Joe's father, on the other hand, could not turn his heart off, could not find the switch. Instead, his heart—raged and rabid—turned on the people he loved. Five months after Kelly's death, Joe's father beat him for the first time. It was a sweltering day in the Valley, and all by himself, Joe decided to make lemonade for his father, just like his sister used to do. He poured in the powdered mix, adding water and stirring it with a spoon, watching the crystals swirl and dissolve. He added large ice cubes to the pitcher, as he had seen Kelly do. He grabbed a glass and carried everything out to where his dad sat in the yard, staring at the half-painted fence. As Joe walked, he tried to hold the pitcher steady, but the ice clinked against the glass with the rhythm of his walking. When his father glanced up, he looked briefly at the pitcher of lemonade, then moved his gaze to Joe with eyes that held not a flicker of recognition.

When Joe felt the pitcher fly from his hands he first thought he had dropped it, that he had let it slip through his fingers. *I'm sorry*, he wanted to say, but there was no time. His father moved at him again, this time striking him hard across the face. Suddenly, Joe was airborne, just a few inches maybe, and only for seconds, but he had been hit with enough force to send him falling into and through the sliding glass door; the glass door he had once spent hours looking out of (watching his father paint the fence, watching sharp-billed birds soar past); the glass door that now was in shatters, its tiny slivers of glass cutting deeply, sharply, into his skin.

§

In the emergency room, he heard his mother tell the doctor, *Oh you know how kids are…he was running to catch a ball his father was throwing to him. They were outside playing catch, and oh, I guess his dad threw the ball a bit too far.* She spoke quickly, almost unable to stop. *He was quite enthusiastic about getting the ball; he is always trying to please his father. I guess he didn't notice I had closed the glass door to keep the flies out.* She giggled nervously.

As they were driving home, after the doctors had pulled the glass from his body and stitched up his wounds, his mother tried to comfort him.

"You know your dad is still grieving a lot. He didn't mean to hurt you. I guess just seeing…I guess he was just reminded of things he doesn't want to remember just yet. You know he would never do anything to hurt you. He loves you. He loves you terribly. We just have to be careful with what we say or do around your dad. Just for a little while."

But the beatings continued. Whenever Joe let slip certain words—like his sister's name—or when he recalled a book his sister liked to read or, worse even, when he was caught one rainy afternoon using some of her old paint supplies (the ones she didn't even like, the ones she had given him permission to use), Joe felt the blows of his father's fists—the sharp, angular bones of his knuckles. He heard his father shout, *shuttup, shuttup, shuttup*; and later, Joe would hear his father's sobs which lasted for hours and the soothing whispers of his mother who embraced her husband to calm his raging heart. Sometimes, afterward, on rare occasions, Joe even heard the muffled sounds of his parents' lovemaking.

Each time his father beat him, his mother promised him it

would be the last time. But Joe already understood what his mother did not. The mere fact he was still living was enough to remind his father that Kelly wasn't. It didn't matter what he said or did. Every time his father looked at him, he was reminded of all he had lost. Late at night, when Joe should have been sleeping, he lay awake and wondered why he had lived and Kelly had died when he wished with all his heart the opposite were true.

§

Things continued like this until Joe met Alice in the children's ward of St. Joseph's Hospital. He told her one day, over tapioca pudding, about Kelly and his dad and how he was the one who should have died, how he felt wrong and out of sorts all the time, like he had won something by cheating. She hugged him and said, "If you had died instead, I would be talking to Kelly right now."

He looked down at his arm, which was buried beneath the hard white layers of a cast. He felt the pain in his ribs at each intake of breath. It was then he understood—if things *had* been different, if he had died and Kelly had lived, then their father would be beating her instead. It brought him great relief to know that in the end, he *had* saved Kelly; he had protected her from this.

From then on, each time he felt a blow against his body, he thought of everything his sister did not have to endure. The more his father beat him, the more Joe refused to let any coldness into his own heart and the kinder, the more forgiving he became. Joe knew that had it not been for Alice, he would not have survived one more day. Alice showed him the truth about how he had saved his sister, which meant Alice, in turn, had saved him. Right then and there he knew he was going to run away with her. And four years later, he did. He left, believing his family was better off. He left, believing he wouldn't be missed. But we were privy now to the details of another heart. We were aware of a different story unfolding.

§

Almost three years after Joe ran away with Alice, Joe's father checked his mother into a health care facility, where she could knit and live out the rest of her days in peace. After dropping her off, Joe's father got back in his car and drove north until there were no more roads to drive. From there, he traveled on foot and an hour later reached the lake where Kelly had drowned. Eventually, vacationers would find his frozen body and report it to the local police. Joe learned of this at nineteen when he finally got up the nerve to reach out to his family again. Unable to find his mom or dad, he called his grandparents. When he heard the news, Joe had assumed his father returned to the lake to somehow get Kelly back, as if he could retrieve her from the cold and bitter darkness. But what Joe saw now, what we both saw, was a man cocooned in grief, not for the daughter he had lost but for the son he had driven away. We observed the last years of his life unfold into one long sweeping search for Joe. Joe's father passed countless hours on the phone with police stations and hospitals from California to New York. Most nights he was unable to sleep, and he drove till dawn through unfamiliar streets and into strange cities looking for his son. Every morning he got down on his knees and renewed his promise to God—*I will give you everything if you let see my son again. I just want to know he is okay.* But God, it appeared, was not listening. Unsure of what else he could do, Joe's father gave the only thing he had left. He walked to the center of the frozen lake, whispering "Joseph," screaming "Joseph," until his throat was as raw and exposed as his heart. Then he removed all his clothes and sat down upon the cold, hard ice, never to get up again.

§

Joe lifted his hand from mine and wiped his eyes. Instantly we were back in his car in the apartment parking lot, children's books open on our laps.

"I never knew. I thought my dad hated me. But he looked for

me every single day. And when he couldn't find me..." Joe choked.

A son.

A father.

A secret heavy, burdened, at last takes flight.

CHAPTER 10

ALICE. JOE. PETER. They were my family. I was 38 and mere days away from the birth of my first and only child. I was finally happy. I finally felt at home in the small apartment I had lived in since graduating from college. Even though I was co-owner of a small chain of flower stores and making enough money to afford a down payment on a home in a slightly fancier neighborhood, I remained where I was. It was safe and clean, and I felt comfortable living close to my new friends. Unbeknownst to me, my small, two-bedroom apartment (with a window facing the parking lot and a small oak growing in a little patch of dirt) would also become the birthplace of my son.

§

During the last months of my pregnancy, I read a lot about labor and birth. I read testaments from mothers who described being in labor as "easy" while others groaned at the painful memories. Truth be told, there is no such thing as an "easy" labor. Some might be long, lasting over 24 hours, while others are short, just under 60 minutes. Some are less painful than others, but none is ever "easy." There is always pain and the ripping (or cutting) of flesh. And no matter how much you want this child, no matter how long you have been waiting for this one moment and all the moments to follow, no matter how many books you have read and parents you have consulted, there is always a nagging feeling that you are bringing a brand new person into this world who is altogether dependent on you, and you, in turn, will always be ill-equipped and under prepared for the task.

My water broke on a Thursday, sometime around 1 a.m. I called out to Alice, who was asleep in the spare bedroom-turned-nursery. As my due date grew closer, she and Joe took turns spending the night at my place. "August is due for his debut any day now," Joe told me. "We can't miss it."

Alice was at my side instantly. She gently stroked my arm with one hand, while she dialed my doctor's number with the other. Then she called Joe and Peter.

"Okay. Your doctor will be at the hospital when we get there. Joe's getting the car now. Don't worry, the doctor says we have plenty of time."

But August, my sweet August, had plans all his own. Qualified to handle whatever might lie before him, he decided he would not be contained for one minute longer. Like a bird slipping smoothly, freely from clutching hands, my son would burst forth into this world.

Alice took one look at me and, in her infinite wisdom, knew. Seconds later, the door opened, and Peter and Joe walked into the apartment. Joe was smiling the way he does—a smile to make even my cold heart flutter. "Are we ready?" he asked.

"Joe, there's no time. I think the baby's coming now. We need an ambulance."

§

August's birth began with a drop, a drop of liquid, of water, of blood. It started with a drop of music, a pin drop, a constant drop of leaves against a white and empty sidewalk, a dropping of hands in acquiescence, a drop of chocolate on the corner of upturned lips licked away by a foreign (but welcome) tongue, a drop of everything we ever imagined or hoped for, a drop of everything all at once. It began with a dream and with pointed and sudden pain, like a sharp-legged insect excavating her tiny nest between the bones of my spine. It began with a sudden urge to push and with long needles, like fingers, kneading the insides of my body. It began with the sounds of laughter and encouragement, and with comforting, familiar smells: the rose-hip perfume Alice always wore, the scent of coffee lingering on Joe's breath, Peter's salty-sour smell, even the powdery smell of Puppet. They were here. They were all here.

It began with a trembling, a rising, I thought, from the hollow between my legs and moving quickly through to the cartilage in my knees and the tips of my toes, a quaking between my breasts strong enough to rattle my teeth. It moved to the end of my bed, causing it to bounce and jump from the floor as if in celebration. At the time I believed the earth was shaking in salute of a new life, and I wondered if I was the only one who felt it. But slowly the rumbling grew in strength and intensity, like a thousand giant birds lifting off from the ground as one. It moved throughout the house, sending dishes crashing to their porcelain deaths and threatening the windows, which shook with uncertainty. Car alarms blared from the parking lot, and the street lights, which normally streamed into my window, went black. All the while, Peter was crouched and rocking, one hand covering his head, the other firmly gripping Puppet, and whispering, "Whoa, whoa."

I heard Alice whispering too, and Joe breathing in my ear. I felt his warm breath against my cheek and was comforted.

Then I felt Alice's hands on my thighs.

Somewhere, a far off voice said, "He's coming now."

I heard someone lift and drop the phone back onto its cradle (Joe, wondering why the ambulance hadn't arrived yet). I heard the calm emanating from Alice, and I heard six singing hearts, yes, even Puppet's tiny feline heart with its dreams of mice and greater things, all beating in synchronicity. And then, there were other heartbeats, hundreds maybe or perhaps only one or two. I couldn't tell. I could no longer distinguish between any of them. They were like coyotes calling in pitches and whines, yelps and howls, never quite starting or ending at the same time.

I knew what was coming. I closed my eyes and waited for it, for the tingling sensation along the base of my neck, for the temporary dark, and then those comforting holes of light. And they came, this time hundreds of them. I saw hands, young and tan, beating against the well-worn dashboard of a car, beating out a rhythm: *thump-shuffle-whisper-thump* as road and land and sky stretched before them in unending invitation. I saw a record player's silvery needle bounce up and down along the thin grooves of a record after it had reached its end—the disk spinning though there was no more music to be heard, only the dull *thump-shuffle-whisper-thump* where needle and vinyl met. Somewhere I saw a couple dancing, unaware the music had stopped.

I saw hands reaching across an otherwise empty bed. I saw a pale moth beating its wings against a silvery screen. I saw a smooth, flat stone bouncing once, twice, three times off a lake just as flat and just as smooth. I saw a young father laughing, an intertwining of chocolate smudged fingers and lips, children running through dried leaves falling. I saw a pale and shapeless bird settle its feathers in the night.

Then I saw my son for the first time. I saw him crying—those first necessary breaths. I saw everyone in the room with me. And at the last, at the very last, I finally saw myself—a mother, a friend. Someone, perhaps, worthy of being loved.

§

When I next woke up, I was in the hospital. Joe and Alice were by my side. August was wrapped in a tiny blanket like a burrito, snug in Alice's arms.

"Hey, sleepy," Alice smiled and passed my beautiful son to me.

I spent the day in the hospital, sleeping and holding my son whenever they would allow it. I nestled my face in his hair and inhaled his warm, clean smell. I pressed my ear to his chest and heard the erratic, tinny beats of his perfectly imperfect heart.

Joe and Alice and Peter popped in throughout the day and
spent as much time as they could with us. They brought me stacks
of the day's newspapers, scissors, and a large scrapbook.

"Just as you requested," Alice said and squeezed my hand. "We
have to go, but we'll be back in the afternoon to take you home."

Alone, I began pouring through the day's newspapers, searching for articles to cut out and save; articles of events which coin-
cided with the day of my son's birth, chronicling the world as it was
in that moment. I grabbed the *L.A. Times* first. I skipped the front-
page news, the news of wars and greed and all of man's crushing
foibles. No. August would learn about those things soon enough. I
read over articles of health care laws passed, of prizes won, of an
up-and-coming artist who used clay and stone to create wildlife
sculptures. I found an article about the passing of a music legend I
had never heard of.

There were many stories I found interesting but only three reso-
nated with me. I sliced the thin blades of the scissors through the
flimsy newspaper print then pasted the clipped articles carefully
into a scrapbook. I would keep them along with photos of August,
a copy of his birth certificate, and the stamps of his tiny hands and
feet. This was my way of giving some small piece of the world to
my son.

The first article was about the earthquake, which hit at 1:44
a.m., the exact time of August's birth. The accompanying photo was
what first caught my eye. It was of an old woman peering into the
camera with a soft smile; her hand rested on an old record player,
safe and intact, though all around her were shattered remnants of
picture frames, porcelain figurines, and other unidentifiable fragments—mementos of a life I sensed had been well-lived. Though
I did not know who she was, or even her name, I recognized her
immediately. I had seen her for the first time the night of August's
birth: her age-spotted hands which had been smooth and lightly

tanned once upon a time, her warm eyes with thin, nearly transparent lashes, her feet clad in sensible shoes. I had watched as she danced with her husband, who she lost long ago. I remembered this dance as her ghosts, temporarily, became mine.

The article read,

TREMOR ROCKS SAN FERNANDO VALLEY

Northridge – Valley residents were shocked out of their slumber in the early morning hours when a 6.4 earthquake hit at 1:44 a.m. on Thursday. Despite the intensity and duration of the tremor, residences and other infrastructures sustained only minor damage such as broken windows and items falling from shelves. Some roads were damaged, making road travel and emergency vehicle access extremely difficult. Though there were no reported injuries or deaths, over 500 people within a five block radius of the epicenter called 9-1-1 while the quake was happening. All 517 individuals reported chest pains and quickening hearts. When emergency vehicles were finally able to arrive on the scenes, however, they found not one actual case of a heart attack.

In a bizarre twist of events, all 517 witnesses also claimed to have had strong, almost lifelike visions of friends and loved ones coming to visit them at the exact moment the earthquake hit.

Helen Yu, lifetime resident of

```
the area, says she dreamt she was
dancing with her husband who has
been dead for over 15 years. "I
woke up this morning smelling his
cologne and our favorite album
was on the turntable. I haven't
used the thing in years." When
informed about other residents
who had reported similar visions,
Mrs. Yu stated, "I know it sounds
crazy, but maybe we all caused the
earthquake. Can a memory be pow-
erful enough to shake the world?"
```

The article went on to talk about the causes of earthquakes and the infamous San Andreas Fault, but this was of no particular interest to me. I re-read the words of Mrs. Helen Yu, as I set the clipped article aside. *Can a memory be powerful enough to shake the world?*

It is true—earthquakes are nothing if not violent upheavals thrusting us out of sleep or comfort. But perhaps our own emotions, our own ghosts, instead of being weightless and transparent, are solid and heavy with the weight of all things. Perhaps all these memories of lost loves happening at the same time, all these memories brought to the surface by the beating of my son's heart, really were enough to move the earth.

§

The second article I cut out read,

```
"MIRACLE" MOTH AT ST. JOSEPH'S
            HOSPITAL

Burbank - On 12 October of last
year, James B. Wilkes suffered
a debilitating stroke that left
him in a coma and on life sup-
port. After months of waiting,
with little change in his fa-
ther's condition, his son, Mark
```

Wilkes, 42, and daughter-in-law, Mary Jane Wilkes, made the decision to remove their father from life support. Friends and family gathered around as the doctor unplugged Mr. Wilkes from the machines and waited for him to die.

Witnesses said the room grew quiet as the machines shut off one by one, until they were all left in silence. It was then when they noticed the tiniest of sounds, "a thunk bop - like someone lightly tapping from far away." When Mark looked up in the direction of the sound, he saw a large moth fluttering its long wings against the window.

He was so distracted by the creature, he later stated, that he did not notice his father had awoken until Mr. James Wilkes stirred slightly, opened his eyes and said, "What's all the noise about?"

Word quickly spread of Mr. Wilkes's miraculous recovery. People afflicted with their own terrible diseases or just plain believers from all over came to visit James in the hospital, to see for themselves the moth capable of saving a man's life. Some claimed to see the face of the Virgin Mary in the patterns on its wings; others believed they felt "something" when in its presence. The situation became riotous, and the hospital had to hire three new temporary security guards to manage the inflow of Mr. Wilkes's guests.

Two days later, Mr. Wilkes was
discharged from the hospital.
Though Mr. Wilkes himself stated
emphatically he did not believe
in miracles and called the critter "just a plain and ordinary,
every-day moth," on the day he
left the hospital he took the insect home with him in a jar, pro-
claiming, "You can't be too careful."

Upon his arrival back home, Mr.
Wilkes let the moth go inside his
screened-in porch. Two weeks later, Mr. James Wilkes passed quietly in his sleep. The moth was
nowhere to be found.

When asked by reporters at a press
conference after his father's
death if he believed a miracle
had occurred, Mark answered, "I
had two more weeks with my father. Two weeks I never expected
to have. Two weeks the doctors
claimed were impossible. I don't
know what a miracle is, but this
sure felt like one to me."

§

The last article I cut out was a short write-up accompanied by a
grainy picture of a bird with long white wings and wingtips so dark
they almost disappeared against the backdrop of night.

FIRST RECORD OF WANDERING
ALBATROSS IN SANTA MONICA COUNTY.

Malibu - To the delight and amaze-
ment of local birders, a juvenile

Wandering Albatross (*Diomedea exulans*) was spotted on the rocks at Malibu Beach in the cover of night, by local and avid birder Paul Gregory.

The sighting was later confirmed by other local experts who flocked to the beach as soon as they heard of Mr. Gregory's report on the Rare Bird Alert. Over the two days it remained in the area, many people were able to see the bird and capture images of it.

"I took this as a sign," said Mr. Gregory, who freely admitted to having suffered from emotional distress over the years, leading him to make two failed suicide attempts in as many months. "I don't really sleep," he said. "I sit on my balcony all night, every night. Hearing the waves crashing against the rocks and sand reminds me life is violent, but persistent, and beautiful. So every night I sit, waiting for sleep or acceptance, whichever comes first."

It was on a night like any other when Mr. Gregory noticed a flash of movement in his peripheral vision. Lights from other nearby houses illuminated the white figure alighting on the rocks. The bird stayed long enough for him to grab his camera and snap a picture. Then it flew.

"At first I thought it was an angel," Mr. Gregory stated, "but then, think about it, a Wandering

Albatross, here, in Malibu? Perhaps it was."

Though a special sighting indeed,
others are a bit more skeptical
about Mr. Gregory's interpreta-
tion. Margarita Jimenez, biologist with the Point Reyes Bird
Observatory, said, "While this
is truly exciting for anyone interested in birds and rare bird
sightings, the truth is this happens quite often. Birds get lost
or blown off course and end up
somewhere none of its kind has
ever been before and perhaps will
never be again."

I stared at the picture now tucked safely in August's scrapbook—this photo of the albatross stepping boldly out into the darkness, wings spread wide as if to capture the night. I wondered if it
really was all an accident. Had strong air currents, storms, or simple
inexperience thrown this young bird off course? Or, every so often,
could it happen on purpose. Could these feathered wanderers with
their strong hearts and their light, hollow bones venture out of the
regular, out of the expected in the hopes that we humans will one
day do the same?

§

Not all the faces I saw on the night I gave birth to August were
present in the day's newspapers. I suppose only a few of their stories could be considered newsworthy. But together, they were powerful enough to move the earth, to throw a bird off its course, to lure
a pale-winged insect out from hiding.

I thought then of Alice and Joe and Peter. I wondered if it was
not only they who were drawn to me, pulled in by my son's heart,
but whether I too was being drawn to them. Perhaps my son's

heartbeat led me to these people with their stories, their secrets, so I would know I was not alone. Perhaps their stories were revealed, not only for their survival but for my own.

§

Still, in all that time, I never told anyone I had a secret, too— a memory locked in the cadence of my son's heart. And though I recognized its particular inflection, its syncopated beats—it was as familiar as the pattern of my own breathing—I couldn't remember where or when I had heard it before. Eventually, though, I would remember the source of this sound that had been buried so deeply in my past (the man and the dead-not-dead bird). I would remember all of this nine years later, and this memory would save my life, even though I was dying.

• • •

SHE IS STARTING to remember me. I don't know how I know. I just do. All I can say is I was dead and now I'm not. Like the proverbial tree in the forest, which falls with no one around to hear…if no one was around to remember me, had I ever really existed at all? I had been dead, but more than dead, I guess. But I'm here now and it's because of her. And I'm getting stronger every day. I feel as if my bones have suddenly been reconnected, teeth and nails and eyes popped back into grooves and sockets. Skin laid down nice and smooth. I have spent too long as ashes in a coffin and now I am…if not whole, at least living and breathing again.

In my new life, I find myself spending a lot of time trying to remember her. There are papers all over my house with drawings I have made, trying to capture the exact details of her. The one that comes the closest, I think, is tacked up on my refrigerator with a Semper Fi magnet. I pass way too many minutes staring at it, wondering what she'll remember about me.

I've made a list in my head, in no particular order:

1. the day with the boys and the bird who was dead but wasn't

2. the day we first met and how she stopped the bleeding

3. the day I disappeared

And if these memories bring her back to me, there are things I'll have to tell her, things she may or may not understand. I'll have to tell her I knew who she really was all along, and I'll have to explain why I left. I'll have to tell her how my father died and why I'd still kept my faith. And I'll have to tell her about the girl with the heart on the outside who stole my faith away.

I'll have to tell her all of these things and hope she'll love me anyway. I pick up a pen and paper.

I write, "The day I signed up to go to war was the day you told me you didn't believe in miracles."

Part 2

four chambered hearts

In all things there is beauty. In the glint of dew clinging to the strands of a spider's web; in the way the setting sun winks off shards of broken glass; in the rainbow forming in the soap suds in a sink full of dirty dishes; in a blade of grass which manages to force its way, with patience and time, through the all too willing grasp of sidewalk cement. It is in the faded brown of leaves, turning, twisting against their fate, as they fall to the ground, light and dry as brittle bones, and in the bare, thin-tipped branches, denuded by a change in season. It is in the way a stranger's laughter cradles you if you let it. It is in the intricate scars of a lover's back and in our upturned eyes when we ask for forgiveness. It is there, in the death throes of a pelican—its wings spread flat and wide against the sand, its four-chambered heart unwilling to beat, the dimpled skin of its eyelids closed against the world as the mulling vultures prepare for their thieving feast. And it is there even, somewhere, in the deaths of our friends; in the sadness relieved by a coarse and determined rope; in the pictures packed and shipped neatly; in the sacrifice made for those you love; and in the emptiness left behind. A desolation we try to fill with cooking and eating, with sleeping and waking, with working and bathing and dreaming—all those ordinary, everyday things, that become something else entirely in the face of grief.

In the tears that pool, threatening to fall as we push through a burning heat threatening to suffocate our hearts, there is beauty. And even though I learned this from my son when he was just four years old, it would not be until my own death when I would finally understand that in all of this, there indeed is beauty, reaching out its hand to us. Willingly giving of itself. If only we are brave enough to accept it.

CHAPTER 11

THE FIRST FEW YEARS after August's birth passed by
gracefully. I continued to work in the flower shop, bringing him with me most of the time. I felt, finally, at home
with myself, and I enjoyed spending quiet moments with my
co-workers; and though Brinda, Mariam, and even her husband
Amal seemed to enjoy spending time with us, both Brinda and
Amal remained unknowable, unreachable, and somehow just beyond my grasp. On the days Amal picked Mariam up from the
store, I would notice a passing look of sadness on his face each
time he played with August while he waited for his wife to gather
her things. Mariam had mentioned once they were still trying for
another child, but their failure to do so felt more and more daunt-
ing—widening the already substantial gap between them. As for
Brinda, she visited the store less and less, and when she was there,
she worked in the shadows like a phantom of herself, an appari-
tion absent to the touch.

When I wasn't working, Peter, Joe, Alice, and I spent all of our
free time together. These people had become the love I had longed
for my entire life, and I was all the more proud because August and
I had created this family together, had built it up brick by brick, and
its foundation was unshakable. But while Joe and Alice were moving forward, studying for the GED and browsing the classifieds for
jobs, Peter seemed to be falling backwards, to be caught off-guard
by the forward motion of time. He was restless and commented one
day, "I never realized how fast time moves, but seeing how big August is getting...I realize how long it's been since I've seen Quinn."

He took to repeating this phrase often.

Alice, Joe, and I did what we could to comfort Peter, and in truth, most of our days were good ones. The four of us talked for hours or wiled away warm summer days at the beach, watching the pelicans soar above the sea just out of reach of the pounding waves. We had lunch together often, sharing stories and laughter. And we marveled at how quickly August grew and at the simple joy one life can bring to another. For me, though, my happiest moments came at the end of the day, after hugging my friends goodnight and making plans to see them the next day. Then I would spend a few quiet moments with my son—walking beside him as he rode his bike around the block, watching him color quietly in front of the window, tucking him into bed, telling him I loved him and hearing him tell me he loved me too. Then, as always, he would ask, "Can we read from our book?" And how my heart would leap!

Every night I read him passages from the journal we kept, our *Diary of All Things Beautiful* as we liked to call it: a simple spiral notebook with a plain blue cover that held magic between its pages, a reminder of my son's ability to pull long and powerful strands of beauty from even the darkest moments.

§

It began as an accidental game between August and me—this finding of beauty. One afternoon, when August was four years old, we were pulling into the parking lot to pick up some ice cream for Peter, when an SUV swerved ahead of us and stole the last parking space. Normally, I am not bothered by such trivial things, but that day was different. On that day in particular I had needed to see just one small display of human kindness. On the news were stories of a little boy gone missing, of a bombing of an embassy on a distant continent. But worse still was the dread I felt much closer to home.

I had just picked up August from school after spending the morning with Peter. From the moment I had seen Peter that day, I could tell from his behavior, from the strange look on his face that something inside him, the thing that had held him together all these years, had somehow loosened. He ignored Puppet, and he seemed overwhelmingly sad. For the first time since we had become friends, he didn't open up to me. He wouldn't tell me what was wrong. I tried to persuade him to come pick August up with me, but he refused. As I left his apartment, I called Joe, who promised to check up on him. Perhaps I already knew what might happen, or I was just being overly protective, but I felt a real and gripping fear for my friend.

So, perhaps it is understandable why I felt such outrage when somebody stole my parking space.

I closed my eyes and tried to remain calm.

Gripping the steering wheel I chanted to myself "In all things there is beauty, in all things there is beauty," in an effort to quiet my nerves.

August looked at me. "Where, Mom?"

I was unprepared for the question. "What?" I asked.

"Yooouuu saaaiiid," he began in his sing-song voice, his tiny legs kicking slowly out in front of him, "something is beautiful. I want to see." He sat up straight in the seat, his tiny fingers wrapped over the half open passenger-side window.

I turned to look at him. I studied his body. Though he was twisted away from me now, I could imagine his face, open and anxious. I knew without having to see—his eyes were wide with excitement, searching for beauty like a tourist at Yellowstone hoping to catch a glimpse of a bison or maybe a bear as it disappears into the forest. Only August wasn't a tourist. He didn't want a photo or a trivial glance. He wanted the real thing.

"Where, Mom? Where's the beauty?"

"Well, I don't know…I didn't mean…"

And when he looked at me, disappointment and confusion clouded his face.

"Well...um...there for instance," I said, tapping my finger gently on his chest where his heart raced at a speed few other human hearts could keep up with, "isn't *this* a beautiful thing?"

He let out a giggle and clutched his chest.

"Okay, my turn," he said.

He looked around intently for several moments.

"Right there!" He pointed his small finger to an old man with shaggy, dirty hair and ragged clothes. He was sitting on one white plastic bucket, slapping out music with his palms on another bucket. An old cowboy hat lay upside down at his side like a hungry mouth waiting to be fed nickels and dimes from strangers' pockets.

"Are you talking about him?" I asked

August nodded. "I like him making music with a bucket."

§

When we got home, August insisted I write about the man we saw.

"I don't want to forget him," he said, "not even when I'm a hundred years old."

So I pulled out an old notebook and wrote, just as August instructed.

Beautiful Things
1. The man who makes music from a bucket

It became our favorite game. Whenever we were together, whether stuck in traffic or taking a walk or playing in the park, August and I played this hide and seek with beauty. As August got older and learned to write he took over the responsibility of keeping a notebook full of the beautiful things we found. He came home with a dead spider and pointed out the patterns of colors across its back; he found a yellowing leaf with its thin bulging veins; he mentioned a woman with fuchsia-colored hair because it reminded him of his favorite stuffed bear. He followed the trail of an ant crawling across our curtain as the sunlight shone through just right causing the ant's silhouette to grow larger and smaller as it picked up shadow and lost it in the folds of the curtain. All these things he carefully logged into the notebook with my help.

Every day, he made sure to show Joe and Alice, Peter and even Puppet his journal of beauty, and the notes he had carefully written in his crooked script:

*ANT STEPS
ONE YELLOW LEAF*

Each time we made an entry in his diary, I was amazed at his ability to take the tragic, the hurtful, and the mundane and turn them into something beautiful. Even turning the words themselves "in all things there is beauty" into something *other than*, into something much more powerful than I had understood them to be.

"In all things there is beauty" was a sort of mantra I used when I was feeling particularly wronged or impatient with the general way of the world. I first picked up the phrase from my foster mom, Annelle. She used to say, "in all things there is beauty," though she usually meant it in the ugliest of ways.

"In all things there is beauty, Lord. Please, help me find it in this child," she would implore, arms stretched toward the heavens, eyes gazing upwards as if God were to blame for bringing me into her life, and therefore owed her an extra dose of patience and understanding. Each misstep I took, each mistake I made—a dirty glass left in the sink, an unmade bed, a question I couldn't answer—caused her arms (surprisingly toned and tanned despite an inordinate lack of any physical exercise) to rise and her eyes (blue like summer sky, blue like Caribbean sea, blue, blue, blue peering out from long, dark lashes) to silently plead to a God who was in her debt.

It had not started out that way. In the beginning we had been, if not friends, then at least on the verge of camaraderie. There was a tenuous comfort between us. I was one of three other foster kids living in her home at the time, but I was the youngest and the only girl. This inspired her to take me into her confidence.

"I can tell you this, Penny," she would say, "because I know you won't really understand. But don't feel bad. The Lord made us all with special gifts and talents. Yours are just better hidden than most."

I heard stories about her life, mostly about the men who had come and gone, about loves which had left her cold and empty (hollowed out like a decaying log); unrequited loves so deep they were in danger of turning to hate at the slightest push.

"Just be glad you were born plain," she said. "It will save you a lot of trouble with men. Being plain is so much better than being pretty. Shit, you're actually lucky no man will ever want to marry you. Marriage ruins your life…"

That was how it went—every story, every secret was accompanied by the slightest jab at my expense. And though I knew she would always find a way to make me feel bad, the connection with someone, this feeling of finally being let in, far out ruled any sadness or hurt I would feel later. I became reliant on her company, such as it was. Though I would cry sometimes at the sting of her words (and wonder— *"Is this really me? Am I not beautiful? Am I not smart?"*), it was always better than being alone.

Late at night, when I thought about how it felt to be taken into someone's confidence, to share a story or a smile, I would gradually forget the parts that hurt. I would try to convince myself she had only been joking, or the small slights were just my imagination or a simple misunderstanding. And I could pretend I was special, that I was her favorite and that one day she could love me like a daughter (even though I was not pretty, even though I was not smart). I would fall asleep with the image of Annelle and me always together. Of me finally being wanted.

So I listened as she told me, first, about Frank.

"He hardly ever comes around anymore. He's married and his wife treats him like a two year old. No wonder he has to look for it somewhere else, if you know what I mean."

I didn't.

Then there was Patrick.

"He's older than me, works construction and had a body like Adonis when I first met him. He drinks too much and curses too much, but boy does he know what to do with his tongue if you know what I mean."

I didn't.

Annelle cackled with laughter, dribbling frothy beer down her chin, a golden stream running down her neck, which she wiped away with the back of her hand.

But it didn't matter. While the foster boys were left to their own devices, I was finally a part of something real. My "brothers," as Annelle insisted I call them, were all under the age of fifteen. They went to school, they kept their rooms neat, but Annelle believed in unlimited freedom for boys. I, on the other hand, had chores to do around the house, though I never minded. That was when Annelle talked to me the most. I mopped the kitchen floor or washed the dishes, and Annelle sat with me, opened a beer or two, and talked-ed. I could always tell when a new man was coming over because she spent extra time on her hair and makeup and always seemed nervous, as if she were worried they wouldn't show, or, worse yet, would be disappointed in her once they got here.

Once, while getting ready for a date, which seemed to make her particularly nervous, she called me into her room and asked me to sit with her while she did her hair and makeup. "Which shade of lipstick do you like better?" she asked. "Should I wear my hair up or down?" "Help me pick out a dress," she implored. As I watched her run a brush through her long golden hair and glide auburn red over perfect lips, she began to tell me about Carl.

"I don't know what it is about him," she informed me while

brushing pale purple eye shadow above her lids, "but I really like him. He's just a young kid—21, 22 maybe. I'm old enough to be his mother. He thinks I'm 32." She winked at me then, with her purple shadowed eye—a butterfly resting its wings.

"I met him at the store. He bags groceries at Albertsons. He always carries mine to the car without me even having to ask." Her blue eyes looked up as she skillfully stroked black mascara onto her already dark and long lashes. "Anyway, we got to talking one day. He's married, with a baby girl. But he and his wife have split up. Well, they had a big fight anyway. She's too young to know how to treat a man. He'll be much happier with me."

She slipped off her robe, revealing a slim, shapely body clad in discount lace and silk underwear. She slipped into the dress we had chosen. "Zip me up, will you?" she turned her back to me, scooping her hair over her shoulder.

I placed my fingers on the zipper, pulling it up, bringing the two pieces of her dress together across her body like the closing of curtains, hearing the teeth and grooves locking one by one. She stood in front of the mirror for a long time. Even when there was a knock at the door she didn't move.

"He reminds me so much of Jefferson," she said, without turning around to face me. "Carl looks just like him. I met Jefferson my sophomore year in college. We fell madly in love, dropped out, got married. We were gonna join the goddamn Peace Corps, come home, adopt a bunch of needy kids and just be happy, you know? I never should've married him. I mean, what kind of asshole gets run over on a quiet street? On a Sunday morning? In the middle of spring? It's just not right."

The doorbell rang again. Annelle was pulled back to the present. She ushered me out of her room and hurried to answer the door.

§

As the months passed, she opened up more and more to me.

Almost every night I heard about her many loves over alcohol or sweet desserts, but mostly she talked about Carl ("he is on and off with his wife all the time, but he always comes back to me") or Jefferson ("only a prick could die like he died") or both ("men love me because I'm beautiful"). Sometimes when she spoke about one, she would accidentally say the name of the other, but most times only I noticed.

§

One night, late, I woke up with a thirst catching in my throat. I stumbled into the kitchen not even bothering to turn on the light. As I stood at the sink, water glass to my lips, I heard something move behind me. I turned to see Carl sitting at the kitchen table. I hadn't noticed him in the dark. He stood up shakily and approached me with a grin that somehow didn't reach his eyes. He was naked except for a pair of tattered, striped boxer shorts. I could make out a tattoo on his arm. It read *Dorothy*. I could smell alcohol on his breath.

In all the time he had been coming to the house, we had never once spoken more than a "hello" to each other. He always came over late at night and went straight upstairs. Every time it was the same. A few minutes after his arrival the bed began squawking like a crow (*rrraak, rrraak, rraak*), then low moans (*oooh* and *pleeeeasssse*), and finally the loud wails (*yesssssyessssoohgggggodddddyesssss*) that signaled the culmination of their sex. I hated those sounds and had to fight hard to keep the image of them together out of my mind.

I wasn't allowed out of the house after dark or to listen to music at a volume any louder than a whisper (lest it creep and crawl beneath my bedroom door or through the cracks in the wall, like a prying, prowling insect into the tunnels of Annelle's bat-like ears). My only escape was to stand in the shower with the water running at full blast—the heat and steam pouring over my head, running between my shoulder blades, dripping down my non-existent breasts, my concave stomach, my skinny legs, running in rivulets down my thighs and across my raised birthmark shaped like a human hand (red, rough fingers reaching to the inside of my thigh). The water would swirl at my feet, drowning out the noise.

Minutes passed.

Hours.

What felt like days.

I would stay beneath the running water until I was sure it was over. I must have been the cleanest ten year old in the history of the world.

But now Carl was standing in front of me, looking at me, as if expecting something from me.

"How old are you now, Pammy? It's Pammy, right?"

"Penny."

"Oh."

"I'm ten," I said.

"I have a daughter, you know. She's two. She loves ducks, can you believe it? I mean, who can love a mallard? I thought most little girls like horses or unicorns, or some such shit, don't they? But she has this thing for ducks. Do you like ducks?"

"I do like ducks," I said, and I did. Even at that age I knew about the secret shine of their feathers, the thin transparent stretch of skin that connected their toes and allowed them to fly through the water with their feet.

"Come sit down."

I pulled a chair out and sat down next to him. I gripped the glass of water in my hands. My throat felt dry, but I did not take a sip.

"Do you want some?" He asked, passing his own glass to me; a dark odorous liquid swirled inside.

I shook my head, *no*.

"Oh, go on and take a sip. It ain't gonna kill ya."

He leaned so close his breath was hot against my face.

"Come on, Pammy, just try it. Most kids your age would jump

at the chance."

I took the glass and tilted it up. I parted my lips and swallowed. It felt like I had inhaled fire, and I coughed into my fist.

"Sshhh…you'll wake Annelle." And in the same breath, "Did you know today is my daughter's birthday?"

"No, I didn't know."

"Don't be stupid. Course you didn't know. How could you? We had planned a party and everything. I even splurged for a fucking cake in the shape of a duck! Do you know how long it took me to find someone to make a cake like that? So after all the work I did, I had a few beers to relax. My wife got pissed at me. She says I drink too much. Yeah, I drink. Who doesn't? We got into this huge fight, and she ran off to her mother's house, taking Dorothy with her. I can't even wish my own daughter a happy birthday. Fuck!"

He slammed his fist against the table.

My heart slammed with equal force against my chest. I grabbed my glass and carried it to the sink. I gulped the water and turned the glass upside down in the dish rack without rinsing it off. When I turned around again, he was standing in front of me.

He put his hands on my shoulders and ran them down my arms. He pulled me to him and held me tight against his naked abdomen. I felt his skin on my cheek, the coarse hairs just below his belly button tickling my nose along with a faint hint of dried sweat and cologne.

I hugged him back, tentatively at first and then tighter. I liked the way he felt pressed up to me. His hands cupped my head, his fingers stroked my hair. I squeezed him hard, my arms just clearing his hips and buttocks, to meet at the small of his back.

For a moment everything stopped.

Minutes passed.

Hours?

Days?

Then, from the darkness came a sharp click (a heavy boot landing on the trigger of an unexploded mine), a deep growl (an unseen predator behind you in the night), and a shadow moving across the room just on the borders of my peripheral vision (a dark-winged scavenger anticipating death).

Annelle.

At the sight of her, Carl pushed me away. He smiled weakly at Annelle. She grabbed his hand and led him upstairs without a word. They left me alone in the kitchen (in the dark), and somewhere in the deepest part of me I understood this: nothing between us would ever be the same again.

§

Carl stopped coming around. I heard Annelle on the phone telling her friend about how he didn't work at the grocery store anymore. All she knew was he had gone back to his wife and was entering rehab. And though Annelle replaced Carl with three new men, none could fill her up the way he did.

She did not speak to me for two weeks. We navigated around each other in silence until one evening she walked into the kitchen while I was washing the dishes. She walked to the fridge, pulled out a beer, and popped the top. She took a long sip, then turned to me and spit out the words, "You slut! Don't you want me to have any happiness at all?"

From then on I woke up every morning thinking, "today is the day she'll send me back to the orphanage," but she never did. In fact, two months after Carl left our house for good, she petitioned for my adoption and though it never came to fruition, it kept me in her house until I was old enough to take care of myself.

She wanted me to stay, I think, to extract the only revenge she knew how to take. She took away the one thing I needed most: the hope of the *possibility* that someone, one day, would love me. As if to make her intentions clear, though we returned to speaking terms, she never confided in me again. All the long talks we used to have were gone. Even when I asked her a direct question about something going on in her life, she told me nothing. When I tried to talk to her about my day, sometimes she would respond, but more often than not she ignored me. I wanted to prove to her I was still worthy of being loved, I was still worthy of her friendship. I began to try even harder to please her. I brought her a beer or coffee when she hadn't even asked for it. I surprised her with gifts I had made in school. But to each gesture I made, she responded with off-hand comments (not even directed to me, but as if she were talking to someone else entirely). She would say, "This beer isn't even cold" or "The coffee isn't hot enough" or "These gifts are childish" or "silly" or "useless." And the most hurtful of all: "In all things there is beauty, but please help me Lord, because I do not see it in this child."

When I brought home a report card with mostly B's, she said, "You aren't working hard enough; you should be getting straight A's." When my next report card was all A's, she said "You think you're special because you got all A's? It isn't attractive to gloat. The Lord sees beauty in everyone, but He does not like a show off."

It didn't take me long to learn I could not please her. Though nothing I did could ever make it right, I continued to work hard in the hopes that one day she would somehow come to love me, or at the very least forgive me. She never did.

But somewhere along the way, I realized I actually enjoyed school and the challenge of learning. My teachers, at least, were not afraid to shower me with praise and to say when they were proud of me. For the first time in my life, I felt like I was good at something.

The work paid off, and I graduated from high school with top honors a year early and moved away to college. The day I left, Annelle barely acknowledged my leaving. I went to her, and though her back was to me, I hugged her and said, "In all things there is beauty. Even in me." Then I walked out the front door and never went back or spoke to her again.

To this day, when things aren't going my way, or I feel frustrated or annoyed, I say, "In all things there is beauty." Even though it always made me feel better, I never really believed it until I began the game with my son. In fact, as he got older, he made the game more challenging, so even in the most mundane things—a smoggy view of the city, a beat up old car—he would find something of beauty: the sun's reflection off a skyscraper, the cherry red color of the car in the one spot where the paint had not faded. In no time he had filled 15 small notebooks, which he kept stored in chronological order on the shelf above his bed as if he could store away beauty and keep it, like canned foods, to feed him in cases of emergency. What none of us knew (and how could any of us have known?) is how soon we would need to dip into our reserves, how soon those emergencies would arise—like cornered snakes, striking with such speed that their arrival was only a blur of light, of colors and of loss.

CHAPTER 12

WHEN AUGUST AND I RETURNED HOME one day, many months after inventing the beauty game (the day we saw the man with music, the day Peter began losing ground, the day my son first showed me beauty in everything), we went straight to Peter's apartment and found Joe and Alice there with him. Peter, lovely Peter, with his kind heart and crooked smile, sat almost expressionless, caressing Puppet who was curled up in his lap. His eyes were those of a man who had given up—a hiker lost in the desert, knowing he will never be found; a fisherman at sea watching the dark clouds of an inescapable storm building on the horizon. I noticed Peter had taken down every picture from his wall except the one in which he was holding Quinn, just a puppy then, in his arms, a forest of trees behind them. They both appeared to be smiling.

A long time passed before anyone spoke.

Finally, Peter broke the silence. "I went to see Quinn last Thursday."

"Peter, that's great!" we all said in unison, happy for our friend.

"Not really. I didn't even have the courage to get through the front gate."

"Peter…" I reached for his hand

"I didn't tell anyone I was going. I took a cab."

"That must have cost you a fortune!" Joe exclaimed. Alice quickly gave him a sharp look, followed immediately by a forgiving smile.

"Yeah, over $200. I used some of the money my parents give me every week. It just sits in a jar in my closet anyway."

"We would've taken you," Alice reminded him.

"I know. But I was afraid of what might happen. I wanted to go alone."

"What did happen?" I asked. "Do you want to tell us?"

"You know, all this time, since the accident I mean, I kinda thought of Quinn as always being young and strong. But now I see how fast August is growing, and it made me think that Quinn must be growing too. He's old now. I wanted to see him because I thought he would finally be like me. Slow and stupid. And then I could take him home because maybe he would be happy just sitting around with me, not wanting to run or chase things anymore. I thought how great it would be to just take him home again."

We all nodded in unison, letting him know it was okay for him to go on.

"But when I got there, I watched from across the street and I saw Quinn running through the yard, barking. He must've been chasing a squirrel or somethin'. He hadn't changed a bit. It was like he was still a puppy. He looked so strong, and he was running so fast.

"So I chickened out. I got right back in the cab and came home. Pretty pathetic, huh?"

"No, Peter, no," I squeezed my fingers around his.

"I guess it just hit me. I'm never gonna get any better than I am now. I'm never gonna be good enough to get Quinn back."

"Don't say that, Peter," Alice begged. "You and Quinn belong together. You always will."

Peter closed his eyes and leaned back against his chair. "I think it's too late."

But despite our protests to the contrary, our words of encouragement, our stubborn refusal to believe it could be true, Peter turned out to be right in all the ways that mattered.

§

It was a Saturday. We had all been spending extra time with Peter, hoping to help him see his way through to the other side. But he was often reluctant to join us, refusing to leave his apartment, except to allow Puppet outside for a few minutes each day.

After much begging, I convinced him to eat dinner with us.

"Come for dinner tonight. Joe and Alice will be there. I'm going to make cookies for dessert," I said.

He promised he would come. He even smiled and seemed happier than he had in a long while.

August and I went to the grocery store to pick up all the ingredients to bake Peter's favorite peanut butter cookies. Mid-way through our shopping, August, a bag of sugar and a jar of natural peanut butter in hand, looked up at me and said, "I don't hear Peter anymore."

I knew without having to hear the rush of his heart, without having to lay my hands on his, without even having to be in the same room with him, I knew what Peter had done. And I knew, with a crushing realization that I, that we, that none of us (despite our best efforts, despite our promises to him, despite how much he knew we loved him) could stop such a thing from happening, could stop what had already been set in motion.

§

A few days earlier, I had just returned home after picking August up from school when Peter had called me outside to watch Puppet (to make sure he didn't fall) while Peter ran upstairs to answer his ringing telephone.

I sat beneath the small oak tree and couldn't help but smile as Puppet clambered among its branches, his sharp cat claws digging gleefully into the bark, his yellow eyes catching every movement: a lizard scurrying in the dirt, a bird preening its delicate feathers, the wind rearranging the leaves.

When Peter returned I noticed he was shaking slightly though he tried not to show it. He scooped Puppet up and into his arms.

"Penny," he said, "will you take me to see Quinn?"

§

Peter, August and I rode in silence, Peter lost in his own thoughts; I not quite knowing if I should interrupt his memories with something as insignificant as words.

When we arrived at the vet's, Jim and Sarah, Quinn's caretakers, were there.

"We're so glad you came," they said and hugged Peter awkwardly. They glanced at August and me and smiled sadly.

"Can we see Quinn now?" Peter asked.

§

We entered the room, unprepared for what we would see. Quinn lay on a metal table; his eyes were open but hazy. His breathing was raspy and harsh. His hind legs lay at odd angles, broken from the impact with the car. Blood covered his coat. But he was wagging his tail unreservedly, and it thumped heavily against the table.

Sarah joined Jim in the corner. Tears now stained their softly wrinkled cheeks. Peter stood unmoving, frozen, his eyes locked on Quinn, looking for signs of life, for signs of recognition, for signs that Peter was forgiven.

"You must be Peter," the vet said a few moments later. "I'm Dr. Vartan. I'm very sorry. Quinn has severe internal injuries. There's nothing we can do for him."

"How long do I have with him?" Peter asked.

"He could live for hours, but he's in a lot of pain. Please, take all the time you need to say your goodbyes, and when you're ready, we will...take his pain away."

The vet left the room after patting Peter gently on the shoulder. When he was gone, Jim said, "I'm sorry we didn't tell you he was missing, Peter. We didn't want to upset you, and I thought he'd find his way home. He's such a smart dog."

"What happened?" Peter asked, rubbing Quinn's coat, trying unsuccessfully to stave off his own tears.

"Last Thursday Quinn just ran away."

"Thursday?"

"I wasn't home when it happened, but the maid said Quinn just went crazy.

He started barking and running back and forth alongside the fence. Then he just jumped. She called me immediately, and I came home from work right away. We drove all over, but we never found him. I didn't call you because I didn't want you to worry. There wasn't anything anyone could do. I put up posters all over the neighborhood. I looked for him every day. I just didn't think he could go very far. I swear, Quinn hasn't moved like that in years. He suffers from arthritis. He's a lot slower and just doesn't get around as well as he used to. I just don't understand it. I don't know what got into his head. I mean, what would possess him to run away after all these years?"

"I think I know."

§

And from what Peter had told me, and from what I knew of Quinn, I too could envision what had happened. I imagined Quinn sleeping on the porch. His old dog bones would be tired and maybe they ached even more in the early mornings when the air was crisper, cooler. Though he no longer had energy for many things, when he heard a car stop and the door slam, he would lazily open his eyes and glance up. Maybe his vision was not as sharp as it had once been and his sense of smell was slowly failing, but he would recognize the figure across the street immediately. I could see him, how he must have pulled himself up onto all four legs, and ignoring the pain in his joints and maybe even a slight limp in his hind leg, he would begin to run. He would run as fast as he could towards the front gate, expecting Peter to walk through at any moment (and from where Peter stood, had it looked as if Quinn were running away from him? Or had Peter's own fears and insecurities kept him from seeing?). Perhaps Quinn barked with excitement or leapt into the air with glee. But then Peter did not walk through the gate, and when Quinn realized he could not hear footsteps approaching and he could barely catch the scent of this person he so loved, he would become frantic. He would run to the fence, the only thing that separated him from Peter. And without any other thought in his head, he would jump.

Quinn must have walked for days. Perhaps he walked first down the winding road of Las Virgenes Canyon, his padded paws slapping hard against the pavement, his chest heavy and heaving though he had not yet gone very far. The salty, clean smell of the ocean would become stronger as he fell into a slow but steady rhythm, the aches and pains of his body temporarily forgotten. Eventually he would make his way onto Pacific Coast Highway. As he walked, perhaps gulls hovered lightly over the crashing waves or flocked in small, loose groups on the sand hoping to find remnants of people's snacks—cold french fries, stale potato chips, bread crusts and, if really lucky, a small piece of chicken still on the bone. Quinn would search for these things, too, and manage to steal a few bites to calm his belly. When he was thirsty he would drink from muddy water in stagnant puddles beside the road. I imagined Quinn continued to walk until he finally, cheerfully, found his way to Peter's front door, to home. But Quinn would not know, could not know that Peter was no longer there, that he had not been there for years. Maybe then Quinn would let out a loud bark or maybe he would scratch on the front door, or whine loudly beneath the living room window, waiting to be let in. But eventually, no matter what, Quinn would face a stranger on the other side of the door.

And then Quinn would realize he no longer knew where he was

or where he was going to go. For the first time in his life, perhaps, he felt real fear. Peter wasn't where he was supposed to be, and Quinn's mind couldn't think of what to do next. Suddenly, things which never bothered him before—the sounds of cars speeding past and the way the wind from these same cars rushed through his fur, the honking of horns, and all the strange people everywhere— would make him anxious and afraid. With his paws cracked and bleeding and not knowing what else to do, Quinn would just walk. He would walk without eating, without drinking, without stopping. And perhaps he was just too tired to pay attention or perhaps fear had caused him to run without looking. In either case, he had tried to cross Sunset Boulevard, and the thing Peter feared the most, the thing he had tried to prevent all those years ago, had happened.

§

Before I could say anything, August walked over and set his hand on Quinn's flanks, right beside Peter's. I placed my own hand on August's shoulders, trying to coax him away, to allow Peter time alone with Quinn, but as soon as I did, Quinn opened his eyes. It had been years since anyone's secret had been revealed to me through my son's heart. I thought after he was born I would no longer be allowed those furtive glimpses into lives that were not my own. After all, our blood no longer pumped through the same veins; my body did not nourish his. Though my heart said otherwise, he was no longer a physical part of me. But now, I once again heard the steady *thump-shuffle-whisper* of four synchronized hearts.

Though Quinn felt groggy and tired, and his hind legs ached more than ever before, and though his breathing was heavy and labored, his thoughts were of Peter (always of Peter). From the day Peter "disappeared" all those years ago, Quinn had thought of nothing else. In his dog mind, it was only a matter of time before Peter returned. Though Quinn felt comfortable with the nice family and the big garden, without fail at each creak of an opening door, at the sound of a car coming to a stop in front of the house, he would perk up his ears listening for the familiar gait of Peter's footsteps; he would sniff frantically to catch Peter's scent. Sometimes, when just coming out of a sleep, curled up on the rug, his back against the sofa, one paw resting over his nose—at those times, in those eager moments of waking—he would be fooled into believing Peter had returned, only to be crushingly disappointed.

So, of course, on that day, more than ever, he ached for Peter to walk through the door of this strange place and take him home. Then, as if wishing and being were one and the same, Quinn picked up the familiar scent, faint at first, but then much stronger, wafting through the walls, under the door and straight to his wet black nose. *Peterpeterpeter.*

And then Peter *was* there, rubbing Quinn behind the ears and whispering that he was "a good boy, a good boy," and Quinn knew he was finally forgiven. He knew, at last, he was going home. Suddenly, all those years without Peter drifted into history and were forgotten. And in that moment, Quinn felt what can only be described as joy—the type of fearless, shameless, carefree joy only dogs and very young children are any good at.

Quinn was so distracted by his own happiness, he did not feel it when the sharp needle entered his body and the killing liquid began to course through his veins. And though Quinn began to feel different, hazy, his senses dulled and flat, he only cared that Peter had come for him. Despite the shadows that fell across his face like dark curtains which seemed to grow thicker with each passing moment, despite the heavy sensation he felt throughout his body and the overwhelming desire to close his eyes, he did not want to let himself sleep. But even though Quinn struggled against it (with thoughts of Peter, thoughts of home) complete and total darkness eventually did come and the blissful beating of his thick tail and that of his canine heart slowed bit by bit by bit, until both, inextricably connected, stopped moving…at precisely…the same…moment.

Peter did not move for a full ten minutes.

He did not hear Jim's apology.

He did not hear the vet's apology.

He only heard his own grief wailing and wild inside him.

Peter moved his hand to Quinn's belly, but he felt no rise and fall of breaths being inhaled, exhaled; he pushed his tear-stained fingers beneath Quinn's thick fur and ran them along the muscles of his breast, but he felt no heart beating there. He lifted Quinn's eyelids to reveal nothing but unmoving orbs.

Then Jim carefully removed Quinn's collar and took off the bone-shaped tag. He handed it to Peter. "This belongs to you. He was always yours."

Peter clutched the tag (weightless and blameless) in his fisted hand. He held it the entire way home and all the way out of a life he knew was no longer possible.

§

So when August, his hand reaching for mine said, "I don't hear Peter anymore," I dropped the groceries I was carrying, closed my fingers around August's, and ran to the car. We rushed home to find Peter's parents pounding furiously against his door, the apartment manager ready with key in hand to open the door should Peter not respond.

Later we learned that earlier in the day, Peter's parents had received a package. Packed neatly inside newspaper, bubble wrap, and a tattered blue and green blanket (the one with frogs on it that Peter had carried around as a child) was a bundle wrapped so snugly it looked like it might actually contain a human infant. When Peter's mother unraveled the layers, she found not a living breathing human but the certain and powerful memories of one; she found stack upon stack of the pictures that had once graced Peter's wall: photos of him winning surfing championships, jumping show horses, learning to drive an ATV in the sandy Colorado dunes. At the bottom of the stack, folded neatly in three equal parts, was a note. His mother unfolded it and read,

I'm giving you your son back.

It took her two and half readings to understand the implications of those six simple words. She told us that when the letter fell from her hand, it landed on the marbled floor with a thud, as if made of lead.

CHAPTER 13

I USHERED AUGUST QUICKLY into our apartment and asked him to please wait for me there. I closed the door behind me and ran up the stairs just as the manager's key was turning in the lock. From the pull-up bar his parents had bought him years ago to encourage him to keep his body fit (even though his mind had deteriorated beyond their ability to recognize) hung Peter. His feet dangled less than an inch from the floor (forgetting, forever, the feel of their own weight). His face was blue and unfamiliar.

I watched as Peter's father cradled his son, and as his mother, feet planted on an up-righted chair, severed the rope (severed her ties, cut like an umbilical cord all those years ago) with a kitchen knife, slipping the noose from Peter's bruised neck. As we turned to leave, I saw August in the doorway, Puppet in his arms, watching us as we carried our friend Peter away (his father shifting beneath the weight of his son's shoulders, I stiffly holding him by his legs). August arranged Puppet in one arm and with the other, grabbed hold of Peter's dangling hand and clutched it tightly all the way down the stairs. I kept my eyes fixed on August, knowing the sight of him was the only thing that would keep me from floating up and away from this spontaneous funeral procession of those who knew Peter, of those who had, in their own ways, in their own time, loved him the most.

We reached the parking lot, where Peter's father and I, struggling beneath the weight (of everything) we carried, finally managed to lay Peter's body into the back seat of the family car. The apartment manager muttered the whole time as he followed behind us, "We have to call the police. We have to call the police."

But Peter's father, his face red with rage, his eyes dry and itchy, a reminder of the tears he could not spill, screamed against his loss, "This is my son! He is *my* son."

Peter's mom stumbled, almost blindly, toward her husband, reaching her arm out to calm him. But when she looked down at her hands she jumped slightly, suddenly realizing she was still holding on to the rope, as if uncertain as to how this course and fraying beast wound up in her lotioned fingers (and I believe all of us were thinking then of all the things Peter's mind couldn't comprehend, and yet, he got the knots right). She quickly tossed the rope into the bushes and wiped her hands down the length of her thighs once, twice, as if she were trying to wipe away the past few years, or better yet, wipe away any memory at all that she ever had a son, that she ever loved someone so much that it caused her physical pain to think of him as he had been in the last few years.

August clung to my leg as I hugged first Peter's father and then his mother goodbye. And in their hearts I saw this: Now finally in death, Peter's father could reclaim the boy he had lost all those years ago. He could look upon the aging body, the pot-bellied man who, when living, resembled his son in only frivolous, unimportant details. They'd had the same hair, the same nose, but the eyes were different. This man's eyes held a vacant look, a look his sharp-witted son would have been embarrassed by. But now that he was dead, his eyes closed, his body, his mind, his heart still and unmoving, once again a father could allow himself to recognize his son.

But at the same time his mother (with the weeds in her heart, with a love so heavy it became a burden) wanted to scream. She wanted to take her husband by the collar and shout, *No, this is not our son anymore.* It was much easier to pretend the man before her was an imposter, someone only pretending to be her son. It made her head hurt and her joints ache to think the corpse in her car could have ever been the same perfect human she had carried in her body for all those months.

August and I watched as Peter's mother stiffly slid into the passenger seat. August passed Puppet to her through the open window. Her husband started the car and they drove off. Inside the moving coffin was a father, perhaps; a mother no longer; a cat (who would be loved like a child); and the inert flesh of a man who used to be someone they once knew, a long time ago, but who had been my friend only moments before.

§

The following day, the four of us watched (I clutching August tightly against the wild beating of our hearts, Joe and Alice with hands firmly locked) as men came to clean the apartment, eliminating any last traces of Peter. We watched as furniture was carried out and garbage tossed: a blender, a lamp, pairs of well-worn shoes crammed into boxes or slipped into bags. All the while, these men laughed and joked, farted, and laughed some more. I watched as August watched. He was silent through it all and did not write in his journal for two days.

As I tucked him in to bed that night I laid my hand against his chest and was comforted by the heart I felt beating against the flat of my palm. "You don't have to go to school tomorrow, you know. We can both take the day off. You can stay home with me if you like."

He shook his head, *no,* and smiled slightly, "We're making bird feeders, Mom."

§

August had only been in school a few hours when his principal called me.

"August won't stop," she told me.

"Won't stop what?" I asked.

"He won't stop making bird feeders. They were making them as a science project, one each, but he has made three already and we can't get him to stop. He refuses to do anything else."

"We had…we lost…his friend died this weekend," I said.

"Perhaps you should take August home, just for the day."

When I arrived at his school, the principal was there to meet me. She walked me to his classroom. "I'm sorry about his friend."

I opened the door of the classroom. Its walls were covered with cheery posters of bunnies and kittens solving simple mathematical equations, colorful maps of the world, and even the famous poster of Albert Einstein with his tongue sticking out beneath a mop of unruly hair. The room was empty; the other kids were at recess. Only August remained, tucked into a corner, his lips pursed together in concentration. Surrounding him were four bird feeders, made mostly out of old milk jugs and wire. Some were painted yellow and green; others were decorated with dried macaroni and old buttons. He raised his head and smiled when he saw me. He stood up, and I hugged my son.

"Show me what you're making," I said.

By the time August put the finishing touches on his fifth bird feeder, the other kids were pouring back into the classroom. We carried all of the bird feeders to the car and loaded them inside. On the way home, I looked at my son and could not imagine a thing he could do, or anything that could happen to him, that could make me stop feeling this heart-breaking love for him. Heart-breaking because I knew I could not protect him from feeling sad or hurt or afraid. I couldn't stop life from happening all around him. I smiled and ran my fingers through his longish hair.

"Do you want to talk about it?" I asked.

"Mom, can we pick up some birdseed on the way home?"

§

We got to our apartment, unloaded three jumbo bags of birdseed and all the bird feeders and left them outside by the front door. As I made lunch, I said, "August, it's okay to be sad, to miss Peter."

"I know, Mom. Can I go outside?"

"Come give your mom a hug first."

Half an hour later, I called to him, "August, lunch is ready."

When he did not answer, I opened the door and stopped. In our tiny oak tree, (the one where Puppet used to sit), August had wound a rope, coarse and dry, among its branches. And on the rope he had hung his bird feeders—the bright red one with the sun painted on it, the one covered entirely in blue and yellow swirls, the one on which he had painted the smiling face of a man and his cat. He had filled the feeders, and already mourning doves and thrushes were descending upon the parking lot, ready for a meal.

"August, it's beautiful. Where did you get the rope...?" Then I noticed its fraying end, the end where the kitchen knife had sliced through it. My eyes drifted to the bushes where Peter's mother had tossed this very same rope only a few days ago. I wondered if August knew where the rope had come from.

But then he smiled at me and said, "It's for Peter," and I knew he did.

We both went inside and watched from the window as little by little, small birds with their delicate feathers and tapered wings perched in the tree or on the rope and snuck beakfuls of seed in the afternoon light. Over the years, we would continue to fill the feeders. Yet, no matter how many days passed between fillings, and no matter how many birds came to feast, we never found the feeders empty. Not once. There was always just enough left before we filled them again. And the front yard was forever dotted with birds, mostly brown and grey, but once in a while a hidden soft patch of yellow or red was revealed as the winged diners fluttered and foraged for food. But more importantly, to me at least, that evening, August began writing in his journal again. His new entry read:

BIRDS SIT ON PETER'S ROPE

CHAPTER *14*

I N LOS ANGELES IN OCTOBER, the Santa Ana winds begin
to blow — warm breezes swirling among dried leaves or plastic
bags that ruffle skirts and bring autumn on their shoulders.
Jack-o'-lanterns begin to grace the front porches of otherwise nondescript homes. Ghosts and red-eyed demons glare at passersby
from drugstore windows. And people from all walks of life prepare for their one-night metamorphosis into super heroes, horror
movie villains, or sexy *anythings*. While I was busy transforming
my son into Charley Harper for his school's early Halloween party, I reflected on the real transformations taking place in our lives.
It had been months since we lost Peter, and our sadness remained
(creeping up on us softly in the night or passing like a cool breeze
against the napes of our necks). But the fact that we had survived it
brought us even closer together. August and I spent as much time
as we could with Joe and Alice, and Joe still spent many afternoons
reading with me, though he had long ago surpassed my help.

Joe and Alice both had taken and passed the GED. Though Alice remained in the same profession, Joe was now attending CSU
Northridge, studying to be a teacher. He had given up his job laying carpet and was busy fulfilling his hours as a student teacher
(but still, always managed to be parked outside the window during
those times when Alice might need him). He worked in a rundown
school in a tough neighborhood and ran an after school program
as part tutor, part counselor, and part friend to a group of troubled
kids. Joe talked about "his kids" often, and I felt like I knew them.

One day Joe came home very excited. That year, as every year, the school director thought it would be a good idea to have the kids put on a holiday play, but as he emphasized to Joe, not a Christmas play or a Hanukkah play—not in these politically correct times when celebrating one's own faith had somehow come to mean an affront to all the other faithful, particularly those who have fought so hard to have the freedom to publicly celebrate their own faith or to have no faith at all. So it was decided. They would produce a non-religious play about religious holidays, and Joe would be the one to direct it. Though Joe was thrilled by the idea, he told me the kids were less than enthusiastic.

"What did they say?" I asked.

"Man, why do we have to be in a stupid ass play?" Joe said chuckling at his own imitation of Marcus, a 14-year-old boy who had been in and out of juvenile hall from the time he was eleven years old.

"So I said, *I'm the director and you're my students. I want you guys in the play."*

He continued to relate the day's events to me as we sat in my kitchen watching August paint.

"Of course, Marcus' comeback was, *It's gonna take a miracle to get me on that stage,"* and I told him, *Well, miracles do happen, you know.*

"But Marcus just laughed. He said to me, *Yeah? Where? And don't give us any crap about the miracle of birth or a fuckin' sunset man. That shit doesn't fly here."*

"Of course, the kids all laughed at first. But then I asked if any of them had ever witnessed a miracle. Their reaction was so strange. They all just stared at the floor and said nothing. It amazed me. These kids are never afraid to say what they think. But they were completely silenced by the possibility of miracles. The irony of it is these kids face real violence every day—and yet they still manage to wake up, get dressed, and go about their day. Which seems pretty miraculous to me."

"Did you tell them that?" I asked.

"I did. I also told 'em about my sister and how her death

changed everything for my mom and dad and me. But then I told
'em about Alice and how she saved my life. I said, *She's the greatest
miracle imaginab*le.

"The kids didn't say anything at first, but then a few of them
started to talk."

Joe proceeded to tell me about Carla, whose cousin, Donna, had
been shot twice in the head. Despite the doctor's prediction that she
would end up blind or maybe brain dead, she healed quickly and
was now in medical school.

He told me about Tyler, whose mom became violent when she
drank, about how she came home one day cursing and screaming.
Tyler and his sister hid in the closet and prayed she wouldn't hurt
them. They could hear her banging her way to the closet door.

"If she had made it through, Tyler believed she would've killed
them," Joe said. "But then they heard a loud thud followed by nothing. When they finally got the courage to open the closet door, they
found their mother—dead from a heart attack."

Joe repeated Tyler's words to me. *She was my mom and all, but her
death was the best thing that could've happened to us. My sister prayed for
it, and it happened. So...miracle or just luck?"*

Joe and I agreed it certainly classified as a miracle.

After sharing a few more of their stories, the kids finally agreed
to write about a miracle of their choice. They would combine them
all together into a play. "I think they secretly liked the idea," Joe
told me with a wide grin.

§

The next morning, Alice needed the car so I gave Joe a ride to
school.

"Come in and meet the kids. They're working on their plays."
So I did.

Once inside, he introduced me to his students. From his de-
scriptions I immediately recognized Tyler and Carla. I watched

them work for a while and was ready to leave when a young kid raised his hand from the back of the class.

It was John. Joe had told me about him. His mother tried to sell him to an undercover cop for heroin when he was six years old. He had lived more than half of his life with his grandfather, whom he idolized, but who was sitting in a home with Alzheimer's racking his brain, unable to recognize the boy who sat by his bedside every weekend but able to remember the passages from his beloved Bible word for word.

"Is it okay to write about something we don't even believe in?"

"Like what?" asked Joe.

"Well, I ain't seen it personally, but my grandpa is always talking about the Bible and shit." Groans came from the back of the class, but this didn't bother John.

"My grandpa says Jesus performs miracles all the time. He even brings people back to life. I read about some guy named Lazarus who got sick and died, and they stuck him in a cave with a stone coverin' it. His sisters begged Jesus to save him, which he did, but only after the dude was already dead and rotting."

"That's fuckin' nasty," commented another kid in class.

"Well, my grandpa asks me to read him the story all the time. And he always says, *That's me. They got the details wrong. I was murdered, I wasn't never sick. But that story's 'bout me.*

"Nobody believes him, of course. It's just the Alzheimer's talking, they say. He's confused. But he shows me the scar on his chest, from where he says he was stabbed. Right in the heart. Either way, it's a mira...it's some freaky shit he's still alive after that."

"What do you think Joe? Do you think it could happen?" a young girl with bright green hair asked.

"Well, I'm not a religious man. I don't know if there is a God, but I believe anything is possible. If you tell me a man could bring another man back from the dead, then who am I to argue? Who am I to say out of all the millions of men and women who have lived through the span of time, that there might not be one with the ability to bring back someone from the dead? Can you prove it didn't happen? Think about it, if Carla's cousin survived with her eyesight intact, against all medical odds, perhaps someone out there has the ability to bring people back from the dead. Or perhaps it will happen. It's the possibility of it that makes it so wonderful."

I felt a surge of pride for my friend.

"What ain't fair," said John, "isn't that miracles happen to some people and not to others. I get it, I guess. But why would God, if there is a God, why would he give only some people the ability to *believe* in miracles? My grandfather had a tough life, tougher than any of us...a rotten mother, a rotten daughter. He worked hard his entire life, and now he can't even remember who I am. A nurse changes his fucking diapers every day. And he still has hope. He still believes there's good. I'm just a kid, and it all sounds like bullshit to me. I don't have faith in anything."

There was silence as heads nodded in agreement around the room.

Then Carla spoke up, "It's your choice to believe or not. You can choose."

"No," replied John. "It's something you either have or you don't. You can't choose to believe in something, just like you can't choose to like the color red or opera or sports. You like them or you don't."

"So, why do you want to write about something you don't believe in?" Carla asked.

"Because my grandpa believes in it. And I believe in him."

So Joe's kids agreed John could write about God. And over the next few weeks they composed their stories of miracles: real ones, invented ones, ones that were hoped for, miracles of life, and miracles of death. And John in honor of his grandfather wrote about a man he didn't believe in, a man he wasn't even sure existed but who his grandfather was certain had brought all of us back from the dead.

§

Six weeks before the opening of the play about miracles, Joe believed he was presented with another miracle all his own—Alice announced she was quitting.

She told us on a Saturday morning. I had just returned from dropping August off at a friend's house, and Joe and Alice and I were enjoying our cups of coffee in my living room.

"I'm quitting," Alice said casually, taking another sip of her coffee. "I see what you're doing with those kids, Joe. How you're helping them. I want to be a part of something important too. I don't know how yet, but I'm ready to find out."

Joe rose, picked Alice up by the waist lifting her slightly off the ground, and hugged her to him tightly. She hugged him back. They stayed in this embrace for a long time. It was finally Alice who said, with laughter in her voice, "You have homework to grade, and I have to look for a job."

§

Alice had been working temp jobs for less than three weeks when I received a strange phone call from Joe. August had just finished his bath, and I was getting ready to read him a bedtime story when the phone rang.

"I need to go out for a while. Can you come sit with Alice?"

His voice sounded odd, hollow somehow, as if he were speaking from inside a deep cave.

"Sit with Alice? What happ…?"

"Please just come," he interrupted.

I gathered a pillow and some extra blankets and walked with August to their apartment. Joe was waiting at the door, visibly upset.

"Alice is sleeping. She's going to be okay. We're going to be okay," he said, and I could see he had been crying. "I put some blankets on the couch for August, so he can sleep too."

Even in the face of whatever this tragedy was, Joe still took care of us, of August.

I smiled at Joe and rested my hand on his arm. "Whatever happened, we'll get through this," I said. I quickly made up the couch for August and tucked him under the covers. I kissed his forehead and left him to sleep.

I found Joe outside. He was sitting on the front step, shaking.

"Joe, what happened?" Worry gripped its sharp tentacles around my heart.

"You know, just today I was thinking to myself how glad I was I didn't have to worry about Alice anymore. She had quit. She was done. I was free. I didn't have to sit in my car beneath the window, listening in case she needed me. I didn't have to worry, because she was finally safe. I thought about this all fucking day. I thought about it on my way home and when I parked my car in any old space. I thought about it as I walked to the front door and even in those few seconds between when I opened the door and when I walked into my living room. I was so sure she was safe, even when I saw the stains on the carpet. You know what my first thought was? It wasn't how those stains got there, my first thought was *the only downside to my new job is I no longer get free carpet cleaning product samples once a month.* Can you believe how stupid I am?"

He covered his eyes and began to weep.

I put my arms around him and hugged him tightly.

"You're not stupid, Joe. We all thought Alice was safe." Though I didn't yet know the details, I could guess what had happened and my heart thudded dully in my chest. I also understood Joe's reaction. It was not that he was unfamiliar with blood and the particular way it had of seeping into carpet fibers. It was simply that his brain could not even fathom the possibility of something terrible occurring in his living room, which most likely involved the woman he loved. It would have been like asking him to comprehend a talking fish or a flying dog. There were things that just did not happen in his world and finding Alice's blood on the carpet was at the top of the list.

"I have to go. Will you stay with Alice?"

"Of course I will. But, Joe, she needs you. Where are you going?"

"I'm doing this for Alice," he said and left.

I immediately went back inside. I checked on August, who was sleeping on the sofa. He looked so peaceful it broke my heart. I walked down the hall, knocked softly and entered Alice and Joe's bedroom. I was not prepared for the sight of Alice, as she was then. Her face was badly bruised. Deep cuts zig-zagged across her lips and cheeks, and one eye was swollen shut. She was curled up in their bed, her wet hair soaking the sheets. Despite the intense pain she must have been in, she had clearly showered. On the floor by the bed was a garbage bag, and I could see it contained the clothes she had been wearing earlier. Blood, like a Pollock painting, across the canvas of my friend.

I removed my shoes, got into the bed and curled up behind her. I wrapped my arm around her chest, nestling my knees in the crooks of hers. I told her we should go to the hospital, we should call the police. But she refused to do either. Her body would heal, and she would not press charges. This was not to protect him, the man who had done this to her. It was to protect herself. She had seen it happen enough times with other girls. She knew it would be his story against hers; and her character would be trashed, her life choices denounced. For every question, for every doubt, for every piece of evidence she had, some slick lawyer would have an answer, a plausible lie that would allow the world order to go unquestioned, allowing everyone to feel safe in their preconceived assumptions:

Him = family man = good

Alice = slut = maybe she deserved what she got or got what she deserved.

She had had to beg Joe not to call the police, and she begged me not to now. Though I didn't want to admit it, I knew she was right.

§

The day Alice was raped began like every other day had for the past two and a half weeks. Late in the morning she and I had talked as she got ready for work. She was working as a hostess at Chin Chin, a trendy Chinese restaurant in Studio City. She told me how she relished dressing up and walking the two blocks to the bus stop. From the way she described it, I could almost hear what she heard—the sounds of L.A. traffic, moaning buses, groaning trucks, the sing-song sound of flashy Mercedes. I could almost see what she saw—colorful people commuting to work (the old man with gray dreadlocks who smelled faintly of aftershave and smiled at her every morning, the bus driver with a scar on his right hand) and all the other people filling and un-filling the fake leather seats at the front of the bus where she sat every morning. She told me how she enjoyed chitchatting with the customers as they waited for a table during the lunch hour rush and the smells of frying onions and exotic sauces wafting through from the kitchen. She particularly liked joking with the chefs and her other co-workers who didn't know her story, who didn't know her past.

"I thought I was beyond this. I thought I didn't have to be afraid. I thought Joe didn't have to worry anymore. I thought…"

"I know," was all I could think to say.

We remained curled together for some time.

Did minutes pass?

Hours?

Days?

When she spoke again, it was to tell me about Mason.

She had come home from work in the afternoon to find Mason, a middle-aged man who had been her client for almost five years, waiting at her front door. Alcohol wafted from his pores. A vein had burst in his left eye and it was hazy with blood. He had been crying.

"Hey, Alice, let's go inside. I need to talk."

Alice told me she hesitated at first, held back by a slight trepidation she felt somewhere in the back of her throat, but she ignored her own better judgment and let him in.

When he hugged her, she reluctantly hugged him back, but when his mouth tried to find hers and his hands groped at her breasts, she pushed him away.

"Mason, I told you, I'm done with that."

Unlike the usually easy-going Mason she thought she knew, he quickly became angry with her.

"My wife left me! She thinks she's too good for me, and now you're telling me you're too good for me too?"

"You've gone through this before with her. She always takes you back."

"This time's different. She filed for divorce. She changed the locks on the doors and got a restraining order against me. She's sellin' the house. My daughters won't speak to me. I'm never gonna see them again."

"Come on, Mason. Let's take a walk," Alice had said, trying to swallow her fear, a fear I was familiar with, a fear which wells up in the mouth like bile.

"I'm living at a goddamn Motel 96! I don't wanna take a fucking walk!"

Then his hand tightened into a fist and he swung, clipping Alice against the jaw. She fell hard to the ground, and he climbed on top of her and his rage did not stop for 22 minutes.

"I'll hold back from telling you the details," she said. For she knew, as did I, that we were both all too aware of the atrocities one human being can inflict upon another.

Once it was over, Mason retrieved his wallet from the back pocket of his jeans, pulled out a wad of money, and let it drop over her. Then he walked out her front door without so much as a glance in her direction.

§

From down the hall, August's voice transported us back.

"Mom?" he called.

I rose quickly and found him standing in the hallway, looking around in confusion.

"I'm right here, honey."

"Can I see Alice?"

I hesitated. Obviously he understood Alice had been hurt, and I knew he wanted to help. But I was afraid of how August would react. Would he be frightened? Would he understand? Did I want him to understand?

Before I let him into the room I sat him on my lap and said, "Alice is going to look different for a while. She's badly hurt. If you feel afraid or uncomfortable, it's okay. We can come back to the living room, and Alice won't be sad or anything."

As we entered her bedroom I braced myself for his reaction, but he did not turn away or look afraid. Without hesitation, he climbed onto the bed next to her. He lay down on his side, facing her, his open hand resting on her cheek, covering the cuts and bruises with outstretched fingers.

"Did somebody hurt you, Alice?"

"Yes, August, somebody hurt me, but I'm going to be fine now," she told him.

"I know," he smiled up at her. I sat on the edge of the bed, my hand resting on August's back, his fingers still touching Alice's face.

Thump-shuffle-whisper.

I looked at Alice and she nodded at me as if in acquiescence, as if she were ready for me to know. I wondered if August would know. Would he see what I saw? Had he always seen? Had he, from the very beginning, understood everything?

CHAPTER 15

A DROP OF RUST-COLORED WATER hit cement *thump*, then the barely heard *shuffle* as a new drop formed, and a *whisper* as it fell, *thump, shuffle, whisper, thump*. From a hole somewhere above, dirty water dripped at their feet. I was hit by the smell of stale urine and the sight of Alice and Joe at 14 years old, stretched out on the ground atop a piece of cardboard and huddled beneath ragged blankets. Not even a year had passed since they had run away from home. The crumbling walls of the abandoned building they were living in did little to protect them from the elements, and I felt the winter wind chilling their bones. I felt the pangs of hunger clutching their stomachs into tight and knotted fists.

Alice lay on her side, one arm draped on Joe's chest. Joe had one arm around Alice, and in the other hand he held a knife. With his thumb, he caressed the blade.

"Are you ready?" Alice asked, without looking up into his eyes.

"I'm ready."

Joe stood and tucked the knife into the pocket of his sweatshirt. Alice rose too, and they both stepped nervously into their shoes. Hand in hand they passed between light and dark as they strolled beneath the streetlights which illuminated the sidewalk in patches. They walked in silence, watching the occasional car roll by on an otherwise empty street.

Suddenly Joe stopped.

"Wait here," he said. "I can't do this with you watching."

"Okay." She let her hand slip from Joe's and watched him walk away.

But Alice was Alice, even then. She gave him a good head start and then followed him.

Joe walked with his head bent slightly down, nervously fingering the blade of his knife and feeling the sharp, cold metal against his thumb. Alice knew what he must be thinking: *what would it feel like to threaten someone with this? What if things got out of control? What would it feel like to plunge this sharp and jagged thing into someone's flesh?* Joe visibly shuddered and pulled the hood of his sweatshirt tight over his head. He watched as the occasional pedestrian passed by in the night, some gliding right by without a second glance, others moving slightly away, for you can never be too careful in a city such as this.

Alice wondered who he would choose. They had talked about it a few days before, when they were lying on the cement floor of the abandoned building where they slept at night, along with a horde of other runaways. Some were permanent residents, like Joe and Alice. Others stayed only a couple of nights then disappeared for weeks or months at a time or were never seen or heard from again. Drugs, unprotected sex, kids of both genders selling their bodies for a couple of bucks, girls giving birth to strangers' babies in tight and shadowed corners—these were the lives of the people who surrounded Alice and Joe. Every night though, they promised each other they would not let themselves get to that point. But they were starving, cold, and they couldn't find real work.

So one day, while most kids their age were debating about which movie to see or which party to go to, Joe and Alice plotted their crimes. The week before, Joe had found a large knife one of the other kids, too wasted to notice, had left behind.

When Joe finally showed it to Alice (its fine wooden handle, the point sharp enough to draw blood when you pressed your finger too hard against it) she took it from his hands.

"Where did you get this?"

"I found it."

"What're you gonna do with it?"

"Not sure yet. Just keep it, I guess."

Alice stared at the knife for a long time—mesmerized by the way it glittered in the afternoon light.

"Maybe you found this knife for a reason."

"Like what?"

"Like maybe we can use it to get some food."

"What are we going to do? Rob a grocery store at knife point?"

"No...not a grocery store."

"Then what?"

So it was decided; they would steal from regular people—nothing serious—just purses and wallets from anyone who looked rich.

"They have to be rich," Joe insisted. "We don't want to take money from people who are just as fucked as we are. Besides, rich people probably won't even miss the money."

"And no old people, no matter how rich. I can't imagine stealing from someone who could be a grandmother."

"Ok. I think I know the perfect place."

They agreed on when (that night) and where (the all night parking garage where nightclub goers and workaholics parked their cars, the former to dance and drink all night, the latter to sit into the wee hours of the morning pouring over briefs or bank accounts).

"I'll do it," Joe said before Alice even had a chance to offer.

"Joe, come on, I can do it. People might not expect it from a girl. Those macho guys will be so embarrassed they probably wouldn't even call the cops or anything."

"I'll do it," Joe grabbed the knife from Alice's hands. "I'm the man, and it's my job to protect and provide for you."

Though Alice found the whole sentiment outdated, she was also touched and didn't want to hurt Joe's feelings. In the end, it was decided. Joe would do it.

But now, as he hung in the shadows among the parked cars, Joe (a heart of gold, a heart—we would later learn—of glass) felt unsure of himself. He knew what he was doing amounted to much more than just stealing a few bucks from a stranger. Along with a wallet or a purse would he also be stealing someone's sense of safety? A little bit of their freedom? Their ability to walk alone at night, to ever feel safe again in the city they called home? Would he take something from these people they could never get back? Even if he stole from someone rich, from someone whose life wouldn't be affected in the least by losing a few hundred bucks—he would still be altering them, changing them forever. Fear does not take bribes. It does not go away quietly.

Then Joe thought of Alice and how hungry and tired she was (how hungry and tired they both were). When a young woman in her early thirties walked by (car keys already in hand, just like they teach in self-defense class), Joe followed behind her. His temples were pounding. All the while, Alice was there, watching.

Suddenly the woman stopped. Fear registered in her eyes as she turned to face Joe.

Now was his chance.

"Are you going to hurt me?" the woman's voice trembled slightly.

From the darkness, Alice whispered, "Come on, Joe, come *on.*"

Joe raised the knife, pointing it at the woman. She took a step back, then stood motionless, as if she were afraid to move.

"Please," she whispered, her throat hoarse and dry with fear.

Joe faltered. Hesitated.

"Oh, no, no, I...uh..." stammered Joe, "I...I found this knife back there. I thought maybe you dropped it. I thought it was yours," he said lamely, his face dropping. He was unable to meet her eyes.

Then he held out the knife to her, flat, on the palm of his slightly trembling hand. "You can take it if you want."

The woman raised her hands up, "No, no, thanks."

She exhaled slowly. "You scared the shit out of me though,"

and she laughed with relief.

Joe laughed too, "Sorry, sorry I scared you."

"That's okay. Hey, do you need a ride somewhere?" she asked, (her trust back, her innocence once again intact).

"No, no. I live around here. Thanks."

"Sure? Okay then."

Joe watched to make sure she made it safely to her car. She gave a short wave and smile as she drove past him. Joe waved goodbye with one hand and slipped the knife back into his pocket with the other.

Watching all of this, Alice was surprised to find she was not disappointed in Joe. She was even more surprised to find that she loved him more right then than she ever thought possible. He couldn't do it, and this fact made her heart leap with joy. She decided then and there she didn't want him to become hard and jaded. She didn't want to lose him, the Joe he was in that very moment.

§

A few nights later, as Joe slept, Alice slipped the knife from beneath the cardboard they slept on and walked out to the street. *I should have been the one all along. I can provide for both of us,* she thought. She had gone only two blocks when a car pulled up alongside the curb. A quick *toot toot* on the horn beckoned Alice over.

The tinted window on the passenger's side rolled down just a crack, and Alice was hit with such a smell of food that she became dizzy. She folded her fingers over the slightly open window and peered inside. In the back seat was a brown paper bag imprinted with large splotches of grease (warm, delectable grease).

"Are you lost?" she asked the driver without taking her eyes off the bag.

He turned off the engine of his car.

"I'll give you five bucks if you suck my dick," he leered at her from behind the wheel. For the first time she looked at him. He was probably in his late forties, balding and overweight. His stomach fell over the belt of his pants and touched his thighs.

Alice's first instinct was to give him the finger and walk away or better yet run. Had it not been for the bag of fast food and its aroma, which hit her stomach like a fist, she might have.

As it was she leaned into the window of his car. "Five bucks and your dinner for a hand job."

The man leaned over and opened the passenger door. Already his hand was in his pants. Alice slid into the passenger seat and closed the door.

The man leaned his seat back and his heavy, sweaty body moved back with it. "Go on, then."

He closed his eyes. Alice placed her young girl's hand on him and made a tight fist. She moved her hand up and down, slowly at first, then faster and faster, in tempo with the sound of his breathing.

§

From the time Alice was a young girl, she had had a rich imagination. Though her childhood was a happy one, she was an only child and once in a while felt lonely for the company of other children. To ease her loneliness, she invented worlds filled with enough brothers and sisters to form a dance troop. In her mind they traveled the world performing for presidents and kings. On other occasions, they had great jungle adventures together which lasted for hours; her mother or father would have to call her name at least three times before bringing her back to her real life. When she did come back, she looked up at the worried faces of her parents and smiled.

"Alice, are you okay?" they would ask.

"I'm fine," she declared happily. "I've just been to the Amazon, is all. And I'm tired."

And, in truth, she *would* be tired from her hike among red and blue poison dart frogs, squawking lime-green parrots and plants with large-veined leaves that were bigger than she was. Absent-mindedly, she would pick out the stringy flesh of ripe mango still stuck between her teeth, as she told her parents about the troops of howler monkeys that bellowed in the early mornings and the large tracks left by spotted cats that hid among the shadows.

By the time Alice was seven years old, she was well-skilled at postponing life's more unpleasant moments. At school, she invented worlds to disappear into during particularly boring lessons; at the dentist's office she became a pirate captured by Spanish imperials; when she was feeling sick, she simply disappeared to another planet where illness did not exist and chocolate fudge banana splits were eaten every day for breakfast. While she was in these worlds, it was not that she did not feel the pain, for example, of the dentist's drill; it was that she turned her pain into something she could understand and control.

At nine years old, when she and her father were returning from a father-daughter canoe trip and a drunk driver careened into their vehicle, sending her to the hospital for several weeks (where she would eventually meet Joe) and her father to the morgue, in her own mind, she did not watch her father die. As they hung upside down in the car, suspended by their seat belts, Alice erased the blood from her father's face and sealed the lacerations on his arms and chest. In their place, she painted on an astronaut's helmet and a blue space suit.

"I love you, dad," she said.

But he could not speak. He was already gone. With eyes closed, breath forever held, Alice knew she would never see her father again—at least not in this world. In this world, she would no longer get to hug him at night or paddle canoes with him along a fast and flowing river; he would never again speak her name, or eat cereal with her late at night when they both were supposed to be in bed. She understood all of this. But instead of a body stuck in the ground to be eaten away at by worms and beetles, she sent her father to another world. A world where she could visit him from time to time—a distant planet where dinosaurs roamed in a friendly way and gave young girls rides on their leathery backs, where father and daughter could swim in the night and understand everything the fish were saying, where someone, somehow had discovered the cure for death.

Alice's mother, meanwhile, became stuck in a maze of grief she couldn't navigate her way out of, so Alice took over the job and mothered herself. But she always allowed herself to drift to another place, another time whenever things became too difficult. And this is what she did in the car, with that man. But do not be fooled. She was aware of him, of her hand on his wretched parts. He too was in the boat sailing across blue waters, right alongside her. If she looked, just for a moment, she would see him—his thick face, his sweaty skin—so she kept her eyes focused on her father, her mother, Joe, and the feast of sweets and breads, cheese, papaya, and fresh tomatoes spread out before them. She concentrated on the orange-leafed trees dripping cool shade onto their heads, the green clouds floating across a mango-colored sky, and the small yellow bird on the shore, scratching up insects or crumbs from the grass, its legs as thin as straws.

§

She allowed herself back into the present only after he had pushed her hand away and was busy rooting through his wallet. He handed her a damp and faded five-dollar bill.

She took the money and the bag of food and stepped out of the car, wiping her hand against her already filthy jeans.

"Hey, I like you," he called after her "and my wife makes a mean turkey sandwich. So, what do you say? Same time tomorrow?"

"Make it two sandwiches, maybe some peaches and carrots, something healthy," she called over her shoulder and kept walking. She was tempted to look in the bag, to see what treasures were inside, but she waited until she made it back to Joe.

On her way home, she stopped at a liquor store and used some of the money to buy a package of condoms (she would stick with hand jobs for as long as she could, but she knew, eventually, more things would be required of her. And, just like Alice in every situation, she wanted to be prepared in all ways possible).

She pocketed the change.

When she made it back, she found Joe pacing the floor, worry in his eyes. When he saw her, he ran over and hugged her.

"Where were you?"

"Getting us dinner," she smiled.

They tore open the greasy bag greedily. Using the knife, they split the double-decker hamburger and the apple pie exactly in half. They shared the large order of fries and the milkshake, licking the grease from the paper wrappers and sucking the last bit of liquid from the cup.

"Where'd ya get this?" Joe asked once they had finished eating and their stomachs were moderately full.

"I held up a guy and got some cash. It was easy," she shrugged, lowering her eyes. Alice had wanted to tell him, had planned on telling him. She had never lied to him and didn't want to start now. But when his eyes met hers, she knew it would destroy him to know what she had done (what she knew she would do again. And again).

They had made a pact when they ran way—they would wait until they were both 15 before they lost their virginity together. It had been Joe's idea of course. *We have to be responsible, act like adults. Fifteen is a responsible age. I'm going to plan everything. It's going to be perfect.*

But Alice already knew she wouldn't make it to her 15th birthday. And, though she held out for as long as she could, one month later she lost her virginity to a stranger in an alley a mere four blocks from where she and Joe slept. She continued to lie to Joe about where the cash came from, hiding most of it, so he wouldn't question her too much about it. After each job, she cleaned herself as best she could in the sinks of public restrooms or dirty hotel bathrooms.

And on her 15th birthday, as promised, Alice came home to a surprise. Joe had saved a bit of money from panhandling, and with it he bought candles and a new used blanket at the thrift store. He had even found some old flowers someone had tossed into the garbage behind a flower shop. They were wilted and brown at the edges, but the centers were yellow, clinging to life.

"You did this for me?" she asked.

"For us," he said. "I told you it would be worth the wait."

§

Almost a year passed before Alice told Joe the story of the man in the car and what she had done. By carefully choosing which words to use and which to omit, she led Joe to believe it had happened just the day before. She retrieved a bit of the money she had been hiding and showed it to him.

"He gave me this," she said. "We can make enough to eat, maybe even one day get an apartment, get off the streets."

Joe looked at Alice. "I trust you."

Alice, for her part, was relieved Joe did not try to stop her but respected her decision. From that moment on, there existed a silent pact between them—they would always do what they had to do for each other without question, without doubt, without hesitation.

Then, I watched as Joe took Alice's hands in his. And again, "I trust you," he said. With those words another heart entered the tale. And we were privy, then, to its secrets, too. We heard the strong beats of Joe's heart (a twin to Alice's, a heart of equal love and of equal sacrifice). Though he never talked about it, though the words were never spoken aloud (to this day, it has been the one thing they could not really talk to each other seriously about), Joe already knew what Alice had done. He had known the entire time. And he understood she did it for him. For them.

The first day, when she came to him proudly carrying a bag of fast food in a grease-stained paper bag, he had felt such relief at first. All he wanted to do was fill his empty stomach. When she told him how she got the food, however, he saw right away she was not being truthful. But it was only when she kissed him that he smelled something foreign (something frightful) on her body and he realized what had happened. But Joe was Joe, even then. He kept silent to protect the person he loved most in the world.

§

I let my hand slip from Alice's and felt my heart calming, steadying, returning to its natural beat.

"Oh my God! Joe knew? He knew and he never said a word. All this time..." Alice wept, "I thought I was the only one making real sacrifices. I thought I was the strong one. But Joe, he's sacrificing everything."

She sat up in bed, panicked. She clutched my arm. "Penny, you have to stop Joe. Please, don't let him leave."

"Alice, he's been gone for hours."

CHAPTER 16

A FTER A LONG WHILE, Alice succumbed to sleep. August slept by her side. I waited up for Joe to come home, which he did a few hours before dawn. His clothes and his right cheek were tarnished with blood. When he walked through the door he saw me and smiled sadly.

"How's Alice?"

"She's resting. She's going to be okay, Joe." I took his hand. "But, I'm worried about you."

"Seeing Alice like this…so damaged. How could I have let this happen? We promised we would always do whatever we had to, to keep each other safe. I let her down. I had to make it right. I had to."

"What did you do?"

He told me that before he had called me to come sit with Alice, he had walked to a payphone on the corner (so as not to wake her) and called every Motel 96 in the greater L.A. area.

"I prayed over and over, please, God, let him still be there," he said, and I envisioned his hands flipping through the phone book, his fingers dialing the numbers, the clink of the coins being fed to the machine.

Good evening, Motel 96, may I help you?

Yes, can you connect me to Mason Brenner's room, please?

I'm sorry, no one by that name has checked in yet.

Motel 96, how can I help you?

Hello, Motel 96. What can I do for you?

Over and over until, *Can you connect me to Mason Brenner's room please?"*

Let me check...okay, yes, hold on please...

Not waiting to be transferred, Joe dropped the receiver back into the cradle and slowly walked home.

§

Joe told me that when he left his apartment again that night, he already knew what he was going to do. By the time he arrived to the motel parking lot, he had a plan formed in his head. He parked his car, slipped on a pair of leather gloves and then pulled a knife (*the knife from all those years ago*) out of the glove compartment. There were few other cars in the parking lot and Joe did not know which, if any, belonged to Mason. So he waited some more.

"Joe," I placed my hand on his shoulder, "what happened?"

When Joe next spoke, his words came like a flood, raging and strong, words that felt like a drowning. He didn't know how much time had passed, he told me, before a charcoal sedan pulled up in front of one of the rooms. But when he saw it, Joe's stomach tightened. He watched as the car door opened and a man's leg emerged, planting itself firmly on the ground.

In those few seconds, as Joe stared at the shiny black shoe (a man's shoe), and the light-colored sock visible just below the cuff of the pant leg, everything stopped. Everything went silent and dark as if God had inhaled and sucked the entire world into His great and mighty lungs, leaving only Joe and the possibility of Mason. If cars passed by, Joe did not see them. If Joe's heart beat, he did not feel it. He was only aware of that foot, in that black shoe, with that white sock. There was nothing else.

The man stood.

It was not Mason.

From the other three doors, a woman in her mid-thirties and four kids all under the age of fifteen came pouring out.

God exhaled.

Laughter and chaos immediately erupted in the parking lot as suitcases, pink backpacks, a slightly worn stuffed elephant, a red cooler, and a hockey stick were loaded up and carried to the hotel room door. The family entered, one by one: the twin girls first (who, to Joe's relief, were not dressed in matching clothes) then the oldest boy who was tall and lanky with longish, greasy hair.

"He was a good-looking kid despite the acne," Joe said.

Next, the youngest boy entered the room, cradled in his mother's arms. The dad entered last and shut the door quietly behind him.

Joe had been so distracted by the family, he hadn't seen the man who was walking lazily across the other side of the motel parking lot until it was almost too late. Joe recognized Mason immediately from the times he had seen him slip quietly out of Joe and Alice's apartment.

"You know, in all those years Mason never once looked at me. He never noticed me sitting in the car outside the apartment, and he didn't notice me waiting for him at the hotel, either. "

Just as Mason opened the door to his room, Joe took him by surprise, pushed him inside and quickly followed behind. Mason calmly took out his wallet.

Look, man, I don't have lots of money. Take what you want and get out.

I'm not here for money.

What the hell do you want, then? asked Mason.

My name's Joe. Alice is my girlfriend. You remember Alice, don't you?

Joe told me that Mason's face went pale at the mention of Alice. He stumbled back, tripping onto the edge of the bed. He lifted his hands, palms up in surrender.

I didn't...I didn't mean for it to happen...fuck...I'm sorry, man. I am so sorry, Mason muttered.

Me too, said Joe.

And without another word, Joe pulled the knife from his pocket and leveled it into Mason's abdomen, once, then pulled it smoothly out. The force knocked Mason to the ground. Joe dropped the knife and began to hit and hit and hit.

Please…, Mason managed to choke out.

And to his own surprise, Joe did finally stop. He wasn't sure why. He didn't know if it was because of Mason's weak efforts to fight back or because of his pleas or all that blood and the sickening sound of flesh pounding into flesh. He wanted (had planned) to continue to hit him long after Mason had taken his final breath, long after the cries stopped, long after his heart lay still inside his chest, but Joe couldn't bring himself to do it.

He scrambled away from Mason and sat on the floor beside him. His entire body heaved as he fought the dizziness, the pounding in his head.

I too had to fight against the sickness rising in my belly as I listened to Joe's story.

Joe and Mason sat together for a while—neither moving, neither saying anything. Finally, Joe grabbed the telephone from the night stand and set it on the floor next to Mason.

It's not too late. If you call 911 now, the ambulance will get here on time. I'll stay with you.

Here finally was a bit of the Joe I recognized, the Joe who, despite everything, would not let a man suffer alone, who was prepared to face the consequences of what he had done.

But when Joe looked into Mason's eyes, he saw only uncertainty. As if Mason perhaps wasn't so sure he wanted to be alive to begin with. Or maybe he was too tired or too weak to make such a big decision—whether he should live or die. Maybe he was leaving it up to God. Maybe he was waiting for a miracle.

§

With a slow, almost sickening realization, it dawned on Joe that Mason was not going to call for an ambulance. He was going to let himself die, and Joe would really have killed him, would really have taken a person's life.

"I thought I could do it," Joe told me. "I thought I could do it for Alice. I owed her that much, but…"

"What happened?"

When he couldn't take it anymore, Joe knelt on the floor next to Mason and picked up the phone. He put it to his ear and listened to the deep, comforting hum of the dial tone, the sound representing his freedom. He didn't have to make the call. He could sit all night listening to the *hmmm* of the phone, or he could hang up and leave and no one else had to know.

Joe dialed 9…1…1.

Give…me the…phone, Mason stammered weakly.

Joe passed the phone to Mason, feeling a torrent of relief. Mason was going to live and Joe would somehow find a way to make up for this terrible thing he had done.

But when the 911 operator answered, Mason said, *I'm already dead. Don't bother…rushing over. The guy who killed me…grey hair… blue eyes…five-nine, 161 pounds…scar under his right eye, an eagle tattoo on his left arm.*

Then he dropped the phone and whispered, *Go,* softly enough so Joe could barely hear. *It's ok. Go.*

So Joe went. He drove his car to the 7-Eleven parking lot across the street and waited.

By the time the ambulance and police arrived, Mason was as good as his word: already dead. Joe watched them wheel his body out already covered in plastic, tucked safely away in a body bag (as if trying to keep death hidden from the rest of the world).

§

"I'm gonna take a shower," Joe said to me then.

I didn't know what to say to him. I didn't know what reaction I should have or what I should feel. I sat, stunned and barely able to breathe.

He returned fifteen minutes later, newly clean, newly washed, but somehow not the Joe I knew. He was carrying the garbage bag that contained Alice's clothes. He tossed the knife, his dirty clothes and the gloves he had been wearing into the same bag. So much blood, so much pain.

"It's over. It's over," he said.

I hugged him hard.

"Will you tell Alice?" I whispered, though I already knew the answer.

I silently prayed for Joe and Alice, for them to still be themselves, to still be *Joe and Alice*. But I feared that what he had done might be too much for him. I feared life might have finally damaged his spirit to a point unrecognizable, to a point beyond even Alice's ability to fix.

§

Over the next few days I watched the news carefully and scanned the local papers for stories about Mason's death. In Los Angeles, over 45,000 violent crimes are committed every year, and the majority of them never make it into the headlines. But the nature of this crime and the fact that the description Mason gave of his murderer was, in actuality, a description of Mason himself, created enough of a mystery for the news programs to report it. Why had the victim described himself as the murderer? Why had he been killed? Images of Mason flashed across the TV screen—a photo of him as a much younger man, smiling and holding a young girl in his arms (Mason, portrayed as an innocent man; Mason, an accomplice to ruin one night in a place which had once held so much happiness).

The television reports talked of police conducting the requisite search for and interviews with witnesses (no one saw a thing) and of sweeping the hotel room for clues. One particularly enthusiastic reporter pointed out that most hotel rooms, even the fanciest ones, are really not very clean. In this case, fingerprints, hairs, even bodily fluids—all the sorts of things needed for evidence—were left behind by dozens of guests who had traveled through over the past few months. It would take the police a while to sort out the evidence.

Meanwhile, reporters had tracked down Mason's wife and were camped outside her home, hoping she would be able to offer some clues as to what really happened on the night of Mason's murder. When they finally cornered her for an interview, she stared dully into the camera. Her eyes were puffy, and she hunched her shoulders as if trying to hide from the world. The reporters asked, "Who do you think did this to your husband?" And "Why didn't he describe his killer to the police when he had a chance?"

As I waited for her to answer, I wondered if she knew what Mason had done. Had he called her to confess his crime? Would she know who Alice was or where she lived? Could she trace all of this back to Joe?

But when she spoke (as if in a final act of letting go of something, perhaps, already long gone) she only said this: "He's not my husband anymore. He hasn't been my husband for a long time."

It only took three days for the story to fade—to make way for other (more interesting) tragedies. The last report I saw mentioned the police still had no real leads and with hundreds of other brutal murders on their hands, they would seal Mason's case and file it as unsolved. I imagined it as I had seen it on countless TV shows. The scant evidence the police had collected would be placed in a manila envelope, labeled, and shelved. There it would remain, gathering dust and mold, eventually forgotten by almost everyone. But for the few who could not forget, it would be a like a wound which does not close—always painful and always threatening the all too real possibility of infection.

CHAPTER 17

THE SCHOOL AUDITORIUM smelled of mildew and incense. It had a small stage bordered with a dusty red velvet curtain, a domed ceiling painted white with clouds against a dark blue sky, and brown birds with wings outstretched in flight toward the heavens. It reminded me of an old church Charlotte took me to once. It was one of the few happy memories I had from growing up.

The rows of chairs began to fill as friends and family members idled in to watch the show. Their voices, the sounds their bodies made as they settled into chairs, the general murmur of a room filled with the living echoed around the small room. Above the voices, I heard a sudden fluttering like stacks of paper in the wind. I looked up and saw a small brown bird flying frantically around the ceiling, as if it had escaped from the painting fresh and feathered or was trying in vain to return. It continued to fly nervously around the room as patrons entered, as children laughed, as props were noisily moved across the stage. Only when the lights faded and darkness took hold did the bird stop its anxious searching and land softly upon a light fixture.

Music streamed in from a boom box at the corner of the stage. Cellos moaned, violins sang taut and fine, and flutes melodied with melancholy sighs. A spotlight illuminated the center of the curtains, the light danced off dust particles swirling in the air like flakes from a first snow. A young girl walked onto the stage.

"The production you are about to witness is a play about miracles. What is a miracle? Is it simply the magic of a life saved against all odds, a body that heals despite the dark outcome predicted by doctors? Perhaps it is indefinable, and we only know one when we see it. But what if we go through our whole lives and never witness anything even close? Why are some people allowed the grace of miracles and not others? Is it random luck or a part of nature that science just can't explain? Is it part of something greater or simply a prayer answered? Do we have the power within each of us to make our own miracles?

"We don't have the answers to any of these questions and this short play doesn't seek to find them. Instead, our play tells the story of five different events we consider to be miracles. Some of these stories you already know; others have never been told before. Some of them are true, and others we only wish were true. Either way, we leave you with no answers. Only possibilities."

She walked off the stage.

The curtains opened and the miracles came. We watched the story of a woman named Donna—shot and left for death and blindness, played by a young girl with a tattoo of a single wing floating along the inside of her wrist; we saw the tale of two children, huddled together inside a closet, praying for someone to save them; we witnessed stories of lives won and wonders accepted. And finally we watched the story young John had written for his grandfather (about his grandfather?)—the portrayal of a man risen from the dead.

We watched the young actors in a mock fight. We saw as the boy playing Lazarus clutched his chest and fell to the floor, stabbed with a fake knife, bleeding fake blood (though for the briefest of moments, I had to look away to remind myself it was not real). On stage, the other actors feigned mourning of a made-up sorrow. They placed a white sheet over "Lazarus" and the fake blood, a crimson dye, seeped into its fibers like tears.

From stage left, another performer walked on stage—Jesus commanding Lazarus to rise from this fake death, not once but

three times. "Rise, Lazarus, rise," he commanded. But when the ac-
tor beneath the sheet still didn't move, August stood up on his chair
and shouted, "Get up! You're supposed to get up now!"

The audience laughed lightly.

I held August's hand and pulled him to me.

"August, it's okay," I whispered. "It's only make-believe, like
on TV."

On stage, "Jesus" bellowed for the fourth time with more force,
"I command you to rise." On cue, the young boy feigning death
stood up on two strong and living legs.

"See, Honey, they were just pretending."

"Mom," August pleaded, "make Joe get up."

The audience clapped.

"What do you mean, Sweetie?" I asked, those words catching
on my tongue like hooks.

§

On hands and knees, I pressed my head against Joe's chest
listening for his heart. Students behind me were crying. I felt the
pressure lift from my body, and in the commotion no one noticed I
was rising—physically lifting—from the floor. Only August saw. He
reached his hand out to me. His tiny fingers grabbed my elbow and
pulled me back to earth.

One of the mothers, a nurse, joined us backstage and began
to give Joe CPR. She breathed into his open mouth. Her fingers
pinched his nose. Her other hand pushed gently upon his chin, tilt-
ing his head back. With each exhalation of her breath, his chest rose
and then sank again. Once. Twice. The nurse, with her muscular
arms, pushed violently upon his chest (*oneonethousand, twoonethou-
sand, three...*) pleading with his heart to beat.

The whole time Alice whispered in his ear, something private,
something I prayed would be enough to bring him back.

Minutes passed like hours, like days.

Eventually the nurse grew tired. Other lungs breathed his breath; other hands beat his heart; one by one until there was nothing more anyone could do except place a white-stained-red sheet (the prop from a fake death moved to an all-too-real one) over his body—heavy like regret blocking a vacant heart.

§

When the paramedics came (slower to arrive in this neighborhood, as if death were less of an emergency when it happens to the poor), I removed the sheet from Joe's body. I held it tightly against my chest. I felt the dampness on my palm where the fake blood had soaked through. It hadn't even had time to dry. His body was lifted onto a stretcher by men in crisp white shirts and dark blue pants with flawless creases that ran perfectly down the center of their legs.

I watched as those men carried Joe away through the double doors, past the staring crowd. The bird, which I had forgotten about until now, flew out those doors, behind Joe (with Joe)—gaining her freedom through our loss. And suddenly I was alone, faced with those kids, *Joe's* kids, who hadn't moved from their spots on the stage. They held each other, crying.

Alice.

August and I.

Joe's kids.

We were all lost in a grief so deep and solid, I did not know how we would climb out from its smooth, high walls. Even in Hollywood, God does not allow for re-writes or second takes.

§

When the results of the autopsy finally came back, the official cause of death was heart failure (failure of his heart to act, to react, to go on beating), caused by the (almost) inexplicable presence of a large shard of glass wedged inside his heart. It was a mystery to the doctors as to how this glass ended up there, but not to us. Because we, the ones who loved Joe, the ones who knew him, we understood clearly what had happened. We knew of the hot summer day when the sound of ice clinking incessantly against a pitcher of lemonade drove a man who had lost his daughter to also lose his mind; we knew of the young boy tossed effortlessly through a sliding glass door and how this glass embedded itself under his skin, cutting deeper than anyone could ever imagine.

This piece of glass (the size of an infant's thumbnail? an apple seed? the round painted body of a fattened tick?) had entered sharply into Joe—a small hole in the soft yielding flesh of his thigh. Alice told me about the scar on his leg, where the glass had entered. It remained in the same ineffectual spot for a while – thin layers of scar tissue growing in upon themselves to protect and shield the body. But after a time, this glass must have dislodged and began to work its way deeper into his body slowly, with a restrained grace, like an earthworm writhing in the soft, moist dirt beneath an upturned stone. It traveled, undetected by all of us, through the rivers of his body, floating along like a leaf or a hollow twig, carried by the current of his veins until it lodged, (gently, willingly, without resistance) into the walls of his heart. There it remained for all these years, where it grew like a sharp edged pearl in the delicate mantle of an oyster. For the very same reasons a pearl forms—a hard substance surrounding an invading parasite, growing in size as more protective layers are added—it must have been with Joe. This tiny shard absorbed all the detritus from his life: each blow from his father, his parents' death, everything Alice had done, everything that had been done to her, causing the glass to physically grow, to expand its blade-like edges inside the walls of his heart. By the time of his death, this once small fractal had grown to the size of a walnut, a fifty-cent piece, the clenched fist of a newborn child.

And on the night of the play, as the scene unfolded before us on the stage, we the audience saw something very different from what Joe saw.

We saw a fake fight between two actors. We watched as one ac-
tor pulled a rubber knife and thrust it inconsequentially (so lightly it
would not even cause a bruise to form) into the belly of another. We
saw corn syrup and red food coloring seep through a young boy's
fingers as he stumbled and fell to the floor, pretending at death.

But what did Joe see? Joe, who in truth, was only a few years
older than some of these kids. Did he see only his own fist thrust a
knife (sharp and ruthless) into the soft and bruising flesh of Mason's
abdomen? Did he feel the sticky wet and inhale the sharp, rusty
smell of Mason's blood? Did the shard of glass (dark, toothed, and
biting) in Joe's heart finally shift beneath its own sudden, unbear-
able weight (the final push, the last straw, the point of no return)?

On stage, a young boy was brought back to life.

Somewhere out of our view, a curtain closed over Joe like a
shroud.

§

That evening I asked Alice to spend the night at our house, but
she refused. She said she wanted to be alone with her memories of
Joe in the home she had shared with him. Back at our apartment, I
put August to bed and tried to sleep myself. But sleep would not
come. Sometime in the pre-dawn hours, I found myself sitting in my
living room, still clutching the sheet (the one which covered deaths
both fake and real). I carried it into the bathroom and stood at the
sink and turned on the water to full blast. I held the damn sheet beneath the running water. I poured soap over the stain and scrubbed
and scrubbed until my hands became numb with cold and effort.
But I did not stop. I would not stop until all that red (red like blood-
shot eyes, red like something lost, red like untended hearts) was
washed away, disappearing in liquid swirls down the sink.

§

A few days after we brought Joe's ashes home (wrapped in plastic and set inside a small box), Alice told me she had been hoping she would feel something, anything—some suggestion of his being present in the little that remained of him still. The ashes themselves were sturdier than she had imagined—weightier, darker, capable of hiding small pieces of bone—but it was not enough. She told me how she carefully unwrapped the thin tie that held the plastic bag closed. How she put her hand inside and rested her fingers on the vestiges of Joe. She felt nothing, she said. She re-wrapped the bag carefully and slept with the ashes beside her pillow, hoping he would come to her in a dream. She spoke to his ashes for hours throughout the day hoping for a response, but none was forthcoming.

So early one morning, after days of trying, Alice packed up everything which held the slightest traces or inkling of a memory of Joe (their letters, the painting he made of her, photographs) and left everything else (furniture, books, music) behind.

Including Joe's ashes.

We found them on the kitchen table nestled tightly inside the plastic bag, inside the plastic box. Beside them was a vase filled with wilted white and yellow daisies.

"Joe gave these to Alice. Can I keep them?" August asked, cradling the vase in his arms. I nodded and picked up the ashes. For several moments we just stood there listening to the refrigerator's continuous hum (food from well-meaning mourners slowly growing mold inside) and the clock still ticking away the days as if nothing at all had changed. We marveled at how empty the apartment (and our hearts) felt without them.

§

The following morning, I awoke to find August playing beneath the oak tree outside. He had never stopped placing bird seed in the bird feeders, and now mourning doves, thrushes, and sparrows waited patiently on nearby bushes—allowing my son his time beneath the tree—before they returned to feed their fluttering lives.

"What are you doing, Sweetie?"

He turned and smiled at me. I noticed the plastic box that had contained Joe's ashes at his side. It was face down—and empty. August was busy piling the cinders in small mounds at the base of the oak tree. Traces of Joe clung to his palms and stuck beneath his fingernails. I watched as one by one he placed the daisies he had taken from Alice's house deep into the yielding grey. The flowers were shriveled on the edges and the petals were turning brown and soft. I knew they would last only a day or two longer, but said nothing when August, finished with his planting, brought out a pitcher of water which he poured over them.

When he was finished he smiled up at me. "I think Joe and Peter are together now."

"I hope so, Sweetie," I said. "I hope so."

§

The next morning while August was still asleep and the sun was just peeking out over the tops of distant buildings, I took a few minutes to stand outside among the flowers and all the birds either feeding or perched lazily on Peter's rope—the beauty my son created from the remnants of death.

Every morning thereafter, I awoke expecting the flowers to be dead. But after a week, they still had not died; on the contrary, they looked fresher than they had on the day August planted them there.

One morning, with a cup of coffee in hand, I walked outside and stood for a long time beside the oak tree. I set my mug on the walkway and crouched down onto my haunches. I carefully pushed my fingers into the ashes, searching for the flowers' stems, searching for where they merged with the earth. And somehow I knew even before I felt their moist stems anchored to the soil that all of those flowers, each and every one, had taken root.

• • •

I WRITE PRETTY MUCH for five days straight. I throw away whole pages and cross out entire paragraphs trying to find the best words I have in me to say what I need to say. All in all, I write 17 pages. I'm sure a more eloquent man than me could produce something a whole lot better, but I hope these words will be enough. They have to be. They are all I have. This is my letter, my letter to Penny Rose: a prayer, a wish, a hope.

The day I signed up to go to war was the day you told me you didn't believe in miracles.

"As far as I can tell," you said "God deals in life and death and hasn't got the time or the inclination for miracles." Do you remember you said that? Those were big words for such a little kid, I thought. It was the day in the alley with those boys. I told you God had saved us, but you didn't quite see it my way. I remember, after it was all over with, you said, "The bird was just stunned, is all. I know birds. Believe me. It happens all the time. They fly into windows and knock themselves out—but a few minutes later they're just like new again."

That was what you said. And I didn't argue. But you were forgetting I saw the bird, too...its neck bent at just the wrong angle, tiny dots of blood small as pinpricks staining its nares. You know birds, well, I know blood. The bird was dead and then suddenly it wasn't. It was a miracle, and I knew you'd seen it; you just didn't want to really see it, I guess.

And I suppose that's why I didn't tell you about the other thing.

But I'm telling you now, and I hope it isn't too late.

When those awful boys had your poor body pinned down, your pants around your bony knees, I couldn't help but see it. The birthmark on your leg. It was bigger than it had been before, sure, but the shape was same. Unmistakable. I was taken aback for just a second. I saw you seeing me, and I thought maybe you somehow recognized me too. Even though it would have been impossible, I still thought...*maybe*. But when you finally told me your name

I knew you had no idea who you really were.

The story of the first time I saw you comes later. The first time you remember seeing me was soon after my mother died. You'll remember it was not my finest moment. I was walking to school, feeling okay, like I could get through the day. And the next moment I felt such a rage bubbling up inside me I wanted to scream. Instead, I just started punching the first thing I saw over and over. I felt my knuckles crack against the brick wall, my skin broke open but the pain felt good in a way. It distracted me from the real pain I felt at being an orphan at seventeen.

It was 1969, and I was a black man crying and bleeding all over the sidewalk. All the people who passed me by just stared at me with fear or pity or avoided looking at me altogether, but not one stopped to ask me if I was okay or if I needed help. In fact everyone, each and every one, crossed to the other side of the street to get as far away from me as possible. Except you.

You stopped and stood right above me and pressed your hands to my knuckles to stop the bleeding. The first thing I noticed about you, after your kind eyes, were those skinny legs of yours, thin like straws. They were the boniest things I had ever seen. I knew even then you were in danger of losing faith in everything. I mean, you were so skinny I thought even the slightest breeze would pick you up and carry you away, sending you tumbling into the heavens until there was nothing left of you—just a dot on the horizon that could have been anything: a helium balloon, a migrating bird, a twelve year old girl who didn't believe in miracles. I thought to myself, *now there goes a girl that needs to have some faith.* I was afraid the world would swallow you, bit by miracle-less bit, if you didn't find something to hold on to.

It might not make much sense to you but you not believing in miracles, or more precisely my hope that you one day would, was the reason I left. On the day with those boys, when I learned you didn't believe in miracles, that very same day, I signed up to go to war. I believed so strongly in the probability of miracles, I wanted you to believe too. I wanted to prove to you they were real. At the time I truly thought I could save lives, change lives, not on a grand scale maybe, but just enough to make a difference. Then I would find you one day and I would tell you everything, and then you would believe in miracles too. You would have to. And that's why I went. I went so I could save you.

I guess I've been lucky. I've lived my entire life believing miracles were not only possible but at the very least a semi-regular occurrence. My parents taught me that. My dad died in an accident when I was just a kid but he is, to this day, the greatest hope I ever had. My mom died years later from a severe deterioration of her will to live. But I never lost my faith. My dad worked as a mechanic from long before I was born until the day he died. He started off helping out in other people's garages. By the time I came around, he had earned a reputation and enough money to open his own shop.

He was beautiful, my dad. He had permanent grease beneath his nails and a slight scent of oil lingered on him always. Even after a shower, a shave, and a change into clean clothes, the smell never left him. It is still the greatest scent in the whole world. No one worked harder than my dad. But even so, he always had time for me. At night, no matter how tired he was or what time he got home, he always came in to wish me goodnight. And no matter how tired I was or how long ago my mother had tucked me in to bed, I always waited up (struggling sometimes to keep my eyes open, biting the inside of me cheek to keep myself awake) just to be able to wish him goodnight.

On Saturdays, we often stayed up late (my father never worked on Sundays). After dinner, Dad played his favorite records. I, barefooted, stood on his feet (the leather of his boots was cracked but still felt soft against the pads of my feet) and held on tight for balance. My mom wrapped her arms around us both, and we danced like that, all three of us, for hours.

My dad only took one week off a year—the week of my birth-day. Every year, we would pack the car with our tents, our lanterns, our sleeping bags and head east to the Great Sand Dunes. Even though we went every year, it never got boring. It was like going someplace new every time because the winds were constantly shift-ing the sands so that those great mountains did move.

"See, Son," my dad told me the first time I'd noticed the change, "God does move mountains, just not in ways you might've thought. People always expect God to bend to their rules instead of trying to understand Him as He is."

During the day we searched beneath the trees for owl pellets and for rabbit tracks in the mud or the deeply gouged ruts in the trees where deer had rubbed their antlers. At night, we went owl-ing—listening for the unmistakable deep hoot of Great Horned Owls. Sometimes we got lucky and heard a pair of them calling back and forth to each other. "A male and a female, looking for romance," my dad always said. Most nights, the coyotes would call too—with howls and yips and high pitched barks. Then my mother would say, "Listen. Listen to the coyotes' symphony serenading us in the night." She had been a dancer and so had a flare for the dramatic.

After hours of stargazing and spotlighting unidentifiable crit-ters in the dark, we finally went to sleep. Usually, I slept straight through the night, but once in a while I'd wake up to a sound I didn't recognize—a wail or a grunt and once even the boom of a gunshot far off in the distance. The noises sometimes scared me. But when I felt afraid, all I had to do was shine my flashlight on the tent next door where my parents were sleeping. If I saw my father's boots still outside the tent, I knew right away there was nothing to fear. It meant my parents were still inside and, therefore, unafraid of the night noises. If my dad believed we were safe, that was enough for me.

After our camping trips, life would return to normal. Mom taught dance at the high school three days a week. Dad went back to work in his garage just a few blocks from our house. And every day after school I ran down to his shop, just so I could have a few hours with him before nightfall. I would sit on a stool in the garage and do my homework while he worked. On the best of days, I got to help him by passing him greasy tools or pouring him cups of iced-tea or hot coffee—depending on the weather— from the thermos my mom always packed for him.

Though it might sound strange, what I remember most when I think about my father, more than the smell of dark oils or the stories he used to tell or even how his rough hands felt comforting against my cheeks—more than all of that, what I remember most are his shoes. The shoes themselves were nothing much to speak of. They were old black boots with a small patch over the left toe. The heels had been re-nailed and the leather re-stitched so many times, my dad often joked he had a new pair of shoes every six months or so. Even though he could've bought new boots, he saw no reason to. "With a bit of love and care, these shoes could last forever. They've served me well. Why should I get new ones?" he asked my mother each time she smilingly rolled her eyes when it was time to take the boots in for yet another repair.

But their dreary appearance isn't what I think of. I remember only how safe I felt to see them set outside his tent when I woke up frightened in the night or how the leather felt against my bare feet as we danced, or how they stuck out slightly from beneath the cars he worked on so, more often than not, his shoes were all I could see of him all those afternoons as I watched him work. I had entire conversations with those shoes or sat in silence with those shoes. When we did talk—about nothing, about everything—his feet moved, gesturing in conversation like some people do with their hands. After a time, I could easily read his moods just by watching the subtle ways his feet, and by connection, those shoes moved. When he was his proudest—when he finally discovered the source of the mystery sound one of his customer's cars was making and was on his way to fixing it—his feet beat out a rhythm as though tapping to music. When he was frustrated, or concentrating, his left foot trembled slightly. And when he talked about Mom, he turned both his feet in circles, so even when he was silent and those feet turned, I knew he was thinking about her.

My favorite moments with my dad, though, were when we made the long trip north to Denver to pick up supplies for his shop. We only went a few times a year, just my dad and me, so it made the trip even more special. To get ready, we woke up before first light— "with the crickets," my mom used to say—because we were four hours out of Denver, and Dad always wanted to arrive at the supply store right at opening time and be back sometime after lunch. He didn't like to be away from the shop any longer than was absolutely necessary.

He drove and sipped tea from a thermos, and together we watched the road spread like black ribbon before us. Sometimes the car's headlights picked up the bright eye-shine of a coyote crossing the road or the white flashes of barn owls darting into the light after insects. Once, we even saw the clear, distinct shape of a mountain lion as it calmly crossed the road in front of us. We caught sight of it several feet ahead as it padded across the asphalt before finally disappearing into the bushes along the side of the road with a final flick of its long and waving tail.

But on our last trip together, we didn't see any wildlife at all— not a single rodent or lizard, not even a dark tarantula crossing the road on its eight hairy legs. The road was oddly silent and deserted that night.

Perhaps the animals knew what we did not.

Just as the moon—almost full and bright enough to illuminate the landscape—was cresting over the Sangre de Cristo Mountains, we also crested a small hill. As our car's nose tipped over the ridge, we found ourselves only a few feet away from a large brown Dodge which was stopped right in the middle of the road. My father braked hard and swerved to avoid rear-ending it. He pulled the car onto the shoulder. He grabbed a flashlight from the glove box, and we got out of our own vehicle and approached the other car carefully. Right away, we noticed it had a flat tire and inside the car we could make out the heads of two passengers.

We walked up to the driver's window. The interior light of the car was on. At the wheel sat an older woman whose hair was dyed a reddish color I didn't believe could be found anywhere in the natural world. In the back seat was a young girl who looked to be about twice my age.

"Can we help?" my father asked. "My name's Glenn. This is my son Carson."

The woman jumped slightly and looked up and down at my father and then at me. I think we made her nervous. She was white. We were black. This was 1950's U.S.A. From the range of expressions that crossed her face in a few short seconds, I thought she was most likely weighing the pros and cons of her predicament. I imagined the monologue in her head and couldn't help but chuckle: *Here we are*, I pictured her thinking, *two women alone on a country road with a flat tire in the middle of the night and no one around for miles, being offered help from a negro man and his son, who, if they aren't rapists or murderers or both, could probably have us back on the road in a jiffy. Those Negroes do tend to be a handy folk. Well, the man does have kind eyes and his son is just a boy, but still…*

She glanced at her daughter, who let out a slight moan. I saw something shift in the woman's eyes—a look of real concern. After a few moments of deliberation, the red-haired lady grabbed her purse and draped it around her neck, clutching the bag tightly to her chest. Then she exited the car and said, "Yes. Please. Can you help us?" In the same breath she added nervously, "You know, our neighbor Mr. Peterson, he was following us to the hospital. He should be here any minute. He's a big guy—a prize boxer. He's won every fight he's ever been in."

"Oh *please*, Mom," the young girl shouted from the back seat. "Mr. Peterson *was* a boxer, about a million years ago." Then she turned to me and my dad and said "Mr. Peterson is a hundred years old at least. He's probably still in his pajamas, sound asleep dreaming of California. He and his wife are moving there next week. Something about the sea air being good for what ails them, whatever that means. Anyway, the point is, he's not coming." She opened the car door and stepped onto the street and shook my hand and then my father's. "I'm Emma. Don't mind my mother, she's just—"

"Emma, stay in the car," her mother said through pursed lips and a clenched jaw.

Emma, however, had a different idea and like many teenagers all across the globe did exactly the opposite of what her mother asked. Judging by her appearance, this did not seem to be the first time she had disobeyed her parents' wishes. She had long hair, thick glasses, and was immensely pregnant. I was no expert, of course, but the girl was huge. It looked to me like the baby was about three years overdue. I had a vivid imagination back then, I guess, because I found myself picturing the baby stubbornly refusing to ever be born, causing this poor girl to live the rest of her life with a baby inside her. He'd cry, crawl, walk, learn which foods he liked—apples, fish sticks—and which he didn't, learn to read, fall in love, graduate from college, get married, have children of his own, and die a peaceful death all while living inside his mother's womb.

My thoughts were interrupted by the red-haired lady. "We're in a hurry. We were on our way to the hospital. My daughter's pregnant, as you can see. She's only 13. *Thirteen*. Not anywhere near graduating from high school."

"*Mom*," Emma sighed, rolling her eyes and clutching the bottom of her huge belly with her hands, "we've been over this. No one cares one way or the other how old I am or if I'm going to graduate from high school or not. And besides," she said turning directly to face us, "I turn 14 in three months. I'm not *that* young."

"Her water broke a while ago, and the doctor told us we had plenty of time. But now…. We were on our way to the hospital and we got this flat tire and have been out here forever waiting for someone to show up. I don't know anything about fixing cars, as you can see. My husband used to do those things, before he ran off with the neighbor's wife last year."

"Moooom."

"Sorry. She's having contractions every ten minutes or so, so I think there's time, but we need to get her to the hospital."

And, then, as if to demonstrate that her mother was telling things straight, Emma doubled over in pain and let out a loud groan.

"Look, let's just push the car to the side of the road, and my son and I will take you to the hospital. Then, we can come take care of your car later, when there's more time," my father said with a smile.

But I could tell the red-haired lady didn't like the idea. After all, it was one thing to let a black man fix your tire on a public road, where cars, in theory, could pass at any moment and another thing entirely to willingly get in the car with two total strangers and your pregnant daughter. No, that wouldn't do. That wouldn't do at all.

"How long will it take you to fix the tire?"

"It shouldn't take more than a few minutes."

"Let's do that. The baby is three days overdue. It can wait a few more minutes."

But the baby, like her mother, was rebellious from the get-go and had her (it turned out to be a her) own ideas as to how and when she would enter this world.

Emma was suddenly hit with a sharp pain. She let out a loud cry and sank to the asphalt.

"Look, please, let's get her into my car. I'll take you to the hospital. I think this baby is coming now." Noticing her hesitation, my father fumbled quickly in his front shirt pocket digging out a business card, which he handed to her, trying to smile in a way that would put this woman at ease. He shined the flashlight on the card so she could get a better look, but she barely glanced at it.

"See. This is my job. This is what I do. I fix cars. But right now, I think we need to get your daughter to a hospital."

The woman was torn but stood firm. She slipped the card into her purse.

"No. Please, just fix the tire." Then she took her daughter by the elbow and led her to the side of the road.

"Go help the ladies, Son" he told me as I approached to help him. "I got this." And then he winked at me.

My dad got to work. As a mechanic, he knew the rules of changing a tire: safety first. Make sure the car is on a flat surface and make sure the parking brake is on. I watched proudly as my dad pushed the car to the side of the road all by himself. My father was never careless; he never let safety go by the wayside. But I also know he felt pressure to get Emma to the hospital as soon as possible. He began to change the tire with the back end of the car still sticking out onto the road, maybe just a foot or two. A foot or two is all it took.

I walked over to Emma and her mother. Emma was breathing hard and sweat poured down her face. I sat down next to them, unsure of what to do. Emma reached out her hand to me, and I held it. Her mother flashed a disapproving smile. Emma squeezed my hand tighter as she cursed and groaned and pushed. Her mother, clueless as she was, tried to be encouraging.

We were all so distracted, we didn't see the car cresting the hill and we didn't hear the drone of its engine until it was right in front of us. It was like it had just dropped from the sky. I looked up to see metal twist against metal, and bone break against bone. My father was there, and then he wasn't.

I don't remember what happened next, and I don't know how much time had passed. I think I fainted or something. When I heard someone calling my name, the sun was already rising in the sky. At first I thought it was my dad calling me. If anyone could've survived something like that, it'd be my dad.

"Carson!" someone yelled again. I turned to see Emma. Her legs were spread wide, and the crown of her daughter's head was ripping through her skin. Blood oozed onto the dirt on the side of the road. I witnessed the birth of that baby girl, born with all her fingers and all her toes. She was covered in mucus and gunk. She let out a loud cry and kicked her legs. Even from where I stood, I could see she had a birthmark on her thigh. It was the shape of a tiny hand with outstretched fingers. It was raised and rough. It was brownish-red—the exact color of fresh blood against asphalt beneath an unforgiving sky.

The phone rings. I let the letter fall from my hands.
"Hello?"
As I wait for an answer, I walk into the kitchen. With the phone held between my ear and shoulder, I take down the picture I had made of her and toss it into the garbage.
It doesn't look anything like her at all.

Part 3

wings, as if a secret

Why is it no word exists in the English language for someone forever changed by the oppressive burden of grief? You become a widow or widower when your spouse slips from you, whether there was love between you or not, whether married a year or an entire lifetime; you become an orphan when your parents are gone, no matter your age. There is a word for us when we lose our sight, our limbs, and even our minds; but no name is assigned to those who suffer the loss of the one person (lover or friend, sibling or child) or thing (belief or comfort, love or freedom) that made life livable. Though your mind and body remain intact, something within you goes missing. And while to everyone else you may look the same as you always have, you know no matter how much time or what events come to pass (no matter how hard you fight, scratching and screaming, clawing and kicking your way back to the person you once were) you will always be wholly and completely unrecognizable to yourself.

CHAPTER 18

THREE YEARS. ONE MONTH. TWO DAYS. In the hours, minutes, seconds following Joe and Peter's deaths, following the even more sudden loss of Alice, August and I lived without tragedy. We went about our business of work and school, of filling journals with beautiful things. August made friends in school, and they often came to our home for sleepovers or joined us for weekend afternoons in the park. I hired John, Marcus, and a few other kids from Joe's class, who I continued to think of as "Joe's kids," to work in the flower shop on the weekends. Once in a while we brought up memories of Joe, those kids and I. It seemed appropriate to think of him then, to speak his name among all those flowers.

But life, as they say, went on. And though I had been witness to the greatest joy imaginable—the birth of my son—the pain of losing my friends lay heavy on my chest. It seemed, at times, I could barely breathe for its weight. Only a hug or a smile from August could bring me back to this life, to my life. At times it was all I could do to keep my feet planted on the ground. For months after Joe's death, I literally clung to furniture and walls to keep from drifting away. As the years passed, it happened less and less, and I could go whole weeks without worrying about where my feet were in relation to the ground. Once in a while, however, on days when I felt particularly tired or when I was alone, when August was away at a friend's house or at school, I found myself losing my gravity once again. I would be lost in thought and suddenly notice myself hovering, inches above the floor, and I would realize I had let my mind drift to the memories of my friends.

When the headaches started, it was easy to convince myself they were the product of grief. They began gradually (a small pressure behind the eyes, a throbbing at the base of my skull) and hit me most often in the mornings. For the first time in his life, August took the bus to school because I could no longer drive him. The headaches made me feel outside of myself—like seeing a photograph of a perfect stranger who looks so much like you from a certain angle that you believe for a split second it *is* you and your mind goes hazy trying to remember the day you wore clothes you do not recognize, the day you posed with smiling strangers, the day you stood in a place you swear you've never been.

When I began to see patches of darkness or wake in the middle of the night unable to see anything at all, I finally made an appointment to see a doctor.

Alone in the examination room, waiting for the results of the tests I had undergone over the past few weeks, I thought of my son who was sitting in the waiting room, anxious for news of me. Perhaps he was reading a book or simply staring at the strangers who, for a short time, were brought together by uncomfortable chairs, worn magazines, and the possibility that someone they love might be incurably sick.

If I were to design rooms made primarily for the waiting of bad news, I would paint bright and colorful birds in flight across the walls and plant potted lemon and pomegranate trees alongside soft and welcoming couches. I would play sounds of oceans churning or winds conducting orchestras of leaves with their twirling saxophones and sharp snare drums. I would try to provide a small sense of beauty, something to cling to in the face of almost certain loss, to shield waiting loved ones (however briefly) from the inevitable news waiting to emerge from behind the door where I now stand.

And what will become of August? I thought, pressing my hands to the hollowness of my stomach, fingering the familiar bones of my ribs. This boy, who at nine years old, sees more beauty in the world than anyone I had ever known in life or legend combined; who dreams of finding beauty as other boys his age dream of home runs and superheroes. What would become of him?

§

There was a knock at the door. The doctor entered and before she could open her mouth, I held up my hand.

"Wait. Let me get my son. I want him to hear this with me."

"I'm not sure that's such a good idea, Ms. Rose. This news can be, well, it will be difficult for him, for you both to hear. Maybe you should wait a while, think of a more…delicate way to tell him."

"Doctor, my son is nine years old. I do not keep secrets from him. I do not give him false hope. I want him to know everything I know. Please."

§

Side by side August and I listened as the doctor spoke.

"You have a brain tumor," she began. "It's imperative we get you into surgery right away. But, I have to be honest with you, the operation is risky."

"How risky?"

The doctor glanced at me, at August. I nodded for her to go on.

"There's a chance you won't survive this operation. But without it—"

"Without it, how long do I have?"

"Weeks…months, perhaps."

"So with or without this surgery I will most likely die?"

Watching the doctor's slow, subtle nod, I knew what my answer would be.

"I can't risk the surgery. Not until I know someone will be here to raise my son."

"What about family?"

I shook my head. "August is my only family."

"Friends?"

"Dead...or disappeared."

"I understand your dilemma but I strongly urge you to have the surgery as soon as possible. At the rate the tumor is growing, there won't be much we can do if we wait."

"What can I expect? Without the surgery?"

She glanced at August and sighed.

"With non-surgical treatment, we can maybe prolong the time you have. But eventually you're going to get very sick. I can give you medication to help with the headaches, to control the seizures, if they become an issue. The truth is every case is a bit different, and we don't know to which parts of your brain the tumor will spread, but you might start to hallucinate, there could be loss of vision, change in personality, one-sided paralysis. Your symptoms will likely remain mild for some time—the headaches which you have already experienced, maybe some nausea. But then things will get bad very quickly. I'm sorry."

§

On the way home from the hospital, with August still and quiet at my side, my mind drifted back to one of the last times we had all been together, Joe and Alice, Peter, August and I. We had taken a trip to Laguna Beach to swim in the cold, blue ocean, to stare at the endless miles of coarse sand, to feel it rough and comforting between our toes. Joe carried August on his back, and after a day of lying in the sun and swimming in the sea, we decided to walk together over the rocks and look for hiding crabs or exposed mussels. What we found, instead, was a lone pelican—a juvenile by the looks of it. It stood with drooping head, eyes half shut. We could tell this bird was sick or starved but before we could decide if we should try to trap it and carry it back with us or if we should leave it and find someone to come rescue it, it took two hesitant, awkward steps (its wings open and dragging along the rocks), fell forward, and died.

"Look at that," exclaimed Joe. "Look how long its wings are—long enough to cover all of us." And it was true. We all stood side by side in front of the bird, and its wing tips extended just past our bodies, as if, in life, those wings could have shielded us from very many things. But now the poor bird lay with open wings, as if a secret lay hidden beneath those stones that, even in death, it wanted to keep hidden. After a while, with nothing left to do, no life left to save, we returned to our day seemingly unaffected by this death we had been witness to. When we began to pack up our things, I glimpsed back at the rocks and noticed the Turkey Vultures already perched on the railing above. They knew perhaps better than anyone that death, though never pretty, is a necessary thing. And had I thought about it at the time, perhaps I would have taken it as a sign; perhaps I would have been more careful with Peter, with Joe. But as with the death of all strangers or strange creatures, I believed it would not affect my life and simply forgot about it. Until now.

§

Back at home, after putting August to bed (the doctor's words churning in my head), I felt the sudden need to see me. All of me. To reassure myself I was not fading at the edges like celluloid burning in the heat of the sun. In my bedroom I removed my shoes first, then my pants. I slipped my t-shirt over my head, removed my bra, my underwear and I stared into the mirror. Though I did not need its reflection to know what I would see, I looked anyway: my old and vein-riddled hands, my too-skinny legs, my mousy hair, my jutting bones, the port wine stain on my leg which had started out as a small hand-shaped birthmark, but had grown bigger over the years and now looked like a grown man had branded my thigh with his palm (the thumb - slightly stunted and the four long fingers raised slightly and coarse to the touch). These things I had despised about myself my whole life suddenly, from one moment to the next, took on an unexpected grace—and perhaps, even, a subtle beauty, a private beauty, but a beauty nonetheless. That is one nice thing I can say about death. For all its inconveniences, it puts very many things into perspective.

I stared into the mirror and sighed deeply. Why had it taken me so long to see, to appreciate this in myself? The evidence of my journey (one of sweeping tragedy and unmitigated joy, equal parts loss and love and learning simply to survive) was displayed across my body—a body exquisitely and tirelessly betraying me. It was a testament to the life I lived. I wore the scars, the signs. The stories of me were written on my epidermis like words on a page. There were memories in the sag of my breasts, breasts so small they reminded me of plums or apples or any fruit really which is easily bruised. I saw heartache etched in the lines of my palms and surrender revealed in the curve of my legs, legs pale enough to reveal the thick blue veins beneath my skin (highways leading to and from my heart). I found acceptance in the birthmark which curved gently to the inside of my upper thigh.

"Two-by-four," I said to no one in particular, and my voice reminded me of bubbles floating to the surface of a delicate liquid and popping. I stared at my stomach, my hips. There, at last, was joy. I traced the stretch marks, carved like a maze across my belly leading to the fine, dark hairs between my legs. I thought of August, asleep in the next room and wondered, *would anybody be able to save us?*

CHAPTER 19

OVER THE NEXT FEW WEEKS I went through long and torturous rounds of treatment hoping to calm the cancer growing inside me—hoping to extend the time I had, even just a little. My hair fell out in clumps. I felt weak and dizzy and unable to keep any food in my stomach. My already skinny body grew even skinnier. Brinda, Amal, and Mariam took turns coming by to help me take care of August. When I was finally done with the sessions (having poisoned almost everything in me but the very thing they were meant to), I slowly gained my strength back. But I was always aware it was only a matter of time before I would fall sick again; and time was running out.

§

In the evenings, August and I sat together, pouring over his old notebooks, remembering the small moments of beauty shared in our short time together. In the nine years I had known him, August impressed me deeply with his goodness. I marveled at it every single day.

"Mom, how come you have to die too?"

I hugged him to me. "I don't know, Sweetie. But I'm so sorry."

"Do you think you'll miss me?"

"I'll miss you more than you can imagine."

"But I don't want you to miss me," he said, "cause then you'll be sad too."

"We'll be sad together, for a little while, but I want you to promise me you will never forget how much I love you and you will remember, always, to be happy as much as possible."

"I promise."

Together, August and I made a list of all the potential parents for my son. It contained only three names.

§

The first person I thought of, the person whose face appeared in my mind the minute I knew, was Ernest. He was, after all, August's father and, more importantly, a kind man. I searched for him in phone books and on the Internet but each time came up empty-handed. I didn't know where he lived or where he worked, but I could think of one place where he might be.

The next day, I covered my head (still bald—with only patches of fuzz growing back) with a scarf and went to the bowling alley where I had first met Ernest over cold beer in plastic cups and colorful shoes. I returned every day for three days. Whenever the door opened, I expected to see his sad smile, his kind eyes. But he never showed up, and I began to realize with ever-increasing panic that I might not find him. Maybe he didn't come here anymore, or he had moved, or...

"Penny, isn't it?" my thoughts were interrupted by a deep but jolly voice. I turned and found myself staring at George. He was older, his thinning hair completely gone now, his pot belly rounder and wider like an impossibly large egg.

He had come with his grandchildren, who now numbered an even dozen, and some of his children. As they bowled, we talked. I told him about the night I spent with Ernest, about August, Joe, Alice, and Peter. And finally about me dying.

He, in turn, told me about his life, his beautiful grandkids, and the aches and pains in his body which made it difficult for him to pick them up. He told me about his friends. Al had married a woman who was the spitting image of Anita Pointer and became an instant father to her five-year-old girl. "They went to Panama on their honeymoon and loved it so much, they never came back. I get a postcard from him every once in a while."

"Do you miss him?" I asked, thinking of my own friends.

"I used to. But, the truth is, we just weren't spending very much time together anyway," he replied.

"We began coming here less and less. At first it was just a couple of nights a week, then just once a week, then maybe once a month if we were lucky. Al had started dating his future wife. I had my grandkids, and Ernest, well, Ernest, I don't know. It happens. Some friendships just sort of fizzle after a while. It's a perfectly natural thing."

I couldn't help but feel a pang of sadness at friendships so casually let go. I know it happens every day—friends drift apart, their lives pulling them in different directions and the excuse of having children or raising a family or being too busy somehow makes it seem less like a loss. But having August had only emphasized to me how important friendships are and how important it was to fight to keep them at all costs.

"The last time I saw Ernest was right before Al got married. He showed up here one day with a suitcase. He ordered beers for Al and me, and he bowled the best game of his life. 'What's with the suitcase?' we finally asked.

'I'm running away.'

'You're fifty years old.'

'Precisely.'

"We tried to talk him out of it, to convince him he was too old for such nonsense, but he had made up his mind. Have you ever heard of such a thing?"

"Yes," I said, "her name was Alice."

George nodded briefly and continued.

"Ernest was stubborn. He just kept saying, 'I'm running away from home. I know it sounds silly, but it's what I'm doin'. I left everything. Everything. All I have is a few hundred bucks and some spare clothes.' When we asked him why, he said he should've done it a long time ago. He said if he had been smarter or braver, he would have left the day Anne died. But he didn't realize what staying behind would take from him. He said he was afraid to leave, 'cause it would have felt too much like he was leaving *her*. And then he said, 'Plus, I had you guys. I thought it would be enough. But now, things are different. I have been living with a ghost for too long. I feel half dead myself.'

"After we finished our game, he hugged us both, tossed his suitcase into his truck and drove off. That was the last we heard from him. I used to stop by his house about once a week to check on things, collect his mail, water the plants—thinking he would come back one day. But he isn't coming back. I imagine him somewhere in South America or maybe Africa. Wherever he is, though, I tell you this: he doesn't want to be found."

I finished my beer, thanked George, and hugged him goodbye.

I was now down to two.

§

I sat at the kitchen table, looking at the last two possibilities on my list.

Brinda.

Mariam and Amal.

What did I really know about them? I knew Brinda was good to me, but we rarely spoke of personal things. I knew Amal and Mariam wanted a child desperately, but what kind of parents would they be? How could I make this decision?

For most of my life, I had been alone. In less than a decade's time, I had created a family of people who could not be dearer to me and had lost them all. Now, I had to accept that one day soon I would be leaving my son. I would leave him motherless, orphaned, just as my own mother had left me—with one big difference. I wasn't going anywhere until I knew August would not be left to the fickle whims of God. I could not die before I found him a family—a mother, a father, a friend to replace everything I was taking with me. But who, in this world of strangers, would be worthy of raising him? Who would be kind enough? Good enough? Who could be?

I sat for a long time, desperation creeping slowly in, tears of frustration stinging my eyes. I didn't realize August had been standing at the kitchen door, watching me the whole time.

"Mom, what's wrong?"

I quickly wiped my eyes and pulled him up onto my lap.

"We just have to find the right person to take care of you, but I don't know how."

"It's easy, Mom."

"It is?"

"Sure. We just have to listen to their hearts."

CHAPTER 20

I INVITED BRINDA OVER FOR DINNER the following day. I told myself I needed to wait at least until we had gotten through the first course to say what I needed to say; to ask her what I needed to ask. But she had only taken a few bites when I blurted out, "I'm dying."

Brinda set down her fork.

"What? Penny, don't talk like that. There's still a chance. The treatments… "

"The treatments aren't working. They were never going to work."

"Oh, God, Penny."

"I know. It's okay. I just…I need to find someone who'll take care of August after…after I'm gone. I don't know how to ask you this, but…."

"You want my story," Brinda said, "because just asking me and my saying yes, it wouldn't be enough, would it? You have to know if I'm the *right* person, not just *a* person for the job."

I nodded my head.

When I intertwined my fingers in hers, August rested his tiny hand over ours. And it began again, the racing of my heart, the *thump shuffle whisper thump* pounding in my ears and the tingling sensation at the base of my skull. When the darkness dissolved into light, I saw Brinda. She was much younger and dressed in a mini black dress that showed off her tanned, slim legs. She wore her long dark hair pulled up into a loose bun at the nape of her long, straight neck. She stood at the window of a room filled with large, grim paintings hanging along the walls of an old building in downtown

Los Angeles. Two boys were bouncing a basketball back and forth against the sidewalk two stories below: the *shuffle* of their feet, the *whisper* of the ball as it rose and fell, the *thump* it made as it hit the ground. The *thump-shuffle-whisper-thump* like music, and Brinda, a glass of wine in her hand, peering down from above. The sun hit the two boys just right, and the shadows they cast stretched far into the street. Brinda watched the shadows move—weightless, graceful, somehow free. Occasionally, a vehicle appeared on the street, temporarily passing over the shadows—RTD buses, Volkswagen Beetles, and even the shopping cart of a homeless woman who spit unintelligible obscenities to the boys and their shadows as they moved away from her (perhaps a life she was accustomed to, things moving away from her, never towards her, always away).

Brinda took a sip of wine and turned from the window to find herself confronted with a vision so perfectly imperfect it took all her strength to not let her wine glass slip from her fingers (sending glass and red wine, liquid and solid, spilling onto the floor, her shoes, the perfectly worn jeans of the man before her).

He extended his hand. "I'm Santiago, the artist."

She eagerly gripped his hand and shook. Her heart fluttered.

This man gave her such a delectable sensation (like the perfect shoe feels when you slip your naked foot into it, comfortable and right), and she knew she had found her match. Not because he was handsome or because he was *the* artist but because in his every look, in his every gesture he was crying out to be saved. And Brinda, for her part, had been preparing for just this moment since she was seven years old.

As a child, she had decided she wanted to be like her mother—strong, unafraid, and a savior of lost souls. She came to this conclusion on an ordinary Saturday afternoon. She had been helping her mother prepare lunch when the phone rang. At seven years old, it was still fun for Brinda to answer the phone, and she did so the same way every time "Menendez residence, how may I help you?"

Even at such a young age, the tone of her voice, the words she used, often caused callers to mistake her for her mother. She thrilled at the voices on the other end of the line—friends of her parents or her mother's business associates—but the salespeople were her favorites. She loved listening to them espouse the virtues of their products knowing, no matter what they were selling, she already had her answer well-rehearsed. She would politely say, "Thank you very much. While your product sounds lovely, we are not interested at this time. Have a wonderful day."

Then she would hang up, feeling secretly powerful. After all, an adult was asking her for something she was fully within her rights to say *no* to. So on that Saturday, when she picked up the phone on the third ring (always on the third ring so as not to appear too anxious—*especially when you are waiting to hear from a boy*, her grandmother always told her despite her mother's unmasked impatience with these types of lessons) she repeated her well-rehearsed line, "Menendez residence. How may I help you?"

And then she waited, holding her breath, excited to find out the identity of the mystery caller.

It was a weekend and chances were good it was someone wanting to sell them something. These were the days before caller I.D., when your heart still raced at all the possibilities of who might be reaching out to you from the other end of the line. But when Brinda held the receiver to her ear, she only heard harsh breathing from some place deep and dark. Unsure of what to do she repeated her greeting. "Menendez residence. How may I help you?"

Then, from the other end of the line, came a man's voice. "I thought I could stop but I can't. I don't wanna hurt you, but I gotta. I'm sorry."

Brinda remained on the phone, her tiny fingers trembling, her face drained of color. Just then, her mother walked into the room and saw the look on her daughter's face. "Sweetheart, what is it? What happened?"

She embraced poor Brinda and pried the phone from her shaking hands.

"Hello?"

Brinda could only hear one end of the conversation, but she imagined the man's voice and the things he was saying to her mother.

Her mother listened briefly before hanging up the phone hard against the cradle.

"Don't worry, Sweetheart, it's nothing. Someone is playing a very stupid joke on us."

"It's not funny," Brinda pouted.

"You're absolutely right," her mother agreed, "it's not funny at all."

When the phone once again broke the silence with its sharp jolting trill, Brinda froze momentarily then ran straight to her mother. She wrapped her arms around her mother's legs and wouldn't let go.

"Don't be afraid, Brinda. Answer the phone, Sweetheart. Go on. It's okay"

This was the moment that changed Brinda from who she was into who she would become. Reluctantly, she picked up the receiver and greeted the invisible caller with a hesitant, "Menendez residence. How may I help you?"

When Brinda's mother took one look at her daughter's face, she knew exactly who was calling. She took the receiver from her daughter and held it to her breast.

"We have a choice to make," she told Brinda. "We can hang up, unplug the phone and hide away for a few hours until he gets tired of us. Or, we can show this jerk we aren't afraid of him and let him know no one can scare us into doing anything as silly as unplugging our own telephone."

Brinda, suddenly feeling brave, nodded for her mother to answer the call.

"Hello?" Brinda's mother said into the phone, then listened briefly to what Brinda could only imagine were terrible and frightening words. "It's your dime," her mother continued. "If you want to waste it on such nonsense, it's your business, but please don't waste my time."

She listened briefly again, but whatever he said only made her angrier. "You think you have trouble, sir? I live in a world where my daughter isn't even safe picking up the phone! You think you are brave and tough threatening a woman and her daughter? You don't scare us. I have known too many abusive men in my life, and they were all cowards. Each and every one. I would venture to say that you, sir, are no different."

Then she hung up.

Even at seven, Brinda was conscious of the fact that her mother did not conjure up a man as a means of protection. She did not say, *my older brother is a cop. You think you can get away with harming a cop's family?* (this, in fact, was true—even though he worked as a police officer back home in India, thousands of miles away). She did not say, *my husband is home, would you like to threaten him?*

At the thought of her ex-stepfather, Brinda felt a sudden upwelling of sadness. It had been just a few weeks since he had run away with one of his students, and Brinda missed him greatly. When her mother spoke of him, however, Brinda heard something else in her mother's tone—not sadness so much as a sense of deep and complete resignation.

It wasn't his leaving that upset Brinda's mother so much. She understood well the weaknesses of men, but she was angry because he had succeeded (despite her best efforts to the contrary) in turning her life into a cliché. She had worked hard to overcome the predictability of her own story: a young woman gets pregnant during an affair with a married man who promises to leave his wife and never does. Thinking she can escape the mundane, she flees to the U.S. on a scholarship. She eschews everything she had been, lovely and demure, romantic and safe. She begins to study Spanish and majors in Latin American Studies. She crosses the border into Tijuana by herself on weekends to dance with locals in bars at night and to spend her mornings talking with the old ladies selling gum, bottled water, and sweets from small carts along the sidewalk. She cuts her long, beautiful hair (the thing which, apparently, attracted this married man to her in the first place) and styles it daily into a spiky bob. She displays her ever-growing belly unashamedly and feels a small tinge of pride at being the only pregnant girl on campus. But she cannot escape her mistakes from the past and seems, somehow, destined to repeat them. The first night she slept with Dr. Menendez, her Spanish Language professor, she felt exhilarated. They married. She took his name and he raised her daughter not quite as his own but close enough. And they were moderately happy for a time. But eventually, they both grew bored. He found adventure in a fine young thing who could not wrap her mind around the simple differences between *ser* and *estar*. Brinda's mother let her hair grow long again and gave up on her weekly trips to Mexico. She no longer danced in bars, and old women once again stopped her on the street to tell her she was "lovely"— a word she came to despise. It was such an ordinary word. Ordinary, just as she had become all over again.

§

Twenty-seven minutes ticked by without the intrusive ring of the telephone. Brinda's heart calmed. Her mother sat on the couch, pulled her daughter into her lap and held her there. She closed her eyes and breathed slowly in and out, and Brinda felt comforted by the rhythm of her mother's breathing.

But when the phone rang yet again, her mother jumped. Brinda opened her eyes.

Ring.

Brinda slid off her mother's lap.

Ring.

Her mother rose and walked to the phone.

Ring.

She settled her hand onto the receiver.

Ri…

And lifted.

"Hello? I thought it might be you. Listen to me. If you were really going to hurt us you would have done it by now. But since it appears you aren't going to stop calling here anytime soon, why don't you just tell me what you really called to talk about."

Her mother stayed on the line for over two hours, mostly just listening. She never once trembled or showed any signs of fear. Brinda was with her the entire time. They both sat on the floor, and Brinda felt safe wrapped in her mother's arms. She tried to stay awake, to listen to her mother's end of the conversation, but safety made her sleepy. She drifted in and out of slumber, her mother's words occasionally coaxing her back into waking,

"Okay, okay, don't cry. Tell me what you've done."

And later, "I believe God to be a good God. He forgives all manner of sins and He will forgive you."

And later still, "Don't you see? You dialed this number for a reason. So, let me help you. Okay?"

Brinda watched as her mother reached over to the small table and grabbed a pen and notepad, the phone still clutched to her ear.

"Okay, go ahead." Her mother jotted something down.

"I have to hang up now, but I will call you right back. No…of course…of course I promise."

Her mother made two more phone calls right then. The first one was to the police. She calmly explained the situation and read them the address she had copied onto the notepad.

Then she called *him*.

"Hi. It's me. The police are on their way…Of course I'll wait with you."

Brinda was unsure of how much time had passed when she finally heard her mother say, "Is that them at the door? I know you're frightened, but you have to open the door...okay...okay..."

The man on the other end of the line never hung up the phone, and later her mother told Brinda she could hear the police taking him away, the shouts, the scuffle, the door closing and finally the long and unending silence left behind.

The next time the phone rang—two hours and twelve minutes later—it was a wrong number.

From that day forward, when Brinda envisioned herself as an adult, she always pictured her mother. *That is how I want to be. Unafraid. Unafraid and strong enough to give of myself in order to save another person's life.*

§

So when she looked into Santiago's face and saw such sadness there, she could not ask for a better way to prove her braveness.

She could smell the sweet sweat of a man too tormented to bathe with any regularity but who cared just enough so his odor did not overpower those around him. You had to be just close enough, inches from him in fact, to smell the secrets his body was revealing, and Brinda inhaled deeply. When he held out his hand to introduce himself she reached to him without hesitation, without trepidation, and he took her hand fully into his.

§

The first few weeks were characteristically passionate, and at night, as they lay tangled and sticky in each other's arms, he let the stories come. The memories Santiago shared with her on those warm nights made her heart cringe and leap at exactly the same time. Sometimes, when he shared his stories of abuse and fear, he whispered them softly, breathily into her ear. This closeness made her tingle all over. At other times, however (most times if she were to be completely honest with herself), when he spoke, it was almost as if he didn't even know she was there. He was just talking for the sake of it and anyone, really, could have been beside him (or no one at all). It just happened to be her.

"Do you believe in God?" he asked, but without giving Brinda a chance to reply, he continued. "I used to. I used to be so sure He was out there, watching over me. Do you have any idea what it's like to be abandoned by God?"

Brinda opened her mouth to speak, but before she could answer...

"I wonder if all my prayers were useless—a fucking waste of time or if He is there and this is some sort of a bullshit test. What kind of God needs to test us anyway...the ego He must have...is it blasphemous to say it? To even think it? I used to pray so damn hard those nights when my parents locked me in the basement for hours on end. Dad unscrewed all the light bulbs and I had to sit there in complete darkness the whole time. Shit, I was terrified. I have never admitted this to anyone before. I was petrified of the dark. Still am."

At those words, Brinda turned her face to him. Her lips met his and her arm wrapped around him traveling to the small of his back, where it lingered, caressing him gently with light fingers. And she whispered to him, "You are so brave. Look at how much you've gone through and everything you've made out of your life. You're my own personal hero," she said, and he squeezed her tightly. In those moments, they would sleep or make love again. The important thing for Brinda was that they were together, flesh against flesh, protector and protected, savior and the one in need of so much saving.

§

Brinda's slow and steady erosion began three weeks into their relationship. They were at another opening in a small gallery where Santiago's work was being displayed. They mingled over wine and cheese and lofty conversation, but after a few minutes, he left her alone. Suddenly, she was faced with the large dark images Santiago had painted—images of a shirtless boy, mouth and eyes open wide in terror; another image painted in blacks and browns, of shadows falling across unlit stairs, and among the shadows were hands and fingers, arms and eyes, reaching out, it seemed, directly to her. Looking at the painting, she felt a cold wind blow across her heart and had the sudden, inexplicable desire to reach back.

Feeling slightly foolish she nonetheless stretched out her hand and gently touched the rough surface of the canvas.

"You're not supposed to touch the art you know," she heard and jumped back as if burned. A handsome young black man who smelled of laundry soap was staring at her and smiling a heart-fluttering smile.

"I know...it's just...well, I'm the artist's girlfriend if that helps," she said with a shrug and a smile, throwing off the chills which had been there only moments before.

"Ah, I should've known you wouldn't be single. I'm new to L.A. and looking for someone to show me around town. But I imagine your boyfriend is the jealous, twisted type. Most artists are."

Brinda let out a laugh. "And how would you know?"

"I'm an artist too."

"You don't look so twisted," she said and laughed again. And he didn't. In fact, he seemed to be perfectly adjusted to the world and the world, in its way, to him. But even though he was good looking by anyone's standards and smelled nice, Brinda was in no way even mildly interested. After all, this was not a man who needed to be saved. But had she allowed herself, even for a second, to recall the feeling of trepidation she felt at the sight of Santiago's latest dark paintings, she would have realized that she, in fact, was the one who needed saving and that this man—this beautiful, clean-smelling man—was just the person who could do it. And had she been given the time, even a moment of reflection, she might have made a different choice, but right then Santiago appeared. He grabbed her tightly by the crook of the arm, mumbled a pathetic "excuse us" and dragged her off to a dark corner.

"You selfish cunt," he spat at her. "This is my opening, and you're over there ready to spread your legs for any asshole with a smile. How about some support, eh?"

Then he stormed off, leaving her hurt and bewildered.

But that night, back at her place, he wept and hugged her. "I'm so sorry. It's just I get to thinking about my parents...seeing those paintings just brings up all my old shit, you know?"

Right then was the moment for her to walk away—to return to the gallery in hopes of finding the man who smelled of soap, or to simply escape into the darkness on her own.

Instead, she said, "It's okay. It's okay," to the drowning man before her.

And though she felt a small part of herself slipping, she focused only on Santiago and the deep pain she believed she had the power to take away. After all, he had suffered so much. Wasn't he entitled to pass along at least some of his suffering to her?

She enveloped his body in her own and told him, "I'm here for you. That part of your life is over."

As she said it, she truly, in her heart, believed every word. He was not a psychopath on the other end of a telephone line, but a damaged man who needed her. Brinda would not let him down.

CHAPTER 21

IN THE TIME BRINDA HAD KNOWN SANTIAGO, his art had begun to sell fairly well in kitschy galleries across southern California. As he rose in popularity, he gave more and more interviews for art magazines and radio programs, though the focus of these seemed to be less and less about his art work and more about the tragedies littering his life. The latest article to come out told a particularly dark tale of his family life, and as Brinda read it, she was taken aback by the fact that he had never told her this particular story before. In truth, it pained her that her love, this man she had sacrificed so much for, chose to share his agony with the rest of the world before revealing it in private to her.

Only months later would she learn the truth: his stories were not real. He had made them all up. He had started with small lies to garner attention, to be seen as something he was not. Eventually, the lies grew bigger as he began to take snippets from his friends' lives, from friends of friends, or even from stories he had heard about on the news or read about in obscure magazines. Eventually, his life was filled with false tales of abuse and abandonment, with such dark and large skeletons they didn't fit snugly in any closet but raged and pounded against the door demanding to be let out.

He had created the illusion of growing up poor in the slums of El Salvador, struggling just to survive. Yet, in truth, he grew up in Bel-Air with loving parents, a stable home, a life filled with family nights of board games and home-made cookies and summer camping trips on the river with Dad and his younger sister, Irene. His true art, Brinda learned, was not the images of dark despair he cre-

ated with oils and mink hair paintbrushes, but rather the stories he
created about his own life. He was the architect of his own suffering.
He took others' stories and weaved them seamlessly into his own. A
happy life, he decided, was a life without meaning, at least for those
who were true artists. Since he suffered no tragedies of his own, he
stole them from others. Then, as an extension to this art, he painted
great swaths of red or black against a white canvas and gave these
paintings such titles as "Rage" or "Death of a Childhood."

It had not always been this way, however. Santiago, né Manny
(for he was Manny then, Manuel Robles Santiago and would not
become Santiago for a while yet), started off painting forests and
mountains in abstract colors; deer grazing against a twilight sky;
or children racing bikes in polished neighborhoods—happy images
from a happy artist. In college, his professors occasionally praised
his efforts, and he managed to get a few pieces into the university
gallery, but his work went largely unrecognized. As part of a regular radio series at the campus radio station, "You Could Be Famous
One Day" (announced by the host in such a way so as to make you
uncertain as to whether the title of the radio program was a state-
ment or a question), part-time disc jockey, part-time pre-law major,
and all-around loudmouth J.C. Bellman coerced up-and-coming
musicians, writers, actors, and artists from the university to come
on his show. He then proceeded to belittle their work or make jokes
at their expense—in such a way that was certainly humorous to J.C.
Bellman and, one would imagine, the audience, but most certainly
not to the interviewee. People continued to come onto his show,
however, because deep down they believed they *could* be famous
one day, and being on the show was a small price to pay for a little
bit of publicity. So Manny was thrilled when he got a phone call
from J.C. Bellman, asking him to come for an interview the following Friday.

Manny dressed in his best clothes and brought along postcard-
sized prints of some of his paintings (even though he knew it was

radio and no one would see him or his art work during this interview except Mr. Bellman himself). From the beginning, things started off badly for Manny and then quickly and smoothly descended into worst-nightmare territory.

"Aren't you a little bit old to be painting kids riding around on bikes?" Bellman asked flippantly.

"I paint memories, you know? That's me, there," he said pointing to a moppy-haired kid at the edge of the painting, standing with his face turned slightly upwards—sunlight illuminating his crooked smile.

"This is radio, man, the listeners can't see, so permit me to describe it for them," Bellman chuckled. "Norman Rockwell on antidepressants, folks. Trite drivel. I mean, come on, Man, what does your work say to the world?"

"I guess…well…" was followed by the long silence dreaded by radio hosts around the world.

But J.C. Bellman seemed completely unperturbed and quite frankly seemed to be enjoying himself.

"I think the kitty cat has mistaken our artist's tongue for a tasty snack. So, Manny, what do you have to say for yourself? Better yet, what does your art say?

But Manny could think of nothing. What *did* his art say? He painted pictures of his childhood, of good memories, of things that made him smile. But, perhaps no one really wanted art which portrayed a life happier than their own. Maybe everyone wanted to look at something dark, tragic, so they could feel better about their own lives.

After the interview was over, Manny immediately loaded all of his paintings into his car and drove out to Santa Monica Beach. He carried them to the end of the pier and tossed them, one by one, into the sea. After there was nothing left but the steady rise and fall of dark waves, Manny wiped the tears and snot from his face, tore off his clothes and threw them into the sea as well. He walked a full three blocks wearing nothing but his socks and sneakers before being stopped by the police and brought to the station on charges of indecent exposure. His father came and got him out after he had spent all of 35 minutes in a holding cell by himself. Since his father was a highly respected businessman in the community, it was easy for him to persuade the cops to let his son off with just a warning.

The next day, Manny shaved off his hair and got a particularly unoriginal tattoo on his left bicep of a grinning skull with black wings. He tossed out all his department store clothes—beige slacks and colorful polo shirts— and replaced them with thrift store treasures—purposefully ripped jeans, black boots, Led Zeppelin t-shirts, and he began calling himself Santiago. He soon began bragging about his arrest. His fellow students were interested in the details but seemed disappointed to learn he hadn't even spent the entire night in lock-up. Noting that people quickly became disinterested, he began to exaggerate, just a little at first (just to keep them listening), but soon he couldn't help himself and in just a few weeks he became known as the guy who had been in and out of jail for most of his adolescent years and who was "seriously messed up." It helped that he had had very few friends before all of this, so most of his fellow students hadn't known his name. Even the professors who did know him didn't seem fazed by the sudden change, so he transitioned almost seamlessly from Manny to Santiago his sophomore year. Those who had been his friends were so unpopular anyway, no one really paid them much attention. When they tried to address him as Manny, he would reply, at the top of his voice, "Manny's dead. He drowned. I saw it happen, Man. It was one of the toughest things I have ever had to witness, and I have witnessed a lot of heavy shit."

After not too long, he became so good at these stories there were no errors in his telling. Each detail was perfect no matter how many times he told it. He never forgot a single name, a single date, a single event—even though each and every one had been invented in his own mind. And perhaps like all those who suffer of themselves, he began to believe these stories himself. By the time he had graduated from college, he started going to therapy and had stopped speaking to his parents and his sister, who were unsure of what they had done wrong.

His family, exhausted from trying to reach out to him, to understand what had happened to their sweet Manny, reluctantly and sadly gave up on trying to win him back. For the most part, they were no longer in contact with him, except for when another interview, another lie was printed for the entire world to see. Then his father would call him. He would yell, weeping, *"Que quieres,* Manuel? You want that we should have hit you? Would that have made you happy?" But Santiago, at the sound of his father's voice, hung up the phone every time.

By the time Brinda learned the truth—that as a child, Santiago hadn't suffered more than a few scratches from falling off his skateboard, or a bruised shin from tumbling out of a tree—it was too late. She already loved him.

§

Late one morning, after Santiago had gone to his weekly therapy session, Brinda lay snuggled up in his bed, the sheets tangled around her, a cup of coffee steaming on the nightstand. She was reading the latest piece about SANTIAGO (his name in print was always written in all caps), which told in even more graphic detail a particularly scandalous account of life with his parents. She was scanning the article, looking for any mention of her name (he never mentioned her), when the phone rang. She let it ring once, twice, three times. She wasn't going to answer it. She knew he didn't like for her to answer the phone, but it kept ringing. Seven, eight, nine times. Finally, just to stop the incessant noise, she picked up the receiver.

"Hello?"

"This is Humberto Robles, Manuel's...I mean *Santiago's* father. I need to speak to him."

Anger rose in Brinda's throat. Here he was, the man who had caused so much pain and suffering in Santiago's life.

"Why would he talk to you?" she demanded, her voice rising, "after what you did to him? How dare you!"

"Hold on...just hold on!" Then his voice became softer, pleading, "I know what he tells people. What he tells everyone. But his mother...his mother and I...we have never hurt our son."

"Well, he isn't home now anyway."

"Have you been with him for a while? I mean...are you his girlfriend?"

"Yes."

"We would love to meet you. Please, come by. Get to know us and you will see. We are not what he says we are. *Por favor.*"

"Sure, next time I'm in El Salvador I'll be sure to stop by."

His father let out a strange, gurgling sound, and Brinda could not tell if he was laughing or crying.

"We live in Bel-Air. My father came to this country from El Salvador as a young man. He worked hard and made a good life for his family here," he said.

With slightly trembling hands, Brinda jotted down the address, took a quick shower, and dressed. She dashed off a note to Santiago to tell him where she was going and drove 45 minutes to meet the parents of the man she still believed she could rescue.

§

The house was nothing as Brinda had imagined. It was large and clean. A crystal blue swimming pool cast shadows of light in strange, elongated shapes against the back of the house. The garden was lush and tomatoes and green peppers grew in pots along its edge. This was not the home of rotting wood, corrugated tin roofs, and over-sized cockroaches that Santiago had filled her head with over the past two years.

At the door, Santiago's parents greeted her. She could tell both his parents had been crying. Once inside, she met Irene, Santiago's sister, who was about seven months pregnant and radiant.

While his mother and sister made lunch, his father gave her a tour of their home. All along the walls were family photos—photos of Manuel (he was still Manuel then) and Irene, maybe at nine or ten years old, on the Santa Monica pier, arms around each other, grinning and holding giant pink balls of cotton candy. There were photos of family picnics around the pool, high school graduations, and framed ribbons that Manuel had won when he used to jump horses.

To Brinda, it was like being in a stranger's house. These pictures told stories of a man she did not know, of a person she had never met. She had never heard any of these stories: the ones involving tasty snacks, blue ribbons, sleek and shining horses, and cool swimming pools on warm summer days. But still, she knew, abuse is sometimes hidden beneath the prettiest of pictures.

"Can I see your basement?" she asked. For this is where Santiago had told her all of the abuse had taken place...underground, secret, hidden from the rest of the world.

"We don't have a basement, dear."

Brinda felt as though she had been kicked in the gut. She thought she might faint.

"Come sit. Lunch will be ready soon," Santiago's mother called from the kitchen. Humberto led her gently by the arm back to the living room. Though she felt nauseous, her appetite gone, she forced herself to swallow the lunch spread out before her. As they talked, she nodded politely and smiled. She answered their many questions and listened to their stories. Despite herself she grew to really like this family. Just as she was beginning to feel comfortable in this space, with these people, consuming their food, the front door opened forcefully and Santiago stormed into the house.

"What the hell are you doing here, Brinda?" he demanded.

"How the hell could you sit here, eating some fucking sandwiches with these people?"

Brinda shot out of her chair, accidentally knocking her glass over. Wine spilled everywhere, but no one seemed to notice or care. There were messier matters at hand.

"Manuel, please...why are you doing this to us?" his mother pleaded.

"My name is NOT MANUEL! We're leaving, Brinda. Now."

"NO," yelled his father. "No. You can't do this to us anymore." Then his father rose from the table and stood face to face with his son. "Please, Manuel...Manny...you are breaking our hearts. *Por favor, hijo.*"

Tears welled in Humberto's eyes as he spoke.

Santiago, however, was unmoved. "I'm not your *hijo*," he said, staring his father directly in the eye.

And then his father, who had never hit anyone in his life, who believed there was too much violence in the world, particularly in most sports, movies, and presidential debates, balled his hand into a fist and punched his son across the jaw.

Santiago fell to the floor as his mother and sister looked on in shock.

His father stood over him then, rubbing his knuckles and yelled, "Is this what you wanted? Is this how you would have liked to grow up? Would you be happy, would you act like our son, if we had done those things you say we did?"

Brinda felt the sudden urge to run as fast and as far away as she could. But she knew she never would. She loved him, this man weeping on the floor at her feet. She loved him, God help her, and there was no going back. Though she knew, for the first time ever, she wouldn't be able to save him, and, most likely, he was incapable of being saved at all.

§

For a few days, Brinda tried talking to him about his life—his real life—but, instead of talking about it, he began picking fights with Brinda over the smallest things. He called her ugly and commented on the unflattering way in which she chose to wear her hair (which he used to love) and on her form-fitting wardrobe (which he also used to love). He called her incompetent and complained that the apartment was not clean enough or, conversely, that she spent too much time cleaning and not enough time giving him the attention he needed. He called her lazy and worthless and complained every time they ate out but mocked her attempts at cooking and refused to eat what she prepared. He soon began demanding solitude and silence as he worked. And worst of all, he allowed his once casual drug habit to escalate into a full–blown addiction.

And still Brinda stayed with him, giving to him of the only thing she had left—herself. Soon, everything she was went to him: her heart, her courage, her femininity, her forward thinking, her sex appeal, her love of literature, her ability to laugh at her own foibles, and all the other small details that made her who she was. She was building him up with her own reserves and though she had started with plenty, even the most abundant resource will become exhausted or die out if used irresponsibly. By the time Santiago died of an accidental overdose, Brinda felt such a strong hatred for herself that when she looked in the mirror she saw *Stupid, Ugly, Unlovable* written all over her just as surely as if someone had actually scrawled those words onto her forehead in permanent black marker. She felt as though there was just barely enough of her left to stay alive. She was half a person—a shell struggling to fill itself up.

After Santiago's death, his father gave Brinda a large sum of money. "This was his inheritance. He wouldn't take it from us, but it was rightfully his. I want you to have it. You've earned it."

Brinda took the money and used it to open the flower shops. She believed, at first, that she could find herself again among the flowers: her sex and desire hidden within the pistols and stamens of burgeoning buds; the particles of her soul mingling with the yellow, scented pollen; her very heart nestled between the smooth under-bellies of rose petals; her innocence lurking in the scentless white buds of baby's breath. But, she would later come to realize that no part of her was to be found there. They were just flowers after all. They held no real magic for her.

§

At this point, some people might have turned to drugs or al-cohol, but Brinda, being wholly and proudly American, began to eat to fill in the emptiness. She stocked up on curries and samo-sas but also on cookies and ice cream, potato chips, and frozen piz-zas. Slightly embarrassed by her purchases, she made comments to the cashier about a daughter's sleepover party or the fictitious Girl Scout troop she was feeding. She did her grocery shopping at five different supermarkets, rotating throughout the month—some-times driving miles out of her way for fear the clerks would begin to recognize her and grow suspicious of the large quantities of food she was buying only for herself. Once at home, she pulled whatever came first out of her grocery bag—chips, microwaveable popcorn, pints of ice cream, apple pies. She ate those things quickly, standing up in her kitchen. And from the moment she took the first bite, she felt a wave of serenity pass through her—an instant calming affect that lasted only as long as she could taste the food in her mouth, feel as it dissolved beneath the weight of her chewing (her dainty teeth, her warm saliva) and thrill as it finally washed down her throat, filling her stomach. It was such a relief for her to be able to feel com-plete again, for unless she felt a constant fullness in her belly, she felt fearful of the world around her, as if one more harsh word or rough glare would be enough to push her completely out of herself and she would be lost forever.

As the months passed she gained visible fat and her flesh stretched, though her body never registered any weight on any scale.

The first time she weighed herself was just after she had been forced to buy a new wardrobe for the second time. She stood in the bathroom and peeled off her clothes, purposefully avoiding looking at herself in the mirror. Once naked, she stood upon the scale, cradling her breasts (now large and cumbersome) in her hands so she could see the numbers more easily. When she bent over to look, dreading what she would see, the red needle was resting comfortably at zero. She stepped off and then on again, bending over quickly, only to see the needle dip and dive then come to stop once again on zero. She stepped off one more time, wrapped herself in a towel, walked to her bedroom, and grabbed three books off the shelf. She placed these on the scale. The needle moved to 5.2 pounds. She moved the books aside and stepped on the scale and—nothing. She ran to her bedroom again, this time grabbing two more large books. She set all five on the scale. It registered 9.3 pounds. Brinda, stepping on the scale again, still appeared to weigh nothing.

She quickly dressed and proceeded to weigh everything she could: a tall potted plant (7 pounds); the television set (30 pounds); the microwave (26 pounds), until she was exhausted. In total, her scale accurately weighed over 47 household items. But when she stood on it zero was all the damn thing could muster. She went through the exact same procedure with nine different scales (bought over a period of two weeks and now stashed away in a corner of her garage) before she came to accept this fact: despite the rolls of fat on her body, despite the pounds of food she consumed each day, she weighed nothing. She had given away so much of herself it was if she never existed at all.

§

I released my hand from hers and she smiled sadly at me. "You know I would raise August if you asked me to, but I'm not the person, am I?"

I shook my head. "I'm sorry, Brinda."

"Don't be sorry, please. I've spent my whole life trying to get back to being the woman I wanted to be at seven years old." And after a moment she added, "Have you thought about Mariam? She is always talking about how she and Amal are trying to get pregnant."

"Actually, they're next on my list."

I was down to one.

CHAPTER 22

FROM EARLY ON, I HAD KNOWN MARIAM'S STORY. I knew how much she wanted a child. I also knew that every week, on the days her husband picked her up from work, he surprised her with a small gift—a bouquet of white lilies, a book, or tickets to a play or a concert for her and her girlfriends.

"Just so she knows how much I appreciate her," he said to me once.

Amal seemed devoted to his wife, and maybe they would love my son as their own.

But I had to know for sure.

Amal, unlike Mariam, did not yet know about August's ability to pull secrets from closed hearts. And I knew if Amal was not willing to give his secrets, August would not be able to force them out. But I also knew we had to try.

The morning after our dinner with Brinda, I brought August in to work with me. We waited outside for Amal and Mariam to pull up. As Mariam exited the car, she greeted us and walked to the shop entrance. August and I stayed behind.

Before even saying "good morning" or asking how he was, I said, "Amal, my cancer is...well, I don't have much time left. I need to find someone to raise August after I'm gone. I know how much you and Mariam want a child, but..."

Amal stepped out of his car. "Penny, my god, I'm really sorry. Are you asking me if we will take in August?"

"Maybe. But I need to know something first. This is going to sound crazy, but I have to know August is going to be taken care of and really loved. To be sure, I need your secrets. Is that okay?"

"What are you talking about, Penny? What secrets?"

August reached out his hand and gripped Amal's fingers. I rested my hand on August's shoulder.

And this time—the *thump* of a taxi driver's thumbs beating against the steering wheel, the *shuffle* of the driver's tongue clucking out a beat against the roof of her mouth, the *whisper* of a well-tuned engine idling in traffic, and the silent tears (important to the telling, as silence often is) of a man returning home with a secret which both lifted him to the heavens and crushed him to dust; a secret which already changed everything, whether it remained hidden in the dark crevices of his heart or was exposed to the light. A moment later, everything went black and silent—a dark hole swallowing this memory. I opened my eyes and noticed Amal had pulled his hand away.

"Penny," he said, "if what you say is true, if you really saw what I think you just saw, you must know already I'm not the right man to raise your son."

I nodded. "Yes. Thank you for giving me the chance to know."

Amal began to get back into his car—then stopped. His back was still to us. "When you see these secrets, do they remain that way? I mean, do you ever tell anyone what you see?"

"Not once. Nor will I. Ever."

He turned to face us then. "What if I wanted you to see my secret, anyway, even if I'm not the person to raise your son? Would you do that for me?"

"Of course. May I ask why?"

"The truth is, I'm exhausted. Keeping secrets is more tiring than I ever imagined. I think I just need someone to know. I'm ready for someone to know."

Hand in hand in hand, three hearts beat.

We each heard the *thump, shuffle, whisper* of the taxi driver playing her musical beat, marking the passage of time in L.A. traffic.

Amal sat in the back of the cab, resting one arm across his suitcase, the other hand rested on his chest, trying to steady his anxious heart. He leaned his head against the pleather seat and looked out the window. He shifted his weight, flinching in anticipation of the sharp pain he was expecting. But, in its place, was a dreary ache, which could have been from the operation or from the steadily creeping fear that Mariam would discover what he had done.

§

It had been a simple surgery, just a snip (a severing) and an occlusion (an obstruction, a closing off), that rendered him unable to give Mariam what she most wanted—another child. He hadn't meant for it to happen. He hadn't planned on it—the side trip to the hospital, the vasectomy. He had gone to New York for three weeks to give a series of lectures at a medical conference and visit a brother he hadn't seen in years. But on his third night there, as he sat in his brother's living room and watched his brother's happy family—a wife who touched her husband gently in greeting (with love, with affection), a couple that laughed easily together—he suddenly felt brittle and hollow (like the paper-thin bones of a heron, scattered by scavengers and left too long in the sun). He was happy for his brother, he *was*, but it only made him understand more deeply what he had lost.

After all, had it really been so bad what he did all those years ago? Sure, he had worried too much about what his family would think if he had been the one to stay home and raise their son while his wife went on to become a respected surgeon; and he regretted that he had stolen so much from the woman he loved. But was it really so bad? Did this one decision made so long ago mean he now deserved a wife who hated him and barely spoke to him?

Even now, ever since she decided she wanted another child and had started to come to him at night, she still rarely said a word to him and often wouldn't even look him in the eye. But even so, for him, these were the moments that truly counted. Because it was then that he was able to hold her again, that he was able to touch the only woman he ever loved, the only woman he ever wanted.

With a cold jolt to his heart, he suddenly realized if she got pregnant again, she would stop touching him, would stop needing him, would stop letting him in. He would forever lose the feel of her against his body; the scent of her would disappear from his skin. He knew then he couldn't let it happen. Once more, he set about to steal the thing she most wanted.

The next morning he picked the first name he found in the phonebook. It was easy enough to get an appointment and had been an easy enough surgery. And Mariam, at least for the next few years, until she gave up on the idea of having a baby or the possibility of it was taken from her by time—by age, by menopause, by the surrendering of her own body, her own biology, to its diminished ability to create life—until then, she would be his. And somewhere in his heart he believed this would buy him enough time to gain her trust, her forgiveness. All he needed was time and she would return to him, back to the soft and empty chambers of his heart, where she used to live.

§

And yet, as he sat in the taxi, going home from the airport, the conference long since over, the inner workings of his body changed forever, he couldn't stifle the overwhelming urge to cry. And at his doorstep, he watched the taxi drive away and the moon rise higher over the cityscape. After almost an hour, he gathered the courage to unlock his door and go inside.

Mariam was already in bed, reading a book on tips for getting pregnant over 40. She didn't look up when he walked into the room.

"How was the conference?" she asked without averting her eyes from her book.

"Fine. Long. I think my paper was well received." He noticed her tense up slightly.

"I'm ovulating." She set her book down and undid her robe, revealing small breasts and a thin stomach. Amal paused. He opened his mouth to speak, to tell her what he had done. But then...

"Come *on*," she said.

He knew if he went to her then, if he didn't tell her right away, it would be a secret he would hold with him every day for the rest of his life.

"Please," she whispered, an unreadable smile itching at the corners of her mouth. "Please."

Everything went dark. Amal let his hand slip from our grasp.

"I'm glad someone finally knows," he said.

We were down to none.

§

We made another list.

§

We listened to other stories.

§

But no one was right. We did not choose any teachers from August's school, or any of his friends' parents. We did not choose my apartment manager or the neighbors who had taken over Peter's or Joe and Alice's apartments. We did not pick the mailman or my doctor or any of the nurses. We did not select any one of the anonymous strangers whose lives touched ours every day—a customer buying flowers, the man at the gas station taking my cash, the gentleman who opened the door for us at the bank, or the woman who smiled at me as we stood together at the crosswalk. I even searched out my first OBGYN—Emelia, the once young girl who had loved a young boy. But at the hospital they told me she had long ago moved to Brazil and they didn't know how to contact her.

We were down to none. Again.

Until one evening August pulled himself onto my lap. "Mom, I think there's one more heart we should listen to."

"Whose, Sweetie?" I asked, tears of desperation in my eyes.

"Yours."

•   •   •

"HELLO," I REPEAT over and over. I can't hear anything on the other end of the line. Even so, I know it is her. It is almost like I can feel her breath in my ear.

When the line goes dead, I pick up the pages of the letter, grab my pen, and continue to write.

I heard the ambulances long before I could see them but they brought me no comfort. I could only see my father's unrecognizable body, motionless, breathless, his legs bent at odd angles. The driver of the other car held one shaking hand to his forehead; blood seeped from between his fingers. Somewhere far away, I heard voices, the man from the other car, Emma, her mother. Later, I watched as uniformed men lifted my dad's body and placed it into the wide, swinging doors of an ambulance. I followed. From the small window, I could see Emma being shoveled into another ambulance identical to mine. As we drove off, sirens whirring, scenery blurring past, I stayed by my father's side. A white sheet—now stained red—covered him so I couldn't see his face. I couldn't see his hands. Only the tips of his boots stuck out. I never took my eyes off them.

At the doors of the hospital emergency room, they rolled my father away. A nurse ushered me along to the cold, impersonal embrace of a waiting room.

When the doctor finally came to talk to me I wasn't expecting much, but still I was shocked by his mumbled words of apology, his attempts at explaining what had happened, as if I hadn't been there firsthand to witness the death of my father. As if being a doctor allowed him to know things that a son did not.

He handed me a brown paper bag and patted me lightly on the head before turning to leave. When he was gone I opened the bag. Inside were my dad's belongings, all covered in blood: one blue shirt, a pair of brown trousers, two dark socks, one leather belt, white underwear, one leather wallet, his wedding ring, which I slipped into the front pocket of my jeans, and at the very bottom his

shoes. I pulled the boots out and set them on the floor. I set everything except his ring back into the bag and threw it into the nearest
trash can. I then removed my own shoes and tossed them away,
too. I pulled my father's shoes onto my feet one by one. I tightened
the laces around the ankles as taut as possible, to keep my feet from
slipping out. I touched the top of the boots and pressed the spot
where my toes began, just like they do in the shoe store, feeling all
that empty space. His shoes, of course, were several sizes too big.
I stood. I walked. I felt my feet slip and slide against the leather. I
shuffled to the stairs outside. I waited for my mom to come take me
home.

From then on, I wore my father's shoes everywhere. I wore
them to his funeral where I looked down onto his sleeping face,
his folded hands. They'd bathed him and dressed him in a suit he
rarely had occasion to wear until now. They'd removed every inch
of grease from beneath his fingernails. He smelled sweet like flowers or cologne. On his feet was a pair of brand new shining shoes I
didn't recognize.

I wore his boots to school despite the kids' teasing and the
teacher's protests and even on weekends when, months later, it finally felt okay to run and play again. I ate with them on; I even
sometimes fell asleep with them on. I took them off only to take
a bath—and then reluctantly. I would set them neatly by the tub,
side by side facing out, ready to be slipped into once my feet were
cleaned and dry again.

My mother, for her part, was understanding enough. She made
me special insets so the shoes fit better on my small feet. And every
night, before I went to bed she told me, "I know how much you love
your father. I know how much you miss him and these shoes, well,
I understand why you need to wear them. But your father was hard
on his shoes and you know they won't last forever, sweetheart. One
day they will become so worn out you won't be able to wear them
anymore. I want you to be prepared for that day."

"I will be, Mom," I always reassured her.

As I got older, of course, my feet got bigger, but no matter how much I grew, and despite the fact that I was taller than my father ever was, I could never fill his shoes. At my tallest, they were still two sizes too big.

But even today, to this very day, as I write this, I'm still prepared for the day to come when his shoes become so worn they'll no longer stay on my feet. But I will tell you this: despite wearing those shoes every single day for decades they remain exactly as they were on the day my father died, just as my love for him remains as strong and the loss I felt remains as sharp.

Four months after my father's death, we packed up and moved to L.A., partly to be closer to my aunt but mostly because my mother just couldn't escape the memory of my father.

"My tired old heart just can't take so much goddamn beauty. It reminds me too much of your dad," my mother said on the morning she told me we were moving to Los Angeles. It was as if everything beautiful that nature contained represented my father and served as a continual reminder to my mother that he was irreversibly dead. So we replaced the mountains for skyscrapers, the sand dunes for concrete.

We moved into a small, two-bedroom apartment. My mom found a job teaching ballet at the YWCA, but she'd lost her spirit. She returned to our old house in Colorado just once, more than a year later. I stayed behind with my aunt so as not to miss school. She collected the mail that had accumulated at the post office and gave away everything we couldn't keep. She found renters for the house, so we wouldn't have to sell it. My father's garage she did sell, though it broke her heart to do so. She came home weeks later with some photographs, a handful of keepsakes, a few letters—one, in a pink envelope covered with red hearts was addressed to me—and little else.

The mere memory of my father wasn't enough to sustain her.

She began to develop migraines that kept her in bed for days. Her dancer's legs grew thick and heavy. Less than ten years later, she was dead. She was only 47.

On the night she died, I sat with her for a long while. We both knew she wasn't going to make it through the night. Turning her head weakly, she glanced down at my feet, at my father's old shoes, still intact after all those years, and smiled. "Look at that," she said. "Your father never let you down. He stayed with you in the only way he could. But me...I've failed you."

I hugged her and I said, "No. Not once."

I kissed her goodnight.

The day of her funeral, I moved into my aunt's house. She was a widow herself, and her kids were all grown and living in far off states.

The following morning, I was on my way to school. That was when I saw you. You were this skinny white girl walking all alone. And then you stopped and helped me. You pressed your fingers onto mine and stopped the bleeding.

The day I joined the Marines, the day with those boys and that bird, I went home after school and switched on the TV. I was immediately faced with images of the war—impenetrable jungles; bespectacled young men, some with cigarettes hanging from their mouths; guns I didn't know the names of yet strapped across their shoulders.

"Those poor boys need a miracle," my aunt said to me. "In fact, I suspect we all could."

"You're right," I told her. "You're right."

At the recruiting office, war protestors shouted, son-less mothers wept, but it wouldn't stop me. Those people didn't know about you and those boys. They didn't know that a grey-backed pigeon was dead one moment and then suddenly wasn't. They didn't know about a girl who needed a miracle.

I believed God brought the bird back to life to save us just as I believed God would save people through me in the war. It might sound ignorant or arrogant, but I was neither. I simply had faith, and it was you who further cemented this faith in my heart. So I went, but I couldn't bear saying goodbye to you. I didn't want you to worry. I didn't want you to know what I was doing, until I had already done it. So I left without saying a word.

But over there, I lost everything. So when I came back, I didn't want to find you. I was afraid to admit you'd been right all along.

I sit back.
I hold the letter in my hands.
I take a deep breath and try to calm my heart.

Part 4

blood feathers

Every living thing must (at its own pace, in its own time) move toward another: roots to earth, predator to prey, sex, ultimately, to sex. So it came to pass that I too would have to move in an attempt to keep on living. And my approach (my propulsion, my momentum, my migration forward) was the culmination of every secret combined. It was the tune of a favorite song; the beat of a funeral drum at the wake of my past; it was the sound of a young boy's heart calling forth my dreams.

CHAPTER 23

THERE WAS A TIME WHEN I DIDN'T KNOW HIS NAME; I only knew his footsteps—the familiar *thump- shuffle -whisper-thump* of his feet as they carried him forward, towards me. There was something odd and wonderful in the rhythm of his long strides, in the irregularity of his feet as they beat against the pavement. It was not a limp—his strong body did not hobble—but there was a strangeness to those footsteps which held such power over me. They were as calming as a favorite song or the sound of rain falling on the roof while I slept. It was as if he walked in regular time, but I heard him in slow motion. I could distinctly hear the slight separation of his foot from the shoe as he lifted one leg (*shuffle*), the reconnecting of his insole as his foot made contact with the inside of his shoe (*whisper*) just seconds before it hit the sidewalk (*thump*) and started all over again with the opposite foot.

I walked to school alone every day. I was 12 years old and had no true friends. I was living with Annelle at the time. Carl had already come and gone from her life, so she no longer spoke to me of anything that really mattered. My only company each morning on the walk to school was the sound of the cars rolling past or the thundering wing beats of pigeons as they startled from the eaves of buildings, or the sometimes light, sometimes heavy foot falls of passing strangers (women in high heeled shoes that made their calf muscles bulge, men in black wingtips polished to a shine, the *click click click* of a dog's toenails as it ambled up the street). Perhaps out of loneliness or something more, I began to look forward to hearing his footsteps every morning as I walked to school. They began, always, faintly—like an outside noise (a dog barking far in the distance, a soft wind whispering at your door, the light laughter of someone you love) that incorporates itself into your dreams as you sleep. But when he turned the corner and took up pace behind me, his footsteps, naturally, became louder, and my heart sang just as loudly. As he got closer and closer (my own footsteps slowing, almost unconsciously, so he could catch up with me more quickly), his footfalls eventually matched pace with mine as we fell into step. We would walk together for a few blocks. We never spoke a word to one another. We never snuck glances at each other. Our hands never accidentally touched. I always kept my eyes downward, so the only part of him I really knew well was his boots. After a few weeks, I realized why his walk was so distinctive. The leather work boots he wore were noticeably too big for his feet. I never asked him why he wore such big shoes, but at night, I slept to the rhythm of his walk playing over and over in my head like a favorite song. After too short a time (a mere few blocks), we would part ways. The sound of his footfalls would begin to fade once again as he walked one way and I another.

I spent most of my school hours thinking of him. To me, he was the most beautiful man I had ever seen, though I only knew four things about him. I knew he went to the high school two blocks down from my junior high, and that he played sports. These first two facts were given away by the lettered jacket he wore (the high school's colors—blue and silver and the school mascot, an open-mandibled eagle bearing its fierce talons, its gold eyes staring up at me from his lapel) on the first day we met. The third thing I knew was he was probably the bravest man I had ever met, and fourthly, I knew, just like me, he walked alone.

§

The first time I met him I was on my way to school and had just turned a corner. The first thing I saw were his impossibly long legs—like a curlew's—splayed out on the sidewalk. When I got closer, I saw he was just as beautiful as his legs foretold. His back was propped up against the wall of an antique store whose doors wouldn't open for at least another hour. His eyes were red from crying, and blood dripped from his skinned knuckles. He didn't seem to care that he was crying and bleeding with the whole world watching. To me, this made him strong, unafraid, and confident— the exact opposite of everything I was.

I was 12. He was 18. I was small and pale with eyes so mild I awoke every day surprised I had not gone blind in the night. To me, he was the size of mountains or of a god, equally unreachable from where I stood. He was black with eyes like granite and steel. I believed nothing could touch him, no harm could ever befall him, no scars could ever mar his beauty.

He looked up at me.

I rummaged in my bag for a tissue or something absorbent and soft. Finding nothing useful, I pressed my hands to his knuckles. I wiped the blood from his fists with my fingers. Then I sat on the sidewalk beside him and rested my head on his shoulder. One by one he lightly threaded each of the fingers of his right hand into mine. We held on. I lifted my head and our eyes met, briefly. We sat together for a long while, both knowing we were going to be late for school but not really caring. Finally, without a word, we stood up. I brushed the dirt from my pants and picked up my bag as he watched. As we both began to walk, I noticed we were perfectly in sync, as though we had been walking together our entire lives.

§

Of all the people I knew, he was the one I most wanted to tell about the boy. I knew he would understand. I knew he would tell me what to do. But I was afraid if I did tell him, he would see me not as a brave kid who walked alone to school but as a weak child who couldn't take care of herself. So, I didn't say a word. I simply thrilled at seeing him each morning. After our first meeting (without discussing it or planning it), we had begun to walk the few blocks to school side by side every day – until, inevitably, our paths diverged. When I sensed him walking away, I would close my eyes and listen until his footsteps got so far away I couldn't make them out anymore, until he had blended so deeply into the landscape it was as if he never even existed at all.

On my most difficult days (when the kids at school were crueler than usual, when Annelle was particularly spiteful), I sometimes wondered if I had invented him. Was it really possible to feel safe with someone whose name I didn't know? Whose voice I hadn't heard? But the next morning he would be there, and I would be reassured once again. But like all things in life, this would not last. Events (both minute and grand) over the course of one day (but brewing, bubbling, building for longer than we could have imagined) would bring us closer together and then separate us for the next three decades.

CHAPTER 24

I WAS IN THE SEVENTH GRADE and had already been given my unfortunate nickname, Two-by-Four. The teachers ignored the name-calling, and on some days it escalated to such a point that I took to writing my name over and over again in my notebooks at night. *Penny Rose, Penny Rose, Penny Rose,* I wrote, falling asleep with the pen in my hand and the notebook propped up against my knees, a flashlight held between my teeth, filling line after line, page after page, just to remind myself I did have a name. I was not *Two-by-Four*. I was, for better, for worse, Penny Rose. Apart from the name-calling, which occurred mostly on days when the kids were bored, I went about my school life in relative obscurity. I got good grades but not yet good enough to stand out. I had one friend who sat with me, reluctantly, and then only when *her* best friend, Marlene, was out sick or pulled from school for the day because out-of-town relatives were visiting.

Everything changed on an ordinary Tuesday afternoon. During our final recess, I was in the bathroom at the same time as Shannon Barnes and Heather Mei, two of the school's best known trouble-makers. They wore gaudy makeup, strong perfume, and clothes that revealed too much midriff or exposed too much of their supple teenage thighs for the school's taste. They were constantly being called to the principal's office for ditching class, talking back to teachers, or neglecting to turn in their homework.

At the end of recess I had walked into the girl's bathroom to find them puffing away on cigarettes and drinking something from a bottle hidden inside a paper bag. They looked at me with bored eyes as I entered the room. A few seconds later, Mrs. Peretti, the eighth grade math teacher, stormed in behind me.

"You can smell the smoke from down the hall, young ladies. Dump the cigarettes and give me the alcohol," she said holding out her palm with exasperation.

"Shannon, Heather." Then gesturing to me, "what's your name?"

"Penny."

"Fine. Shannon, Heather, Penny, you will meet me and Principal Wilson after school to discuss this. Now get to class."

I didn't protest or try to argue. I had never been held after school in my life and usually left the grounds as soon as the last bell rang. I didn't linger at the lockers with some of the other students or hang out with the packs waiting for their parents to pick them up. I always headed straight for the exit and was on my way home by no later than ten after three.

In the principal's office, I was eventually cleared of any wrong-doing and allowed to leave, but I didn't make it out of there until 3:29. It was only a 19 minute difference and yet, time enough to change everything.

A few blocks from school, I walked toward a bus stop I passed every day, and almost every day, it was void of people. But on that day, I saw Mike Cullins waiting impatiently for his bus, which, according to the schedule, should have come a while ago. Mike was popular with the kids at school, a cool boy with just the right amount of attitude so the teachers secretly feared him and the kids openly respected him.

The first time I became aware of Mike Cullins, I mean really aware of the heavy weight of his being, the feeling that he could consume me if I let him, was that day. I passed his bus stop on my way home every day, normally minutes before he even arrived. If the bus had been on time or if I had picked a different girl's bathroom, our paths might have never crossed. But that was not how things were meant to be. When I walked by him, he was sitting on top of the backrest, his feet resting on the empty bench. In his hand, working back and forth, he held a small knife, which he used to scratch against the wood. It made a dull, grating sound (sorrow itself cutting against the dry bones of memory). When he saw me coming toward him he folded the pocketknife, the whole thing about the size of a grown man's thumb, and stuffed it into the front pocket of his jeans.

"Hey, you're Two-by-Four, right?" he asked. And instead of being insulted by the nickname, I felt a moment of elation—Mike Cullins recognized me! One of the coolest kids in school knew who I was.

"Why does everyone call you Two-by-Four? Does your dad beat you with a two-by-four, Two-by-Four?"

I didn't say a word but shook my head, *no*. My inner voice whispered *my mother killed herself right after I was born because my heart is hard and flat*.

"Do you kill anything, like kittens or stray dogs, by bashing their bodies to bits with a two-by-four, Two-by-Four?"

I shook my head, *no*, but again the voice, *I saw Charlotte die in a pool of blood on a white linoleum floor, and I never once cried because I am wood*.

"Maybe they just call you Two-by-Four because that's your name, Two-by-Four."

I thought, *I have never been able to love anyone*.

He stood then, stuffing his hands deep in his pockets. In the distance, a bus came rumbling down the street. As it squeaked to a stop he said "Hey, Two-by-Four, can you keep a secret?"

He did not wait for me to answer but hopped onto the bus, disappearing behind the *whoosh* of closing doors. Once he was gone, I looked to see what he had scratched into the wood. At first glance it appeared to be an indistinguishable mess of lines, but as I looked more closely, I could make out the outline of a single wide wing.

I thought no more about him and continued home. No one was there to notice, or worry, that I was almost an hour late.

§

The next day, I saw Mike in school, but he didn't even look at me. He never acknowledged we had spoken, and I was perfectly content to let it stay that way. But after school he was there again, his young body perched atop the back of the bench, his feet upon the seat. His head was down and his dark hair hung low over his face, obscuring the details, but I knew. I knew he had come early to wait for me.

"Hey, Two-by-Four, what do you know about God?" he asked jumping from the bench and taking stride beside me. He flicked his hair back, his hands once again shoved deep into his pockets. I did not look at him but thought about the question.

"I think God might have too much say sometimes," I said. "Other than that, I don't know much."

There was a long moment of silence, perhaps three minutes went by. He walked beside me trying to keep pace with my shorter legs.

"Well, sometimes," he said, "when I get bored, I take my mom's lighter and burn up ants when they're all together walking in those lines like they do. Not all of them, though, ya know? Some, I just let go by. No reason, really. I mean, sometimes I let whole bunches go by at a time. But sometimes I burn the whole lot of 'em right up. It just depends. On those days," and here he looked at me and smiled, "I remind myself of God."

§

From then on, every day after school, I would find him waiting for me with a question or a story or sometimes a gift. The first present he gave me was wrapped carefully in a sheet of lined notebook paper, folded neatly, its creases hard and pointed.

"This is for you," he said, nonchalantly.

I turned the folded paper over and over in my hands, unsure of what to expect.

"C'mon open it," he said.

I unfolded the flaps one by one. When I saw what lay there, my heart took an unexpected skip and my breath hiccupped in my throat. Balancing the paper in one palm, I reached down with two fingers and plucked the object—red, green, blue—from the page. It was a feather but one with so many colors I could not believe it came from a real bird—at least not one which existed in this world.

"It's beautiful." And it was. It was like nothing I had ever seen before.

"I collect feathers, and I don't have anything like this. How did you know?" I asked.

"I just thought you would like it," he said.

"I do. Very much."

I folded the feather back into its papery cocoon and carefully slipped it between the pages of my math textbook. We walked a ways in silence, a smile forming at the corners of his mouth. A few blocks down, he caught his bus. He took a seat at the window and waved to me as the bus pulled away from the curb. I waved back.

§

Days later, he passed me a note in English class. This was the first time he had ever made contact with me in school. I opened the note. Tucked inside was another feather, identical to the one he had given me the day before, and a drawing of me, labeled "2x4" (so I couldn't be mistaken), and a pile of feathers, or what I took to be feathers, raining down around me. I turned to look at him and smiled. He had been watching me the whole time. I mouthed the word *thanks*, but he didn't respond. He was looking right at me, but it was as if he didn't see me. Suddenly, I felt a tingling in my throat, my tongue felt dry and pasty. I swallowed hard once, twice, pushing down the uneasiness until it lay in the pit of my stomach, a dull ache that I convinced myself to ignore.

As we walked together after school that day, I turned to him and asked, "Where did you get the feathers?"

"My mom has a pair of Lovebirds. Birds molt their feathers, you know."

"I do know," I said, and I felt better, comforted somehow, because he knew this simple fact.

§

The following day, he wasn't in school and didn't show up for the rest of the week. I found myself torn between wanting to see him again, watching for him in the hallways and in class, and a huge sense of relief when I did not see him among the crowds of my fellow teens, when his seat at the back of the class remained empty long after the bell had rung.

On Thursday of that week, though I had not seen him in school, I spotted him at the bus stop, again etching something into the bus stop seat. He stopped when he saw me, folded his knife, dropped it into his pocket and hopped off the bench.

"You weren't in school today?" I asked.

"Nah. I just came here to see you."

"Why?" I asked and saw something dark like a shadow sweep across his face (hurt, humiliation), and then it was gone. Had I imagined it?

"I was waiting for you. I have something," he said.

He handed me another folded piece of paper. It was bulging and wrinkled.

I unfolded the paper and inside were feathers. Many, many feathers. One in particular caught my eye: it had a thin grey shaft around much of its length. It was a new feather growing in to replace the old one being molted out. A blood feather. Then I noticed several more like them. Too many.

"Mike, how did you get these? These feathers...birds don't

molt feathers like these."

I looked more closely at the other feathers piled haphazardly together—some with tiny barbs of flesh stuck to the shaft. My hands began to shake.

"Mike, are these from your mom's birds?"

"I told you she had a pair of Lovebirds."

"Yeah, but…"

"Look, it ain't no big deal. I killed them. Well, one actually. I killed one. It was just like killing those ants. Except I couldn't burn it with a lighter. I tried to strangle it, but birds don't strangle easy."

"No, they don't," I said.

"So, I had to find another way. It was easy, really, once I thought about it. But you know what I did, don't you? You already know the best way to kill a bird."

I nodded my head and swallowed hard. I did.

"Why did you do it?" I asked.

"My mom says they can't live alone. If one dies, the other one does too. I just wanted to find out if it was true."

I stayed still, trying not to show him the surge of panic I felt. I stood rigid for minutes. Finally I heard the familiar rumbling of the bus heading in our direction. It whined to a stop, and its doors opened. Mike got on and waved goodbye. As the bus pulled away, the wind it generated blew the feathers out of my hands. I watched as they floated around me, settling like a premonition at my feet.

My legs felt weak. I sat on the bench and rested my head between my knees, catching my breath. When I sat up, a few moments later, my eyes were drawn to the spot where I had seen him carving into the wood. This time I could make out the design. It was the outline of a bird with an upturned belly and crooked legs, its wings pitching out at odd angles and tiny x's where its eyes should have been.

CHAPTER 25

I DID MY BEST TO AVOID MIKE CULLINS. I ignored him at school, pretending I didn't hear him or see him. I waited an extra twenty minutes after school before walking home, knowing the bus would have come and gone long before. It worked for two days. On the third day, I found him waiting for me at the bus stop.

"Mike, I can't talk now. I have to get home or my foster lady'll…"

"What? All of a sudden you have to get home? You're 20 minutes late. I missed the first bus waiting for you, and now you won't even talk to me?"

"Mike, please, you're scaring me a little," I chuckled, trying to keep it light.

"You're scared? Of me? C'mon Two-by-Four, please don't do this, okay? I'm sorry. Look, I was just kidding about the bird. I wanted to see how you would react. I mean, I did kill it, but it was an accident. I had taken it out of its cage, just to hold it. My mom doesn't like me to hold them when she's not around, but I did. It was so squirmy inside my hands, I accidentally let go. Then it was loose inside the house. My mom would've killed me if she came home and found the bird had escaped. So I tried to catch it. I got a broom and tried to trap it. I guess I hit it too hard. It fell to the ground and was dead. I didn't mean to scare you. It was an accident. I just made up the other shit to…well, I don't know. It was stupid of me. I wouldn't kill a bird on purpose. I just thought you would like the feathers."

"I did. I *do* like the feathers, but…"

"Look, I said I was sorry. Don't be such a baby."

I recoiled against his words.

He hugged me then and I let him, though his body felt stiff and awkward against mine.

"Tell me you forgive me."

"I forgive you," I said.

Still hugging me, he rubbed his arms along my back, stroking my hair and once again I let him. He rubbed my arm and placed one hand on my waist, and I let him. He brought this same hand up and rested it on my breast. Then he pinched my nipple hard. It was all I could do not to yelp in pain.

§

Over the weeks, I tried harder to evade him. I began to walk a different way home to avoid the bus stop; I spent an extra hour in the school library, finishing all my homework, before leaving school. But he was always there. Somehow, he always found me.

"I gotta get home, and you're making me late," I told him.

"I'll walk you home, then. Come on."

At my front door he pleaded with me.

"Let me in, Penny, come on."

It wasn't even 5:00 yet. Annelle was not home from work and wouldn't be for at least another hour, and who knew when the boys, my "brothers," would be back.

"My foster lady will get really mad if I let a boy in here."

"Who gives a shit?" he said pushing his way in. Once inside, he picked up knickknacks off the shelf, turned them over in his hand, and then placed them back.

"Um...do you want something to drink?" I asked heading straight for the kitchen. He was the first person who had ever come to this house to see me. Under the best of circumstances, I would have been nervous. As it was, I had no idea how I was supposed to act.

I took a few deep breaths and poured milk into a glass, accidentally spilling some on the counter.

Back in the living room, I found him sitting on the couch, with his shirt off. I glanced back to the kitchen, regretting leaving my schoolbooks on the counter. I wished I had them now, to hug them tight against my chest, as if they (as if anything) could protect me from him.

Instead I stuck my arm out as far as I could and offered him the milk, keeping my eyes averted to the floor.

He grabbed the glass from my hand and set it on the coffee table. He patted the spot beside him on the couch. "Sit down."

I sat.

"Kiss me here," he pointed to his chest. With trembling heart, I leaned out and kissed him, my lips barely brushing his skin.

"Now it's my turn."

He pulled up my t-shirt and laughed at what he saw.

"You look exactly like me," he said.

It was true. I looked exactly as he did—my girl's body no different from a boy's. But this fact did not seem to deter him. He kissed my left breast, the one he had pinched, which was bruised and yellowing. Then he kissed the right, his tongue grazing my small, ineffectual nipple. He laughed again, pulled down my shirt and drank his glass of milk. When he finished, he wiped his mouth with the back of his hand, thanked me, and left.

§

Days later, I mustered the courage to tell Annelle about what had happened.

"Sweetie," she said in her saccharine way, "no man is perfect, you better get used to it right now. We can't all be supermodels, and those who aren't can't be too picky. If some little boy likes you, well, I say go for it. If you don't want to be alone for the rest of your life, sometimes you just need to settle. It's not pretty, but that's life."

The doorbell rang.

"Who the hell is comin' here on a Sunday? I'm late for my hair appointment already. It better not be no goddamn salesman trying to sell me hundred dollar encyclopedias that are only good for collecting dust." In a huff, Annelle answered the door.

I heard her call to me, "I'm going out. There's a nice young man to see you."

My heart sank. I ran to the door.

"Annelle. Stay. *Please.*"

"I've gotta get to my hair appointment. You can visit with your little friend but have the kitchen clean by the time I get home," she patted me roughly on the head and walked out the door.

Mike was already inside the house. He closed the door behind Annelle and approached me. He placed his hand high on my leg, his fingers rubbing my thigh. For the first time in my life, I felt grateful for my birthmark and its ugly raised flesh. Because of it, as a young girl, I never wore skirts or dresses (it would be years before I would feel comfortable wearing even calf-length dresses) for fear the wind would blow, or the hem would ride high when I sat and people would see one more defect, one more flaw in me. So, I always wore pants, mostly thick jeans, even in summer. But, even the coarse denim did nothing to block the sensation of his hand touching me. The hairs on my arms and neck stood up as though a cold breeze had blown into the room.

"I don't like this, Mike", I said pushing him away.

"That's good, Two-by-Four, that's good. That's why I'm doin' this. See? You can say no, after all. You're always so goody-goody. Everyone calls you Two-by-Four and you just let 'em."

He began to grow angry.

"As if you have no control, as if you can't just stand up and shout, 'Stop! Stop right now!' But you never do. You just let it go."

He smiled then and calmly continued to speak.

"You're like I was—young and so stupid. I let her do those things to me for so long. But when I finally told her to stop—no, made her stop—it felt great. I pushed her down and squeezed my hands around her throat. I could've ended everything then. Made it all go away. But I didn't. Instead, I killed her birds. They fuckin' deserved it. They knew what was goin' on and did nothing...just squawked and squawked all day long. Shut the fuck up I wanted to shout, but I never did 'cause I was a good boy. I just wanted to be a good boy, but then all of a sudden I wasn't. I left one of the birds on her bed where she would have to see and know what I'd done. But I was never sorry. I won't ever be sorry and you shouldn't be either."

Then he looked up at me and said, as if we had just been conversing about the weather or the latest episode of our favorite television show, "I'm hungry. What you got to eat?"

In the kitchen, I surveyed the mess—the remnants of one of Annelle's parties: dishes caked with unrecognizable food, empty wine bottles, half-eaten bread sticks, and crumpled, lipstick-stained napkins filled the sink, spreading out like a tentacled octopus onto the countertops and floor. I opened the silverware drawer and the only clean utensil was a serrated steak knife. I grabbed it.

I spread peanut butter onto eight slices of bread as slowly as I possibly could. I, sloth-like, sliced thin pieces of banana and placed them one by one on top. I made us two sandwiches each. Before placing the knife in the sink to wash later, I licked the sticky sweet substance from its surface and felt a sharp pain. I'd accidentally cut my tongue on the blade. I dropped the knife onto the counter and felt a warm rush of metallic-tasting blood pool in my mouth. I spat into the sink and rinsed my mouth with water. The whole time, Mike—calm as a summer afternoon—ate his two sandwiches and just watched as I grabbed a paper towel and squeezed it against my tongue to stop the bleeding.

When Mike finished eating, he wiped the crumbs from his mouth, kissed my forehead, and walked out the door, leaving me clutching the edge of my own tongue, blood and saliva seeping through the napkin.

After Mike left and my tongue stopped bleeding, I begrudgingly started to tidy the kitchen, to clean up after the messes Annelle was so good at making. The first thing I saw, like a flag on top of a crumbling hill, was the knife. I picked it up and held it in the light. I could see a few dark stains (my own blood) tarnishing the blade. I washed the knife and dried it. Then I slid it gently into the sleeve of my sweater and cupped the handle in my palm. It rested firm beneath the tight material. The metal felt comforting against my forearm.

I began to carry the knife with me constantly. During class, I hid it in my school bag. But just before heading home, I would duck into the bathroom and quickly tuck it beneath my sleeve once again. I secured it to my arm with two pieces of elastic I took from Annelle's sewing kit. When Mike passed me in the hall, I wondered if he saw the difference in me. When an entire week passed and he hadn't said a word to me and hadn't waited for me at the bus stop even once, I began to believe the knife gave me a secret power. I carried it wherever I went, never imagining I would ever have to use it. Then one morning, a few weeks later, as I was leaving for school, I opened the front door to find him waiting for me. He pushed me back and forced his way inside.

No one else was home.

"My brothers are upstairs," I lied. "You better leave."

He ignored my warnings and instead reached out to me, rubbing his hand against my cheek.

"I missed you," he said.

"You need to go now," I said stepping back from him.

"Just wait," he grabbed my hand and pulled me toward him. "You're always running away from me."

I knew if I yelled to the neighbors to help me (I could see them through the window, going about their lives—picking up the morning paper, taking out the garbage, getting into shiny cars headed to destinations unknown), I would never be free of him. If I wasn't the one to stop him I would become lost in him, in what I allowed him to do to me. So without another thought, and surprising even myself, I slipped from his grasp, pulled the knife from my sleeve and plunged it into his arm. The blade entered smoothly and when I pulled it out blood spurted all over the tile floor. He clutched his arm and screamed. I took two steps back. I couldn't breathe. My eyes focused on the blood trailing behind him and the sight of him as he ran off, crying. I dropped the knife to the ground and vomited my breakfast all over the tops of my shoes.

§

When Mike appeared at school the next day with a bandaged arm his popularity grew. He told everyone he saw an old lady getting mugged and fought off the would-be attacker with his bare hands, getting stabbed in the process. While he was jovial and light, bragging with his fellow classmates, I caught him brooding when he thought no one was looking.

Even so, I was sure I had ended whatever had been between us. I never once considered the alternative.

CHAPTER 26

IT WAS APRIL. IT HAD BEEN RAINING ON AND OFF for three days. The sky was grey and more rain threatened. But in the distance, the sun peaked out from behind dark clouds. I had walked only a few blocks when I accidentally stepped into a small murky puddle. Cold water soaked through the toe of my shoe, wetting my sock. I looked down. At my feet was a pigeon. Its legs were splayed out, and its head lolled to one side. Its softly feathered eyelids were closed. I sat upon my haunches and picked the bird up by the wing. Water dripped from its feathers. I continued to walk to school with the bird cradled in my hands. I was so absorbed with the look of this delicate thing—one wing now tucked and the other outstretched, the intricate patterns of its feathers, the iridescent shine of its back—I forgot to pay attention to anything else around me. When I first heard footsteps behind me I ignored them. I didn't ponder them or consider them (I wonder now how could I have not learned to recognize the sound of *those* footsteps?). I walked along in blissful ignorance, until I felt a hand clawing at my scalp, then pain as the hand closed around my hair and pulled.

Mike.

He pulled me into a narrow alley behind a large garbage bin where two other boys were waiting. I recognized them immediately. One was Tim Krakowski, who always sat in back of class and was most likely failing the seventh grade; and the other boy was named Jason...Jason what? I couldn't remember his last name, but

I had known him from the foster home and he had been nice to me then. We had almost been friends.

Mike grabbed my hair again and knocked me to the ground. My school bag fell off my shoulder, and the bird dropped from my hands. It made an odd-sounding thud as it hit the ground (or was that me?). Its wings and my legs, splayed out on the asphalt as if in resignation of what had already passed, of what was to come.

"This will be much, much worse," Mike whispered into my ear. "If you aren't careful, you may end up like that bird of yours."

Tim pressed his weight on my arms. Jason held on to my feet but refused to look me in the eye.

"Are you sure you're a girl, Two-by-Four?" Mike asked. "You look more like a boy to me. Let's find out."

He laughed but his eyes remained dark. He struggled with the clasp on my pants, yanking them down to my knees.

"Gross. What the hell is that?" he scrunched his face at the sight of my birthmark. And at the same time, as if his hands and eyes were seeing two different things, his fingers groped between my legs.

I turned my head against the feel of him, and kept my eyes focused on the bird. It was so close I could almost touch it.

§

We all heard it at once—the *thump-shuffle-whisper-thump* of approaching footfalls (those I *could* pick out from a thousand others). They grew louder as he, the man with bleeding knuckles and eyes like granite, my companion in silence, walked toward us. But my relief at the thought of being rescued was quickly overtaken with shame. Believe it or not, I tried to will him away with my mind. I repeated over and over in my head *keep walking, keep walking. Keep walking*. I did not want him to see me like this. I did not want him to know. I struggled to get up, but the boys would not budge; their knees and hands pinned my arms and legs.

When I stopped struggling for a moment, I realized I could no longer hear his footsteps. He must have gone, passed us without ever knowing I was there. I was filled equally with gratitude and terror.

Then, from somewhere above me, I heard a voice say, "Let her up." It sounded as loud and deep as thunder.

I felt Tim and Jason's grips relax.

But Mike, in his best bravado, bellowed, "Who's gonna make me?"

"Let her up," the voice said again. And I saw him walking toward us as if he were simply strolling along the beach on a lazy afternoon. I didn't meet his gaze. I didn't want to see the pity he must have for the poor girl who got herself into such a predicament.

Mike, where his boldness came from, I don't know, pushed harder down onto my chest. He looked the man in the eye and barked, "Fuck off."

"Let her up. Let her up," the man repeated until he was almost upon us. The other boys let go of my arms and legs. But Mike did not.

"Let her up."

"Fuck off," Mike said again, but this time with a tremor in his voice. Tim and Jason were standing a few feet away from the scene as if any amount of distance could separate them from what they had done.

The man looked down at me. I could have sworn, for a moment, a look of surprise or shock passed over his face. Had he seen my birthmark and been horrified too? Was he sorry he had come to rescue someone as ugly as me? But then the look was gone, and all I could see was kindness.

"Let her up." Over and over he said it. "Let her up."

Mike stood suddenly. Surprised at how light I felt I shot to my feet. I pulled my pants up, fumbling with the zipper, and then bent down to retrieve my bag. When I looked up, I was more surprised at first, than scared, to see Mike was a holding a gun.

But my friend didn't seem flustered at all.

"Holy Shit, Mike!" and "What the fuck?" were Tim and Jason's last comments on the situation before running way.

"I *will* shoot you. They'll call me a hero. I'll tell everyone you were attacking Two-by-Four here."

I cringed at the sound of those words, that *he* heard me being called by this name.

"I'll tell 'em I rescued her from you. Who do you think they're gonna believe?"

"And what about her?" he asked Mike, nodding his head in my direction. "What do you think she'll say?"

"She'll say what I tell her to say, won't you Two-by-Four?"

I was shaking, but the man just walked past Mike and calmly, casually, as if he were an old friend meeting me for lunch, put his arm around me.

Mike took a step closer to us, the barrel of the gun so close I could have touched it.

"It's okay," I whispered. "Please go. I'll be fine." And I meant it. No matter what Mike could do to me, nothing could be worse than being responsible for another person's death.

"Don't worry," he winked, as if he knew what I was thinking. "No one's gonna die here today. God has other plans."

"Well, God is the only one who can save you, so He better act quick," Mike said.

And then...

A flutter.

A whispering of wings.

A subtle intake of breath.

We all saw it. We saw the pigeon (the one I had carried for two blocks in the palm of my hand, the one with the lolling head and lifeless eyes) as it lifted, spread its feathers, and took flight in a fury of sound, wings beating the air. It carried itself along the length of the alley before disappearing into the maze of the city.

Mike took two steps backwards and dropped the gun to the ground.

The man, my savior, wrapped his arm tighter around my shoulder, guiding me away. I turned to catch one more glimpse of Mike, the boy I had ravaged just as he had ravaged me. The boy who penetrated me with hands and fingers and bludgeoning words, the boy I penetrated with sharp fear. I stared at the quaking of his lip and the tears filling his eyes. I saw the drooping of his head, the slump of his shoulders. For just one moment he was simply a young boy who carried the weight of another's sins on his (frail and desperate) back.

§

When we were a good distance away from the alley, the man turned to me. "I told you God would save us." He smiled at me, and I noticed how smooth his skin looked. I wanted to touch it. I imagined it would feel like the soft velvet of a queen's dress or the smooth petals of the flowers that grew in our neighbor's garden or, perhaps even, like the soft of an owl's feathers pushing through air as it flies silently like a ghost hunting in the night.

But I knew God hadn't saved me. I had been fooled by death once before. I would not be again.

"No. You saved me."

"The bird..."

"The bird was only stunned. Trust me. I know about birds," I said. What I didn't say was that I also knew about death.

§

We sat together for a while afterwards, finally finding our voices. I learned his name—Carson Deens—and he learned mine. Though we never again talked about what happened that morning, like the moon pulling the tide or a seed carried on the wind, when we moved together it felt like the most natural thing in the world.

Though Mike never again returned to school, Carson insisted on walking with me to and from school every day, and of course, I didn't mind. But then, about a week before summer, he simply disappeared. The first time he didn't show up, I walked extra slowly to school, hoping he was just running late. The second day I waited around for an extra 20 minutes. The next day, when he still did not come, I told myself he was probably home sick. I told myself I shouldn't worry. But when I didn't see him again the next day or the next, I began thinking of all the terrible things that might have happened. Was he hurt or worse? Had I done something to anger him?

On the last day of school, when there was still no sign of him, I pushed him out of my mind for good. I convinced myself I had simply imagined him, and I was too old for imaginary friends. So I closed my heart and my mind to him. Over the years, I had done a great job of forgetting. It was not until I listened to my own heart, beating wildly to match my son's; it was not until I exhaled, not realizing I had been holding my breath; it was not until two words escaped my lips—Carson Deens—that I finally remembered. And with this remembrance came an overwhelming feeling of relief. I had found the man who would be a father to August—the man who had once saved my life and who would now save my son's.

§

I tracked down three Carson Deens living in the Los Angeles area. One was an 82 year-old retired doctor who sounded kind and lonely and surprised to hear I was still alive after I told him about my condition. The second was a man with a deep southern drawl and an answering machine message that said, *Hi this is Carson. Give me a good reason to call you back and I just might.* The third was a woman.

I expanded my search and found 102 Carson Deens living in the United States. On phone call number 43 a man picked up on the second ring.

"Hello?"

Though I had only ever heard him speak a handful of words over 30 years ago, I knew instantly it was him.

I hung up.

I called Brinda next with instructions to keep whatever she wanted from the apartment and sell or give the rest away. By the time we packed everything we needed (toiletries, clothes, and August's 251 notebooks on beauty) it was already late into the night. We piled our things into the car and headed east. We drove straight through, stopping only for gas and a bite to eat. We reached our destination at dawn and were greeted by the rising Tucson sun, which radiated against our backs as we stepped nervously from the car. I held August's hand tightly—his smooth fingers familiar and honest in mine. We stood for several minutes outside the door of 814 Camino Seco Rd, apartment number 39, before I mustered up the courage to knock.

• • •

I FOLD THE LETTER and place it into an envelope. I think of the phone call—the silence on the other end of the line a song in my ear. I hear footsteps on the stairs, outside my window. I hear a knock on my door to match the beating of my heart.

I pull the letter back out and unfold its pages. And because I want to believe that wishing for something hard enough will make it come true, I write this:

But then you showed up at my door, all those years later; you found me at a time when neither one of us believed in miracles,which, perhaps, is a miracle all its own.

I re-fold the letter neatly into thirds and place it into a plain white envelope. I set it on my night stand and walk to the living room.

I open my front door.

Part 5

impressions of flight

Black wheels turn steadily against the hot asphalt (a whoosh, a whir-ring to steady my mind). I can feel my heart pumping again, kept alive by the man who I came to ask for mercy and by August—the child who, against every wish and will in my bones, I would leave behind. As we move, land and sky spread before us in a blur of colors—greens, blues, reds, the indefinable color of life happening at every turn. August—his head up-turned to the sky, eyes wide open— looks first to me and then to Carson and asks, "Is it cheating if I see beauty in everything?"

CHAPTER 27

THE DOOR OPENED. The once clean-shaven young man of my memories now had a head of salt and pepper hair and an unkempt beard that looked as though it could house several small mammals without anyone noticing. Even so, I recognized him immediately. His smile was still bright enough to light up my heart. His clothes were clean and neat. I inhaled his scent. It was just as I remembered. When I looked up into his face I saw the same smooth skin, and it was all I could do not to reach out and touch his cheek, to find out if it was as soft as I had imagined it to be all those years ago.

"Carson Deens," I said, my voice smooth and fluttery as if each word had been carried from my lips on the wings of nervous butterflies—green and turquoise to match my dress and the cotton scarf I wore to shield my head from the sun. "You probably don't remember me. My name is Penny. You saved my life once. I'm here to ask you for another favor. I'm dying. I've probably a few good weeks left before I start to get really sick. I was hoping you would want to raise my son after I'm gone. We've got a car outside, and we're headed north. Just driving, really, seeing what we can see. I was wondering, if you weren't doing anything in particular, would you like to come along?"

Carson's eyes grazed August's and then landed squarely on mine. I saw him take me in.

"I've been waiting for you," he said.

§

Those words, even now, are etched in my mind. I can almost see them written in the silvery streaks of my hair. "I've been waiting for you." Those five simple words, only a few weeks ago, would have sent me into one of my uncontrollable periods of self-induced levitation. But I did not blanch and I did not drift. Instead, I put my hand to my throat and felt the soft, regular pulse there at the base of my neck. I gripped my son's hand more firmly and took one slight but noticeable step forward.

"So..." I said, "Are you coming?"

§

I didn't know what I would have done if he had refused, if he had politely closed the door in our faces, saying "I'm sorry, but no." I didn't know how I would have gotten August somewhere safe, how I would have protected him, how it would have been for him once I was gone. Right then, I didn't know very many things, only this: my life and my son's life were dependent on a man I had known for a few months when I was twelve years old, a man who I was certain I had imagined into existence but who, it turns out, *was* real.

I watched Carson's face, trying to read his thoughts. After what seemed a lifetime of silence, he spoke.

"I just need to collect some things. Come on in."

We entered his apartment and waited on the couch. About twenty minutes later, he came out clutching a large olive green duffle bag and a small wooden box.

"I'm ready," he said.

August walked up to him and extended his hand. Carson shook it and smiled.

"Thank you. I've never had a father before," August said.

"Well, I've never been one before, but I had a great father. I hope I learned enough from him in the short time I knew him to be a good dad to you."

"He died?"

"A long time ago."

"Was he sick like my mom?"

"He died in an accident. Do you want to see a picture of him?"

August nodded.

Carson sat down between August and me and held the wooden box on his lap. He ran the flat of his hand over its smooth surface before opening the hinged lid. From the top he removed an envelope. It was bright pink and covered with tiny red hearts. Despite myself, I felt curious about the letter…was it a love letter? Had he been in love once? Had someone brave and wonderful loved him? From my heart sprung the tiniest sprout of jealousy.

He set the letter aside without mentioning it. He then drew out another envelope, plain and browning at the edges. From it, he pulled out two silver bands.

"These are my parents' wedding rings," he said and handed them to August, who examined them as they sat, side by side on his palm.

Then Carson pulled out a photo of a beautiful woman with short, cropped hair, a smiling man, and a little boy with a grin from ear to ear.

"These are my parents," he pointed to the faces in the picture. "That's me."

He handed the photo to August. Then he pointed to the shoes he had on and said "And these are my father's shoes."

I recognized the shoes instantly—the same loose grommet on the second hole of the left shoe, the same worn heels, even the same tattered laces. I had seen them on his feet every day as we walked together so many years ago. It was easy for me to understand, then, that those boots were a manifestation of Carson's love for his father. And like Peter's bird feeders and Joe and Alice's flowers, these things could never grow empty, could not die, could not wear away.

"If you become my father," August said, "then these will be my grandparents."

"That's right," Carson smiled. "They would have been wonderful grandparents."

"I can tell I would've liked them."

Carson gathered these small remnants of his parents and placed them back into the box, along with the heart-covered letter.

"You would've liked them a lot. I suspect they would have really liked you too."

Then August told Carson all about our friends, our dear friends who were still so close it felt as if they were traveling by our sides at every moment.

"Where are they now?" Carson asked.

"Joe and Peter died," August said matter-of-factly. "And Alice left. And Puppet, well, Puppet was only a cat really, but he was Peter's best friend."

"He sounds like a very nice cat."

"He was."

CHAPTER 28

WE MOVED SLOWLY ALONG THE ROADS TWISTING and winding through the Sonora Desert. Green Palo Verde trees spread their thin fingered branches to a cloudless sky; Christmas Cholla bore bright red fruits like gifts; and coyotes ambled down dry riverbeds which, in times of heavy rain, flowed with waters both raging and impermanent.

We climbed up the curving road of Gates Pass—August, Carson and I—past the forests of cactus with arms spread wide as if to greet us, past the red rocks jutting at odd angles from the soil. We then lumbered on to Hohokom Road—a dirt road leading us deeper into this arid land. I had always imagined the desert as a place that was always in wait, like a parched throat, waiting for the sky to fall in liquid form so sleeping toads and hiding snakes and dormant seeds (so life) could emerge. But as I looked out my window I saw more life than I thought possible.

Carson was driving (before I knew about the girl with her heart on the outside, before I knew what he must be seeing, before I knew of the ghosts he saw mirrored back to him). August sat in the back, his window open, taking in sights he had never imagined existed. As the car jostled along the bumpy road I felt a sudden urge to urinate.

We pulled to a stop. I unbuckled my seat belt and slid out onto the soft dirt. I noticed August writing furiously in his notebook. I couldn't help but smile. Turning my back to him, to Carson, I wandered alone into the desert, the lushest desert in the world they say, but apparently not lush enough to provide me with a secluded place to relieve my bladder. I passed the too short brittle bush, the too skinny Ocotillo, and made my way to a small Mesquite tree. The best cover this landscape had to offer.

I pulled down my pants, squatted down against my calves and released. It was then when I noticed, to my right, a large round hole covered with a grate. When I finished buttoning my jeans back up, I wandered over to have a better look. I had heard there were old mines in the area and was curious.

I peered in. At first, all I could make out was darkness. The hole appeared to be very deep, but was not smooth. Small ridges ran all along the length of the tunnel. Suddenly, a slight movement caught my eye. I got down on my knees and rested my hands on the grate.

From the darkness, a lone barn owl tilted its white, heart-shaped face up to me. Our eyes met. It blinked once and lowered its head again.

I waited, breathless, for a few moments, until it raised its head again. This time its gaze did not leave my face. It was like an angel in the darkness, beckoning me home.

"Not yet," I whispered, "not yet."

If I could not have forever with my son, there was at least one more thing I wanted to witness with my child before I left this earth. I had read about the migration of thousands of waterfowl—Snow Geese with black tipped wings, Sandhill Cranes with their gurgling calls—coming down from the north, from lands of ice and snow, to rest in the Rio Grande Valley each winter. This is where we were headed. Our own migration, of sorts.

§

We arrived in New Mexico the next day. It was late in the afternoon, and we had climbed a small peak overlooking the Rio Grande below. We sat, wrapped in scarves and sweaters, mittens and blankets, and watched. Below us, fields and fields of white geese and grey cranes with red patches on their heads foraged for grubs in the lush wetlands below.

We were silent, content to listen to the cacophony of sounds of wild birds going about their lives—unaware of how marvelous they were to us.

August was the first to speak.

"Carson."

"Yes."

"I put your beard in my book."

"What?" he asked.

"Yeah. See, I have:

54,22. CACTUS ARMS THAT LOOK LiKe HUggiNg
54,23. NighTHAWks BecAUse THeY FLY FUNNY
54,24. TOO MANY STARS TO COUNT
54,25. CARSON's BeARd BecAUse iT MAKes HiM FeeL sAFe
54,26. A gAZiLLiON WHiTe geese LiKe iNside A sNOW gLOBe

"Why would you do that, Son?"

"I want to always remember it."

"I'm not going anywhere, August."

"No, but she is."

"Who? You mean your mother?"

"No. *Her.* The girl with her heart on the outside. She's the reason you're afraid all the time. But she'll get her heart back soon. You won't have to be afraid of her anymore."

Carson looked from August to me and back to August again.

"How do you know about her?"

"I just see things people want me to see. I see her, too, just like you do. But you don't have to worry. You have us now."

Carson looked down at August. August smiled up at Carson. Then August, who was seated in between us, took Carson's hand and placed it in mine. He cupped both our hands in his.

"See?" he said.

§

I heard the *thump-shuffle-whisper-thump*, this time of helicopter blades spinning in slow motion overhead and I felt the heat—stifling and clawing against my skin. I saw Carson then, just as he was when I first knew him: his smooth skin, his clear eyes, courage and strength emanating from him like a strong perfume. The light-colored military fatigues he wore were stained dark with sweat and they clung to his strong body. I felt the weight of his weapon on my back and a deep thirst in my throat. I saw him as he walked. But he was not alone. Twelve sets of dark boots marched in single file, spraying up mud against sturdy legs, a forest of towering trees casting strange shadows above them. After the sun disappeared and night set in, those boots continued to march, through the heat and humidity and through the rain which fell so hard sometimes it seemed as though it might just rain forever.

Despite the horrors unfolding all around, Carson managed, with each grueling step, to appreciate the beauty of the landscape unfolding before him. He admired the large vines, like arms, growing down as if from the heavens and the broad, green leaves the size of a man's chest. He noticed the red in the bromeliads which had taken root in tree branches, and he listened when birds sang their melodious calls to attract a mate or signal the finding of food or warn of a sudden, looming danger.

§

The first time I saw her, it was through his eyes. She was breathtaking—not only for her physical beauty, though true, there was that—but because she was smiling, actually smiling and happy in the midst of all the pain. She did not yet know this story was going to be about her. She was standing with her back to the sun and waving happily as Carson and the other soldiers entered her village.

As Carson's troop marched, their eyes scanned those of the local men, women, and children peering out from the imagined (the hoped for) safety of their homes. They searched out the enemy among smooth child-faces (serious and scared, now, but if given the chance would reveal gap-toothed smiles and dimpled cheeks), in the stern look of frightened and angry women, and in the faces of old men with wrinkles so deep they could hide even the biggest secrets between their folds of skin. No one met the soldiers' eyes with their own. No one spoke, and except for the cries of a few babies and the comforting murmurings of their mothers, everything was silent. Even the air was still, as if it too was waiting for what might come.

But not the smiling girl. She appeared to be in her early teens. She began to run at the sight of the soldiers, her footsteps breaking the silence. At first I thought she was running away, but when her body shifted, I saw she was moving toward the men. When she got close, she slowed to a walk. She was carrying a white goose under one arm, her long fingers disappearing into its white feathers. One of its wings flapped loose. The goose remained calm, bobbing its long neck with each stride.

The girl was laughing and looked Carson straight in the eye. She showed no fear or hatred. She pointed up and then titled her long neck back and her dark hair fell almost to her waist. All eyes turned upwards and watched as a group of five egrets flew lazily across the grey sky, their necks curved into tight S's. For a few seconds everyone stared at those birds, as if they had forgotten why they were there (as if there had been a pause in the war) as if they were thinking, instead, of summer days spent at the lake; of catching frogs hiding in the dark green cover of cattails; of other egrets in other places; of birds so bright they were like tiny individual suns — the smooth beat of their wings reaching out for happier times.

After the birds had long disappeared from sight and the soldiers, one by one, remembered where they were (though few really understood why) the girl finally spoke. Though Carson and his men—speaking not a word of Vietnamese—didn't understand what she said, her voice was soothing like a breeze. She pointed again, this time to a spot in the forest just at the tree line. Only Carson turned to look but saw nothing except the moss-covered bark, the dark green of leaves and the even darker shadows that fell between all the empty spaces the foliage left uncovered.

She repeated her words again, with more urgency now, and then did the unthinkable. She placed one of her hands on Carson's, lightly touching his skin with her fingers. She met his eyes, and this time she grew serious, pointing again to the edge of the tree line. I felt a warm flush through my body. I knew right then, Carson was thinking of *me*. This girl, with her beautiful smile and her bravery reminded him somehow of the 12-year-old girl who had wiped blood from his knuckles and who had walked by his side to school (a girl from too many life times ago).

The girl of this story then turned and walked into the waiting arms of her mother who had been watching the whole time with an expression of pride. But as soon as the young girl met her mother's gaze, the woman's face took on the stern look of mothers the world over, and she quickly ushered her daughter into their home.

The men continued to advance in the direction the young girl had pointed. When they came to the tree line they saw what she had been talking about. Hidden in the tall grass was an egret just as blindingly white as the others. As they got closer, Carson expected it to take off in flight, but it didn't move. It simply stared at the approaching bodies with one yellow-ringed eye (the other eye was missing, now just a hollow grey socket where sight once resided). Its head drooped back, before awkwardly righting itself. One wing hung crooked and low. The bird was injured or sick, or both. Carson looked back and saw the girl watching him. She was waiting to see what he would do. Carson finally understood what she wanted. She knew the bird was suffering, and she wanted him to put it out of its misery.

Here, in the middle of war, in the middle of so much suffering, the girl had seen a way to relieve a little bit of the pain. I watched as Carson steadied his weapon, his index finger rubbing the smooth metal trigger, and took aim. An explosion rang in my ears and the bird pitched back, feathers flying in loose swirls from its body.

Carson turned to look back but the girl was no longer there.

CHAPTER 29

THE MEN RESTED FOR A FEW HOURS THAT NIGHT, their backs propped up against trees or their own large packs. Some tried to sleep, others picked at the tasteless rations the government supplied, but no one spoke. Above the din of the forest—evident when the men fell silent (the humming of stiff-winged cicadas, the slow *drip, drip, drip* of a new rain coming, the scurrying of some unknown critter along the damp forest floor), was the nervous tapping of Private First Class Milner Timms' left leg. He always seemed to get anxious in the company of too much silence, perhaps noise was all that kept his fear at bay. As he tapped his leg, his lips twisted themselves into tight knots, as if he was desperately trying to think of something to say.

Finally, the words fell from his mouth, "Can you believe that kid? Worried about some bird when we could've burnt her whole village to the goddamn ground? She must be retarded or something."

"She's a fuckin' gook. Who knows how those people think," replied Morgan, the oldest in the group who was currently serving his second tour in the war. He had *volunteered* to come back—a fact that equally awed and repulsed the rest of the platoon.

"I think she just wanted to end the bird's suffering is all," Carson said suddenly.

"You mean she wanted *us* to do something about it. Typical. They have a problem and we have to clean up their shit for them. I'm tired of wiping this country's fucking ass!" Morgan said. "It's bullshit, Man."

"Maybe...but it's the right thing," Carson replied. "She isn't any different than anyone else caught up in this mess."

"Here we go again. Next you're gonna give me the 'we're all made in God's image' sermon."

"We are."

"What? You think God's got slant eyes like these fuckin' VC? Or maybe he's a darkie, like you? You think he got crooked teeth and pimples on his ass like Stephens over there? That's bullshit, Man. Bullshit. There ain't no God, and if there is, he's one ugly son of a bitch."

"Well, I thought she was amazing," Carson replied. "Come on. Here's this kid who didn't hate us, wasn't afraid of us. The fact she could smile in the middle of all this bullshit...maybe that's God right there."

"You've been in this jungle way too fucking long, Preacher!" Morgan said and the rest of the group broke out in laughter.

Carson smiled, too. "I think we all have."

§

As the weeks passed, Carson's platoon lost two of their men. Stephens died on a rainless afternoon as they were ambushed by the enemy hiding in elephant grass growing at the edge of a rice field, and Morgan, a week later, was sent home just in time for Christmas with no legs below his knees and a matching pair of fingerless hands.

But for the boys in M Company, Second Battalion, who remained behind, the fighting continued. One day, on a so-called "routine mission" (as if any of this were routine) they were walking, one behind the other. The heat clawed at their backs. Sweat poured down their faces, down their legs. They sweated so much it ran into their boots, dampening their socks. Timms had just pulled a leech from his neck (as if enough blood hadn't been spilled already) when they walked into a patch of sunlight which fell in white streams and managed to penetrate the otherwise dark forest. They walked in silence (except for Timms muttering curses about "goddamn leeches"), alert for any movement or sound.

Suddenly, in one of the rays of light, a white shape moved between the trees. Carson, for just a brief moment, thought he had seen an angel. And from the looks on the others' faces, he wasn't the only one. But as they got a closer look, the men could make out the bright white feathers of a large goose, the bright orange of its bill. It honked and fluttered away from them as they approached.

"What the fuck is a goose doing all the way out here?" whispered Timms, but no one responded.

Only Carson remembered this same white goose in the arms of a certain girl only a few months before.

And because he knew what they would find next (as surely as he knew it had been a mistake to come here, as surely as he knew he had come to this war to find a miracle and was quickly running out of time) he was the first to see it: a body (her body) lying still in the roots of a giant tree.

It was not unusual to stumble upon death in this forest. They were used to seeing the bodies of the enemy, the bodies of their comrades. But Carson knew right away *this* body, tangled among the roots, was not of a VC or a fellow Marine. He recognized the hands—the long smooth fingers that had once touched his.

§

She was face down in the mud. Her arms were splayed open at her side, as if hugging the earth. Blood came from every part of her and lazily soaked into the moist ground. Every once in a while, her body moved, almost in a whisper, as she inhaled, slowly taking in the air around her in breaths so shallow they were almost imperceptible. Then she pushed her hands into the earth and slowly began to push herself up. *Rise. You can do it. Get up now,* Carson urged in his own head, willing her to be okay. Her head and torso lifted, for an agonizing moment, before falling to the ground again.

Carson knelt beside her and gently rolled her over as the other men watched in horror. Her face was covered in blood, one eye sealed shut. Whoever had done this to her had also cut her left breast clean off, as if beginning but not finishing, the arduous task of mining for her heart. The missing breast lay flat on the ground beside her, so the dirt seemed almost alive—Eve forming from the earth before their eyes.

Carson lifted her up into his arms and held her against him. She winced in pain. Carson did not know, or care to think, who could do such a thing—his fellow soldiers or those on the other side of the issue, perhaps boys from her village, or someone she never knew. He held her and watched her and wondered how he was going to save her. It wasn't the ugliness of this place, but the small moments of beauty that broke his heart. He placed his hand to cover the hole where her left breast had been and felt her heart barely beating beneath his palm. Once in a while he absentmindedly swatted the flies away, who, unwilling to wait around for death, had found her already.

§

The first shot exploded into a tree just above Carson's head. Carson dropped the girl to the ground and covered her body with his. Then shots rang out from all around; a couple of his men took bullets as they fired back upon an enemy they could not see.

Timms, on the radio, shouted for reinforcements, but none were on their way.

As Carson rose and fired round after round into the shadows, his only thought was—*how am I going to save her?*

"She isn't going to make it, Man," Timms shouted to Carson.

"I have to get her out!"

"We're all gonna die if we stay here. We have to move now!"

"I can't move her. She's in too much pain. I'll stay with her."
Carson said.

"We're not gonna leave you and you fucking know it! We're all
gonna die if you stay here. Even if we could get her out of here—
look at her. She's in fucking agony. She's not gonna make it."

"I can't just leave her here to die."

Carson and Timms looked at one another and held each other's
gaze, neither saying it out loud, but knowing it all the same.

This was the moment I felt the shift in Carson's heart. This was
the moment when Carson understood what he had to do, understood it was the only thing he could do. This was the moment he
lost all of the faith he had in him. It was like watching the color
drain from a person's face; the change was so obvious. As bullets
flew past his head, as his friends were hit and more blood spilled,
he stared at the girl he thought he was there to save and wondered,
Is it true we are all made in God's image? Is she God?

He thought of Morgan's words—Morgan, somewhere now
with no legs, who had no faith to begin with. If we are not made in
God's physical image, what image of God were we made in? Are
we a reflection of His desires? Are our actions, our hearts, simply
a mirror image of God's own? As Carson thought of the war going
on around him, the deaths and the brutality, he thought, *This is God.*
It was the only thing that made any sense. It wasn't that Carson
stopped believing in God; he merely decided God wasn't someone
he wanted to know anymore.

He knelt beside the girl and squeezed her hand. He whispered,
I'm sorry, in her ear. Tears soaked the collar of his shirt. When he
stood, his whole body trembled. He gripped his weapon with shaking hands. The girl moaned and her eyes fluttered open, meeting
his. "I'm sorry, I'm sorry," he repeated over and over.

And if she could have heard him and understood what he was
saying, I do not know if she would have told him it was okay. I do
not know if she would have thanked him or cursed him to a hell

even worse than what they were living. She only clutched his leg, looking squarely at him, squeezing his flesh with her long fingers.

And I listened hard for her heart, waiting for it (needing it) to reveal its own secrets. And then we did hear it, all three of us. Faint, but strong; a young girl's heart beat once (acceptance) — a heart hoping death is not the end, a heart hoping it will soon be free.

Carson rested his finger on the trigger...

and squeezed.

High above in the insipid sky, three pale egrets disappeared behind a darkening cloud.

§

There was a flash and a strong force which sent Carson's body through the air as if he were weightless. He landed hard against the ground. Everything went black.

From the darkness bright bursts of fire fell all around, shedding flashes of light, like a strobe. Carson could just make out legs running past, arms reaching out. He heard voices shouting but could not understand what they were saying. Occasionally, loud booms echoed in his ears, as if the explosions were taking place in his own head.

From somewhere, above all that noise, a heart was beating.

§

The early morning light cut wide swaths across Carson's bed. His eyes blinked open; he swung his feet to the floor and rested his head in the palms of his hands. It had been months since he left the hospital, since he had been honorably discharged from the Marines and sent home. This was the first morning he had not cried the instant he remembered where he was. And for what felt like the first time (as if he were a child, just learning to walk) he rose by himself (out of his own bed) and showered. He stayed for a while beneath the hot water, letting it pour over his head, his back, his neck. He was afraid to move. For the first time in his life, he was afraid of what lay ahead of him. It was only when his aunt knocked on the bathroom door and called out his name that he forced himself to turn off the water and exit the shower. Naked, he stood in front of the bathroom's full-length mirror and stared at a body he barely recognized anymore. The steam from the shower cast a haze against the reflective surface so that his image was cloudy and distorted. He laid his hand flat against the glass and wiped a swath of the mirror clear. Almost immediately, it began to fog up again, but before it did he saw someone pass quickly behind him. He knew right away it was her. He wiped the mirror clean again and waited. She walked behind him then, her face in profile. She was so close that the hairs on the back of his neck stood up. He turned around quickly to find himself alone with the shower curtain and the slow *drip, drip, drip* of the leaky shower head. But when he turned back to the mirror, she was there, facing him now. Her breast was gone, and in its place there was a gaping hole that revealed her beating heart.

§

Weeks later, Carson left Los Angeles and moved to the desert. He removed every single mirror in his new apartment. When he walked the streets, he kept his head down to avoid the reflective windows of fancy department stores and restaurants, for every time he saw his own reflection she was there, too, staring back at him. And every time he accidentally caught his (her) reflection—in a store's security mirror or in a pane of glass—it always seemed to be when he was doing the most mundane of things (waiting to cross the street; shopping for food stored in plastic containers with happy, smiling people pictured on the packaging; or at the car wash where people paid good money to have someone else wash away the dirt from their vehicles). He quickly grew ashamed of the life he was trying to make for himself. It seemed so trivial compared to…anything. So he began to hide from the world and gave up those things he believed anchored him to it. He bought the minimal amount of food (nothing in packages, and certainly nothing that featured happy, smiling people); he gave his car away, leaving it in the parking lot of the shopping mall along with the keys and a friendly note for whoever happened upon it first. After a time, he let his hair grow out and refused to touch a razor to his face. And for 30 years, except for a few rare, unexpected glimpses, he hadn't looked in a mirror at all. And after all that time, even in his dreams, he could not really remember what he looked like. He did not know his own face; he wasn't sure if he would recognize himself anymore.

§

Now, as Carson, August, and I sat on the edge of a small hill, with the sounds of cranes and geese below, I looked into Carson's eyes and saw everything. He went to war and killed a girl and white birds flashed above him in the sky. He went to war and killed a girl with long dark hair, straight as a pin, cascading like water down the sides of her face. He went to war and killed a girl because her hands were clean and smooth and olive like a fertile soil. He went to war and killed a girl because she was dying, because she hurt; because he could not save her. He went to war and killed a girl and now could not go on with his daily life; he could not shave or comb his hair because something so beautiful had been taken, and because something so frightful remained to always remind him of that place. He went to war and he killed a girl because she was raped and mutilated and left for dead—because they had cut her breast clean off and tossed it in the dirt for laughs. He went to war, and he killed a girl without ever knowing her name.

And it was then I knew I loved Carson all over again. I loved him for his strength, for what he had to endure, for his living, for his being human. I loved him because I wanted his pain to dissipate, to leach from his heart like water from a sieve. I loved him for his faith, and for the fact that in the young girl he had finally seen the eyes of

God and met Him face to face and had come out the other end, tattered, torn, but never broken. As I looked over at him, I knew I had made the right choice.

CHAPTER 30

ONCE AGAIN THE WHEELS OF OUR CAR TURNED. Carson in the driver's seat, August beside him, and me curled up in the back seat. The headaches had returned. They came and went, and I fluctuated between feeling only slightly tired and the all-too-real sensation of knives cutting into my brain. We were heading north to Albuquerque, to the hospital, to see if there was anything that could be done. I was napping, in and out of wakefulness, when I heard August say "Where do you see beauty, Carson?"

August had never asked anyone but me to participate in his game before. I felt my heart swell with gladness.

After a few moments of looking, Carson said, "See that old shed out there?" He pointed to something outside my field of view.

"The way the clouds are formed just above it, and the light streaming around it, that is beautiful to me."

August handed him the notebook.

"Would you write it in?"

"I would be honored." Carson pulled the car over. August passed him his notebook and pen. Carson wrote:

54, 859. The light and clouds against a wooden shed in a field of green

§

That night, we settled into a two-bedroom motel suite equipped with a small living room and kitchenette located just down the street from the hospital. I had been given medicine to ease the pain and it helped, but I knew time was no longer my friend.

It was late, and August had fallen asleep in the car. Carson carried him to bed, prying the notebook from his fingers before laying him under the covers. While he did so, I set about covering up the large mirror in the bathroom and the reflective screen of the old TV.

As Carson made us some coffee and sandwiches he asked, "Where's August's father?"

I liked that he asked me outright and didn't say something silly like "I hope you don't mind me asking" as if we hadn't been through enough together for those types of formalities.

I told him about all the men in my life and finally August's father.

"You never loved any of those men?"

"I think I was afraid to. I was afraid to love them, because I didn't think they would ever love me back. How could they? I was never beautiful enough or smart or strong enough for men to overlook my dullness. Some women, I think, they are so beautiful men love them no matter what. Or they are so smart, for men who appreciate smartness in a woman, that all their other faults are overlooked. I have heard men say about their wives, *she is so strong* or *so stubborn*, with a wink and a smile that betrays their admiration for the type of woman she is. I really believed I had nothing, you see, which would allow anyone to overlook all that is wrong with me."

"You know," Carson said, "when I first saw you, I thought you were beautiful. This beautiful little kid. It made me happy just to see you. That's no small thing. Plus, you are kind."

"People say kind. They mean weak."

"Not me. You are kind, which makes you smart and strong and beautiful."

"No one but you believes it." I said. "I will tell you what though. For the first time, none of it matters. None of it. I have everything I need."

We sipped our coffee in silence for a long time.

I watched as he unconsciously scratched at his beard. The moment felt right.

From my purse, I pulled out a plastic bag and set it on the coffee table.

"Open it," I said.

Carson opened the bag and fished out its contents: a razor, a can of shaving cream, shiny scissors reflecting the florescent ceiling lights.

"Why?"

"Only if you want…but I think, maybe, you're ready to understand how important your life really is…how important *you* are. To me. To us. There's nothing silly or trivial about the way you live each and every day. You saved me all those years ago and you are saving me again; you are saving my son. And you saved that girl. It's time."

§

We pulled a chair into the bathroom. I opened the tap and filled the sink with warm water. I listened to the *rush* of tepid water as it flowed into the basin.

He sat on the chair.

I draped a towel over his shoulders.

We did not speak. The only sound was the water pouring into the sink. Then, the crisp sound of scissors slicing away hair, cutting away the weight he had carried with him all these years. He was the opposite of Samson, I believed. His strength would come from shedding this burden. I felt nervous and fluttery as his hair drifted into piles on the linoleum floor.

When I finished cutting his hair and trimming his beard, I cupped my hands into the pool of water filling the sink. I wet his face. Then I sprayed the cool, soft foam of the shaving cream onto my palms. It felt soft, slippery between my fingers. I brought my hands to his face. Our eyes met. I rubbed the shaving cream against the roughness of his beard, across his cheeks, down his throat, along the ridges of his Adam's apple.

I moved the razor slowly along his right cheek first, then the left—finding, underneath, the face of the boy I knew all those years ago.

Beneath his beard, the skin was smooth on one side, on the other it was pock-marked, scarred from where the shrapnel had ripped into his face like claws. It was the most beautiful face I had ever seen.

I reached out to touch it, and I felt him jump.

"I'm sorry. Did I do something wrong?" But then I glanced up and noticed a corner of the sheet had slipped from the mirror.

I knew by the look on his face.

"You see her," I said.

He nodded.

I moved to adjust the sheet back over the mirror. I felt his hand grip mine.

"Wait," he said. "Look. Do you see her too?"

And I did. She stood before us, one hand rested open-palmed over her heart. With the other, she was waving, beckoning us forward. I wanted to go after her, to follow her across the high grass, the open fields. She removed her hand from her left breast and pointed upwards. I flinched, expecting to see her exposed heart red and beating against the hole in her body. But instead, I saw only her young breasts, her body intact. When I looked up, white birds trailed across the sky. Her sky.

"Can you see?" Carson spoke. "Her heart. It's back where it belongs."

I did not say it, but I thought all of our hearts, finally, were back too, where they belonged.

That night, as August slept in the small room just off the kitchen, Carson and I stood naked in the semi-darkness. We were not beautiful by anyone's standards, perhaps, but our own. I had lost more weight since getting sick, so my breasts, never full to begin with, hung like partially deflated balloons left too long after everyone had already gone home from the party. There was too much skin at my knees, and it sagged strangely.

Carson's body, once muscular and strong, had grown weaker over the years. His stomach stuck out over skinny legs, and his body was covered in raised and ragged scars.

"My breasts are old," I said.

"My butt is flat as a white man's," he countered.

We laughed.

"You're lovely," he said, and I was astounded. Not because he said it, but because for the first time in my life, I believed it was so.

It's not true what they say—that love is blind. Real love sees everything clearly and finds beauty in all of it. In every detail.

"I love you, Penny," he said, "I have always loved you."

There, finally, were the words I had longed to hear my entire life.

"But, I'm dying," I said.

"I know. And I love you."

"I love you too."

We lay in bed, our hands caressing our old bodies, with scars and stretch marks, and muscles that had lost their firmness years ago, rocking and sweating, holding and releasing. When it was finished, we lay in each other's arms for a long while.

I began to tell him everything. As he ran his hands across my breasts, my stomach, touching me gently with his worn and rough knuckles, I told him about my mother's suicide probably brought on by my birth, I told him about my miscarriage, and about Charlotte and Annelle.

"Oh my God, Penny, I had no idea. I had no idea you thought

your mom killed herself. I didn't know you were treated so awfully by that woman, Annelle."

Then he slowly moved his hand to my thigh. Normally I would have flinched, tried to pull away, afraid of how my birthmark might feel to a man. But not this time. I let his fingers wander. I felt beautiful.

He placed his palm flat against my thigh, resting his fingers one by one upon the outline of my birthmark.

"I know," I mumbled, "it's ugly."

"No," he said. "You're wrong. You're wrong about everything."

He hopped out of bed.

I sat up. "What?"

He came back with the box which contained his parents' keepsakes. He opened it and pulled out the letter in the pink envelope, the one with all the hearts. With his other hand he pulled out another envelope, it was plain white and stuffed so thick I thought it might burst.

"I've spent my life wanting you to believe in miracles and it has been in front of us the entire time. I told you my dad died in an accident, but I didn't tell you the whole story. I...here," he said, handing me the letter in the white envelope. "This is what I had to tell you, what I *should* have told you all those years ago."

I removed the pages from the envelope and unfolded them, reading the words written for me by the man I loved.

When I finished, I let the pages fall.

"Carson, I...you...that baby was me? It was me. You knew my mother. And, oh God, I am so sorry about your father."

We sat for a long while in silence, wrapped in each other's arms. I had a million questions, but Carson only had one.

"Can you ever forgive me for not telling you? If I had known... if you had known..."

"Carson, how could you have known about Annelle? About any of it? I never said a word to you. There isn't anything to forgive.

If you *had* told me, maybe nothing would have changed, or perhaps everything would have. What if I had never had August, what if we weren't here together now? My mother didn't die which I am grateful to learn, and she was young so I get it, but it doesn't change the fact that she didn't want me. She gave me away."

"No, Penny. Don't you see? You're wrong about that too."

Then he handed me the other letter, the one covered in hearts. I removed it from the envelope and with it an old and faded photograph of a young girl clutching a tiny baby in her arms. I stared at the girl with her warm smile and saw happiness everywhere: in her eyes, in the way she held her baby to her, in the slight tilt of her chin. Could it be? Was this my mother? I next looked carefully at the baby—her round eyes, her thin legs, and her birthmark, dark and raised - its familiar outline the shape of a tiny outstretched hand. With trembling hands, I unfolded the letter. The handwriting was neat with large and loopy letters, just like mine.

My Dearest Carson,

I wanted to write sooner, but I somehow couldn't bring myself to do it. I wanted to thank you for helping me the day my daughter was born. To say I'm sorry your father died would be an understatement in the least. But what do you say to someone when his father dies? There aren't really words for those sorts of things and when you try to say something meaningful and deep you just end up sounding shallow or stupid or both. But I do know, and you know, he was so proud of you. What father wouldn't be? You saved my life. I don't think you know it. If I had to give birth on that stupid highway all alone with my mother I would have died from her nagging. Can someone annoy you to death? If anyone could do it, it would be her.

At the hospital I stole your dad's card from my mom's purse. I knew she would just throw it away. She wouldn't appreciate what you had done for us. I named my daughter Deena, after you guys. Get it? Deens = Deena. Deena Forester. I gave her my last name. Not her father's. He was worthless. I wanted her to have a strong name. A strong name for a strong girl! I wish you could have met her.

I only knew her for three days but I loved her so much in that short time. I held her and held her until my arms got numb. Of course, I was scared—but seeing her little face made me feel brave. I knew I would be a good mother because I had her as a daughter. I couldn't wait to take her home and show her my room—our room! But on the day we were supposed to leave the hospital, I knew something was wrong the minute I saw my mom's face. "What did you do?" I asked her. "What did you do? Where is Deena?" She said I was too young. She said we were too poor. Finally my mom told me she sent Deena away! I started screaming. I swear to God (excuse the blasphemy) I fell to the ground screaming. I screamed until the nurses gave me a shot to calm me.

I swear I looked everywhere for her, but I never found her. I cry every single day. My mom tries to comfort me. She tells me not to worry, tells me she left Deena a penny for good luck and a rose she bought in the hospital gift shop for love. Can you believe that? A penny and a rose was all she left her grand-daughter? I love my mother but I don't know if I can ever forgive her. Deena is one year old today. I miss her terribly. I think about her constantly.

She was born so skinny and so beautiful. I hope she stays skinny and doesn't turn out to be chubby like her mother. I would love her any way she is, but I think being chubby makes life harder for a girl, don't you? But I think she was born lucky. The birthmark on her leg, it looks just like a hand. I think she was touched by God. I think he left His mark on her to protect her. It was as if He knew she wouldn't have her mother with her for very long.

My greatest fear is she won't know how much I love her. For the whole three days I knew her, I told her I loved her all the time. Do you think it was enough? God, I hope she knows how much I love her. I hope she knows I will only stop loving her the day I stop breathing. And maybe not even then.

Your Friend,
Emma

§

My entire life I believed I was responsible for my mother's death, that she had died—had wanted to die—because of me. To find out now that this was not true, that she had loved me, and that all those things I hated about myself—being too skinny, my birthmark—were things my mother found beautiful, was my parting gift. She wanted me. She loved me.

"We can try to find her if you want." Carson said. "We have her name, her old address."

"I don't want to find her, only to have her lose me again. No. It's enough to know she loved me." I told him.

I then felt myself begin to rise, to float again, as he held me. This time, the force was strong enough to lift us both, so that we lay there, suspended several feet above the bed, like eagles clutching talons, who spin together and release just before hitting the ground. But we were not letting go, and we were not falling. We would never touch ground again.

CHAPTER 31

ON THE DAY I WAS ADMITTED TO THE HOSPITAL, the air was cool, the sky hazy, and the sound of cranes warbling overhead woke us early in the morning. My cancer had spread and there was nothing more to be done. The doctors gave me medicine for the pain, and August and Carson were at my side every moment. I don't know if days or weeks or months had passed. But on the day I died, it snowed.

"Look, Mom, it's snowing!" August clutched his hands together in excitement. He pulled back the curtains to reveal large white flakes swirling outside our window.

"Come on, Mom, let's go play."

I decided then and there I would not die in that room. I rose from the bed, pulling the tubes and needles from my body. I didn't even bother changing out of my hospital gown. I felt light and strong on my feet. The doctors and nurses didn't seem to notice when I ran past them, down the stairs, and onto the street, which was wet and shining with snow. I saw August and Carson up ahead. They were laughing and swallowing the thick flakes that settled onto their tongues. I ran to them, my bare feet pounding down the wet street, the hospital gown open at my sides like wings. I realized then the woman I had seen in my dreams for all those years, the woman with the upturned feet—the woman running, yet frozen as if in a photograph, was not my mother at all. It was me.

§

The wind blew softly around us as we made our way past red rock formations. We were swimming New Mexico, like airborne fish, our feet never really touching ground but resting somewhere in between sky and earth, watching the snow falling heavily now, like baby's breath or daisy petals. As I walked slightly ahead of August and Carson, I felt there was nothing more, nothing more really, to do.

I paused beneath a pine tree, its needles drooping beneath the weight of the snow. A deer skull, still with dark patches of fur matted in places like unfinished art, lay silent in the white drifts. It was all that remained of the deer, killed somewhere nearby. This life fed upon to feed more life.

I crouched down then dropped to my knees. I stared, almost longingly, at the deer's skull. How had it died? What had it seen from its large brown eyes? Had it known, as I now knew, that death is inevitable, if not always welcome? When I picked up the skull, one large, white tooth fell from its socket and lodged itself in the snow by my right leg.

When I looked down I saw something even more amazing, something I had only read about in books—the outline of wings carved into the snow. I inhaled sharply at the sight. A raven had been here, had bathed its body in the coolness. I imagined it now, its dark body (so bold in its blackness it was almost blue) pressed up against the blinding white of snow. It left a perfect pattern of body and wings, its own impression of flight in the snow, glistening now with specks of gold from a ray of sunlight streaking through a part in the clouds. It was as if an angel had lain here, as if to say, *so, this is heaven.*

I sat down beside the pattern of wings, my eyes open and watching as the wind blew particles of snow all around me. August and Carson reached me then. And only then did I realize how weak I felt. How my whole body trembled from exhaustion.

"Penny, you can't be here. You'll freeze," Carson said, supporting my head in his lap. And my boy, my sweet boy, rested his head on my chest and hugged himself to me.

"I don't want to leave," I said.

And so we sat, and waited, in the cold and light watching as the last snowflakes covered my eyelashes, my hair, my hands. I wanted to tell them to not be sad, that everything was all right. I wanted to tell them so much. But instead, I closed my eyes to listen to the sound of the wind and all the beauty it contained.

When I opened my eyes again, I saw blue sky, only blue. The snow had stopped, and the sun shone down on me. I saw my life, not in a flash before my eyes like they say, but in a slow wave of beauty and death, sadness and joy, the rumbling of the earth and the miracles we possess. I thought of everyone I had known with a mounting recognition that I had loved and had been loved by so many more people than I had ever realized. And I also realized this: we are God and God is us. He is in our failures and our successes; He is our fear and our courage. We are Him. He is us. He is everything we are and everything we will become. It is with this knowledge, in this place on this last day of my life, that I could finally forgive myself for being human.

A laugh began in my belly, erupting with such force I couldn't contain it. It emerged from within me, slowly at first like a butterfly unfolding from its cocoon. Then all at once it was like the force of a thousand butterflies, pumping, fluttering their wings, changing the weather patterns of my life.

And August and Carson, they laughed too. We all laughed and we all cried, and I looked up at their faces, framed in blue like halos, and I asked them, through my laughter, through my tears, "Is it cheating if I see beauty in everything?"

But if they answered, I did not hear. For in the distance a raven was calling, and I swear I heard my name.

EPILOGUE

My mother died twelve days after she was admitted to the hospital in Albuquerque. The very last days were particularly difficult. She was in a tremendous amount of pain. The medicine they gave her or the tumor in her brain, or both, caused her to have hallucinations and strange dreams. On the day she died, the first snow of the season fell in large flakes. I opened the window for her, but I don't know if she ever noticed. She had opened her eyes, but I don't think she recognized me.

"Mom, it's snowing," I told her and wanted her to look out the window, but she wouldn't take her eyes from us. Seven hours later she died, speaking of ravens and how they lifted her up on light and splendid wings.

§

We had my mother's body cremated, as she wished. My dad and I drove her ashes to Highway 160 outside of Alamosa, Colorado. We stopped the car when we arrived at the Sangre de Cristo Mountains. Cradling her ashes, we headed for those great peaks. I would love to say we climbed to the highest point, but I was only nine and Carson was old. Instead, we climbed a small ridge overlooking the exact spot where she had been born. We brought her here so she could finally see it, so she could remember that from the moment she came into this world she had been loved. We scattered her ashes onto the dark soil. Above us, a raven called out, and I swear I heard my mother's name.

§

Carson and I didn't have to drive far after that. We found her name and address easily enough. The wonderful part and the hard part would come next: meeting my grandmother for the first time, and having to tell her that her daughter had passed away.

When the door opened, I saw my mother's eyes, the delicate wrinkles which would have covered her skin had she been given the chance to grow old. Then arms like her arms pulled me in and tears of joy, that should have been my mother's, flowed.

Emma Forester.

My grandmother.

My mother's mother.

We found her living not far from the long stretch of road where her first daughter had been born beneath a pending sun.

"You know, after I got out of the hospital, I searched every orphanage in the entire state. Not one ever had a record of Deena. It wasn't until my eighteenth birthday that your great-grandmother, my mother, finally told me what she had done. She had sent my baby to California. She paid our neighbors, who were moving there, to take her to an orphanage. My mother had called and arranged the whole thing. The very next day I packed my things and moved to Los Angeles. The orphanage where she had lived had long since been shut down. I couldn't find any record of Deena, or where she had gone, what her life was like. But I stayed in California, hoping one day, somehow, we would find each other. I hired a private detective, but when she couldn't find any news of her either, I began to fear the worst. I couldn't bring myself to imagine my little girl had died. I preferred to think of her happy, safe, and loved. When I met my husband, we moved back to Colorado. I married a good man and had two wonderful sons. But I never stopped thinking about your mother."

§

Carson and I moved to Colorado to be close to my grandmother and the memories of our families. He took me to the Sand Dunes every year, and we spent Christmases and birthdays with my grandmother and my new extended family. At every gathering she told the same story—how Carson and his father saved her life and her daughter's life.

Three days before my 15th birthday, Grandma Forester died of a brain aneurism. It happened over dessert one evening. She died suddenly, with the taste of vanilla cake with strawberry icing (her favorite) on her lips. She died with a laugh bubbling up in her throat. She died happy.

§

Carson, my father, died peacefully in his sleep the day I got engaged to the woman I would spend the rest of my life with. He was ready to be with my mom and, like her, had waited to make sure I would not be alone before departing this world.

I became an ornithologist, honoring my mother's love for birds. I am married now and have a wonderful son of my own. I continue to fill hundreds of notebooks with beauty and have a whole shelf in my house devoted to them. After my mother died, I was never able to "see" anyone's secret again. She always believed it was me, my heart, that revealed those stories, when the truth is, it had been her all along. Just as it had always been her who truly understood that in all things there is beauty—even if sometimes we have to make it for ourselves.

§

Almost 20 years after my mother's death, she received a letter from Alice. It arrived at the flower shop, which I had inherited. The letter was covered in unfamiliar stamps and the return address was somewhere in Spain. I removed the folded paper from the envelope and scanned the lines scrawled in her neat hand.

Dear Penny,

I wanted to write so many times but I didn't know where to begin. I think about you and August all the time. In fact, I'm enclosing an article I cut out of the paper years ago that I meant to send, but I just couldn't bring myself to write to you. Every time I picked up a pen and thought of you guys, it reminded me too much of Joe. But I was cleaning out some papers the other day and found the article. I took it as a sign.

I know you know, but I'm finally ready to say that I'm so sorry I ran off like I did. I know how much Joe meant to you, too. I just couldn't stay. I couldn't. Everywhere I looked, everything I did, I felt the complete and utter loss of Joe. I'm living in Europe, now, can you believe it? I guess I just wanted to get as far away from my old life as possible. I spent years traveling around the States, hopping from job to job. I've done everything! I was a waitress, a secretary. I even worked on a construction crew. Me! Can you believe it? Ten years ago, I bought a ticket to Spain. I didn't speak a word of Spanish, of course, but it was terrific. I got a job teaching English (again, me! Can you believe it?) and didn't have to talk to anyone about Joe. I refused, for the longest time, to learn the Spanish word for death so I couldn't tell anyone about him, even if they asked. I have since learned the word (la muerte) and find that, finally, I can say it without feeling like my insides are twisting into a thousand knots. It even actually makes me happy to think about Joe. I think he would be proud of me.

I hope you and August are well. I anxiously await news from you both.

All my Love,

Alice

§

I unfolded the newspaper article nestled in with the letter. The page had turned brown and was worn with the years. It was dated the exact date of my mother's death.

VANISHING COLONY OF ALBATROSSES
MAY BE RETURNING

South Georgia – Almost two decades ago, an entire nesting colony of Wandering Albatrosses disappeared overnight, baffling scientists. The discovery was made midway through the normal breeding season when biologists

made their yearly pilgrimage to
the site to band and tag young
chicks. When they arrived at
the island, they found no adult
birds, chicks, or eggs.

The Wandering Albatross is a
long-lived bird – surviving ap-
proximately 80 years in the wild.
It is a highly pelagic species
and, generally, individuals only
return to land for breeding purposes, once they reach breeding
age between seven and ten years
old. They are a colony nesting
species, and most individuals
return to the exact site where
they were hatched to produce the
next generation of albatrosses.

That is why their disappear-
ance all those years ago came
as such a shock to the birding
community. Scientists suggested
a change in weather patterns or
lack of food could be some of the
reasons they left in the first
place. But today, just as inex-
plicably, one of these birds, at
least, is back. This bird's return could signal an improvement
in environmental conditions.

"We are thrilled to see this
bird here again. We know if
she is alive, that others are
too. She has so far raised one
chick successfully, so we know
at least her mate is out there
somewhere," said noted ornithologist James Lee. "We can't
explain why these birds aban-

doned their nesting site in the
first place, or why this one bird
has come back. But her presence
here, her return, gives us great
hope."

§

I traveled almost 48 hours to get here. I stand now with my feet upon the rocks and pull the aging newspaper article from my pocket, sent to me just a few short months ago. The wind is blowing hard against my back. Mist surrounds me. I adjust my eyes to the haze and see...nothing. At my feet, there are some discarded feathers, and the smell of bird feces is sour and heavy on the air. The birds that returned to this place one by one so long ago have once again laid their eggs, raised their young and, without a moment's hesitation, returned to their pelagic life—abandoning solid ground until it is time to breed again. But, in my heart, I know she will come. I have been here for hours. Waiting.

Finally, from the corner of my eye, I see her—a large, dark shape soaring above the sea. Her grey shadow is visible against the even greyer sky. I strain my eyes to see her delicate face, her feathered wings. But I only manage a glimpse, and then she is gone. She disappears into the mist like a ghost—enveloped, perhaps, by the invisible hands of God.

Acknowledgements

First and always, I must thank my family—my mother (we miss you), my sister Maria, my brother Giorgio, and my brother-in-law Tony—for your unending love and encouragement and for supporting me in my dreams, even though they have kept me far away from you for so long.

This novel has benefited from three talented and generous editors: Elisabeth Sharp McKetta whose brilliant insights and genuine passion for writing are an inspiration; Melanie J. Mendenhall whose close attention to detail helped shape this novel into what it is today; and Lisa Bovee of Green Pen Editing (Austin, Texas — Greenpenediting.com) who not only provided excellent editing services, but much appreciated encouragement as well.

I thank all of those who generously gave of their time to read and make comments on the first drafts of this novel. In particular, I owe a huge thanks to Erinn Magee for going first and for her support; to Bill Lee for having read almost everything I have ever written and for always pushing me to do better; to Chris Doyle for taking time away from her beautiful family to read this book; and to Jini Cicero, Silvio Sirias, Helen Kiser, Miriam Butterman, Amy Seidenstrang, and Grainger Hunt for their helpful suggestions and comments. I am grateful to Trish Nixon for giving me permission to use the beautiful sketches that grace the pages of this novel. I also thank Waga Ledezma, Anna Gorin, Jenn Sinasac, and Christine Hayes for graphic design assistance and support.

I owe a special debt of gratitude to Steve Sneed for being a dear friend and for trusting me with his stories.

Finally, I thank those who have shaped my life in so many wonderful ways: those of you at the Bosque del Apache and Sevilleta NWRs (you know who you are) for showing me the beauty of birds, and to the good people at The Peregrine Fund, past and present, for letting me live my dream for so long. I thank Terry and Lori Tadano and the whole Tadano clan for taking me in; Frani Ruch for freeing my wild side; Cris Trevisan and John O'Keefe for their friendship; Ayesha Irani for the gift of yoga; Ana Lucia and Ben Muela, just for being who they are; and finally, Angel Muela for being my family away from family for the seven years it took me to write this book.

ABOUT THE AUTHOR

Author Photo © Angel Muela

Marta Curti was born in Los Angeles, California, and gradu-
ated from Pepperdine University with a degree in Communi-
cations/Creative Writing. She went on to pursue a Master's
in Education and currently works as a biologist and environmental educator for a non-profit organization, splitting her
time between Panama, Dominican Republic and the U.S. She
is the author of two bilingual children's books. *In All Things*
is her first novel.

33791193R00188

Made in the USA
Middletown, DE
27 July 2016